SKIRTING DESTINY

Kay Keppler

SKIRTING DESTINY

Acknowledgments

Many thanks to Beth Barany, Patricia Simpson, and Anne Victory, who did their best to help me make this book as good as it could be. And a special shoutout to that unknown participant in the writers workshop, who, when asked what the young woman in the poodle skirt might do for a living, said, "Maybe she works for the CIA."

Chapter 1

Phoebe Renfrew ripped off the neon-pink sticky notes that bristled like porcupine quills all over the pages of the bridal magazine she held.

"My mother is nuts," she said.

Chase Bonaventure, her fiancé, the former star quarterback of the Las Vegas Rattlesnakes and current CEO of electric-vehicle start-up manufacturer Venture Automotive, glanced away from the heavy Washington, DC, traffic he was navigating and grinned at her.

"Brenda sent you another annotated bridal magazine?"

"Yes." Phoebe scowled. "I don't get it. All through my growing up, she couldn't be bothered. I mean, she practically *abandoned* me. Not that I minded, exactly. It was what I knew, right? And it all worked out in the end. But now all of a sudden, she's turned into some kind of insane supermom or something. It's all wedding advice, all the time. Isn't that weird? Not to mention irritating."

"You think that's bad?"

"*Yes.* Because I've told her a million times, *there's no date for the wedding.*"

She loved Chase with her whole heart, one thousand and ten percent. But they'd only known each other three months, and she was nervous—*very* nervous—about getting married after such a short time. Her mother had a lifelong pattern of going off with guys she'd known only a few weeks, sometimes only a few days—men who'd spun her a line of promises in the cocktail bars where she worked—convinced that they were The One. Brenda would disappear for months at a time and then return home, heartbroken, when the guy left her.

Phoebe didn't know what it would feel like when she knew for sure that her love for Chase was different—stronger—than what her mother felt for the guys she went for, but she hoped that she'd know it when she felt it. In the meantime, Chase had promised that they could have as long an engagement as she wanted.

And that was the other thing. Chase had been married once before—married and divorced in little more than six months. Phoebe wanted Chase to be sure, too.

Although he seemed pretty sure.

And he was annoyingly nonchalant about the pressure her mother was exerting.

"Brenda's probably trying to make up for a lifetime of ignoring you," he said, following the GPS instructions and turning off the busy thoroughfare into a quiet residential neighborhood.

"Maybe. In a way, I suppose it's kind of, I don't know, nice, maybe, that she's trying to act like a normal mom for a change. But she's gone way overboard with this wedding stuff. If this magazine is anything to go by, she wants *bows* on the *chairs*." She shuddered.

"She's happy for you. And maybe she needs a hobby."

Phoebe snorted. "And I hate to say this, because I love your family, but *your* mother isn't helping. She's supposed to be the sensible one. *My* mother runs wild, and Claire *lets* her."

"I don't see how you can expect my mom to corral Brenda, even if she wanted to," Chase said. "Your mom lives in a different state from mine."

"My mother lives in a different state, all right," Phoebe said. "A different state of *mind*."

Chase grinned. "Your mom's in Vegas, mine's in

8

Louisiana, and we're a thousand miles from either of them." He turned the corner onto a narrow, tree-lined street. "Ignore them. When we're ready, we'll elope. Problem solved."

Phoebe sighed. Men did not understand how women went nuts over weddings. Save-the-date postcards. Invitations. Dresses. Venues. Food. Flowers. Photographs. Music. *Bows*.

Not that *she'd* ever be a bridezilla. No. When she and Chase decided they were ready, her best jeans and a justice of the peace would do fine for her. But her mother, thwarted from having a wedding of her own, had other ideas. And Chase's mother had a solid, if unwelcome, idea of how large her famous son's wedding should be, so she went along with Brenda's nutty schemes. For a wedding that might not occur for *years*.

"Maybe they'll calm down once we buy a house," Chase said, cruising slowly down the street, looking for the right address. "With luck, we can do that today."

Phoebe couldn't shake her gloomy thoughts. "And then Mom can start sending me annotated home-decorating magazines."

Chase laughed. "Maybe after we see this place, you can go somewhere and catch bad guys. That'll make you feel better."

Phoebe rolled her eyes and pitched the magazine over her shoulder into the back seat of the car. She wasn't due back at her job as a language analyst at the CIA for a couple of weeks yet, which was a good thing, because they'd need the time to get settled after their move from Las Vegas. And they hadn't even found the right house yet.

She'd met Chase in Vegas, where he'd been the Rattlesnakes' history-making quarterback until a bad hit in the Super Bowl ended his football career. After that, he'd taken over a failing electric-car company that, under his direction, was making a big splash in the industry. She'd been surfing Brenda's couch in Vegas after the agency suspended her because of that terrible, horrible, no-good, very bad day when she'd thought Swedish-Korean terrorists would strike at the

Empire State Building. Only they hadn't.

Instead, they'd shown up at Chase's factory.

The terrorists were caught, and—in time—she'd been vindicated. The agency even offered her a promotion, but that meant returning to DC—and breaking up with Chase. Then he made her a deal: he'd move with her to DC and work remotely if she agreed to an engagement of whatever length she wanted.

She'd never turn down an offer like that.

"The bad guys are safe from my clutches until I go back to work," she said. "Unless we run into some at one of these viewings, which I think is unlikely." She peered out the windshield to see numbers on houses that were set far back from the street and partially, or entirely, concealed by leafy trees and shrubbery. The place had to be here somewhere, but all these McMansions looked alike to her. "Where are we?"

"You don't know? I'm the stranger here. You're the one who used to live in DC."

"In three hundred feet, your destination will be on the right," the navigation system announced.

"I was going to say that," said Chase as Phoebe laughed. He pulled into the circular driveway of a sprawling house with a FOR SALE sign posted behind a flowering bush.

"This is it," he said. "What do you think?"

She gazed with misgiving at the giant house with the elaborate drive and turrets. "Turrets. Will you feel an urge to take up jousting? That's what turned Henry VIII into such a grouch, you know. Jousting accident."

"Won't happen. Anyway, keeping horses in the back-yard probably violates the zoning regulations."

"Maybe not. This is Washington, you know. Plenty of horses' asses in the backyards."

Chase laughed. "I defer to your experience. Well, I could do without the turrets, but the place has six bed-rooms—that's why we're checking it out. We need six if we want to put up my family when they come to visit. Unless we pitch tents for them in the backyard."

"That's what we'll do if my mom comes to visit. No matter how many bedrooms we have."

Chase grinned, opening the car door. "I like your mom."

"I like her, too." Phoebe got out and squinted up at the turrets again. "But I don't want her getting too comfortable at our place, wherever that is."

As they walked up the drive, a tall, middle-aged woman in a business pantsuit emerged from the front door to meet them. Susan McIntosh, their agent. The woman who wanted them to live in a house with turrets.

"Chase, Phoebe. How are you? Did you find the place okay?"

"GPS is a miracle," Chase said, and they all trooped inside.

"So this house has the six bedrooms you want," Susan said, handing them each a sales flyer. "And all the rooms get beautiful sunlight."

"I like sunlight," Phoebe said, willing to be accommodating. If Chase really liked this place, she supposed she could live with turrets.

"This is the great room." Susan led the way into a space so huge the full Rattlesnakes squad could have held practice workouts in it. The cream-colored, flat-weave carpet was cushiony underfoot. A fieldstone fireplace occupied one wall, and two stories of sparkling windows, through which blinding sunlight poured, occupied another. A flight of stairs on the third wall led to a mezzanine, where a skimpy railing hypothetically prevented people from plunging to their deaths below. A chandelier with an enormous fan that spun faster than a jet engine on takeoff dangled from the cathedral ceiling. Phoebe hoped that it wouldn't fall and chop them into bits. They'd never get the blood out of that white carpet.

"Great room?" she asked.

"That's what they call the living room now," Chase said. "Impressive."

"Uh," Phoebe said. *Dangerous*, that's what she'd call it.

"Okay," Susan said cheerfully. "The kitchen's through here. It was just redone. It has a farmer's sink, granite countertops, a waterfall island—"

"That doesn't sound like a good idea," Phoebe said.

"That means that the granite carries on from the top surface down the side," Chase said. "It's not about water."

"Oh," Phoebe said. "Why does it have a farmer's sink? For that matter, what *is* a farmer's sink?"

"It's big and square," Chase said. "With that apron look."

Phoebe nodded. "So it's a style thing."

"Sure," Chase said. "It's all a style thing."

"I'm glad I found that out," Phoebe said. "I wouldn't want functionality to interfere in any way."

Chase laughed.

"It's about style *and* functionality." Susan frowned. "Style adds that wow factor and improves resale value when you're ready to move on."

Phoebe sighed. If they found the right house, she'd never want to move on. She'd want to stay there forever, putting down roots, becoming friends with her neighbors. Building a life—a future—with Chase. *Belonging.*

The problem was, she couldn't tell what the right house was. Chase had told her she could pick the house she wanted, as long as it had six bedrooms. When they'd started searching, she thought that she'd know the right place when she saw it. She'd feel something. The house would call to her. Or at least *whisper.*

But all the houses they'd looked at so far had felt the same to her. They all seemed to be built to the same specs, and she couldn't really tell any of them apart. If those houses called to her at all, it was to shriek *run away.*

Originally they thought that they'd find a place long before she was due back at the CIA. But they'd need a place with six bedrooms by Thanksgiving at the latest, only two months away. She hoped that she wouldn't have to settle for something like this.

"Let's keep moving," she said.

"Butler's pantry is through here." Susan pointed to a door at the back of the kitchen.

"Do we have to hire a *butler*?" Phoebe, appalled, whispered to Chase.

"That's just what it's called." Chase kept his voice low. "It's where people keep their glassware."

"I don't like this place," Phoebe said, still whispering. "It's like I'm following the White Rabbit into Wonderland. I don't understand what she's talking about. I don't know the *words.*"

"Keep an open mind," Chase said as they walked through the butler's pantry. "Think *glassware storage closet.*"

"I hate that you know all this stuff."

"Dad's a contractor, remember?" Chase said. "I've helped. I stay in the loop."

They came out into yet another huge room and more miles of that pale, flat-weave carpet. There must have been a sale at the carpet store to have so much of it everywhere.

"This is the breakfast nook," Susan said.

When the tour was over, Chase led the way back to the car. Phoebe was right about one thing: the turrets were stupid. His brothers would never let him live those things down. But he'd be okay living here. He wasn't fussy. As long as the place had six bedrooms, he'd be fine.

Phoebe, it was clear, would not.

She got in the car, leaned back against the headrest, and closed her eyes. "I'd almost rather read annotated bridal magazines."

He laughed. She'd change her mind on that once her mother sent her another one with those pink sticky notes full of "helpful" suggestions.

"I'm happy to let that place go, but we're running out of options," he said. "At least, if we want to be settled into something before our jobs gear up. And the holidays arrive."

Phoebe opened her eyes and swiveled to glance at him. "I know. I wish I could like that place, but it has a two-story living room. Sorry, *great* room. It isn't cozy. You need scaffolding to dust the corners. And we've got a dog, remember? Trouble would trot across that white carpet *once* with muddy paws and we'd have to replace it. And then you've got that open hallway up there, with only that teeny railing to keep people from falling."

"You think one of us would fall?"

"Yes. Or when your little nieces and nephews come for Thanksgiving. They'd be horsing around, and one of them would go over."

"That would be bad," Chase said, starting the car. "Probably wouldn't happen, though."

"It could. And that house isn't worth what they're asking for it. They want *millions* for it, and it doesn't seem to have *value*. All that cheap carpeting. All that gray paint. In. Every. Single. Room. Nothing's special. Nothing's unique. Nothing says *us*."

"I'm not sure what *us* is in terms of home buying, but yeah, the place was a bit builder's grade. High-end builder's grade, but still. Tell me: What do you think a house like that *should* cost? What is its value?"

"A dollar ninety-nine," Phoebe said promptly.

Chase laughed. "And you still wouldn't want to live there."

"I would not. But I would, if you liked it and that's all there was. But not for millions of dollars. Or anything close."

He knew the value of a dollar—his parents had made sure of that—but he earned a lot, always had, and wanted to enjoy it. And he wanted a big house so his family could all stay in one place whenever they could get together, which was as often as they could all swing it.

But Phoebe had grown up with nothing, and she'd learned—better than he had—how to wring every penny from a purchase. Most women who were temporarily unemployed and up to their eye sockets in overdue school loans would be thrilled to be engaged to a guy who had enough cash to pay off that debt and buy a big house besides. Not Phoebe. She insisted on paying off her school loan herself, no matter how long it took. And now she watched their expenses like a hawk.

Of course, the reason he wanted to marry her was that

she wasn't most women. And she wasn't wrong about the house, either. The price on that cookie-cutter McMansion was high, although not higher than anything else they'd looked at.

"I won't lie to you that I'd like to get our housing situation squared away," he said. "But I said back in Vegas that you could pick the house, and I meant it—as long as you pick *something*. And you know the price on that place is ballpark for what we want, right?"

"No, I get it. And I agree with you in principle. But it's so much money for such an ugly house. And it isn't easy to overcome twenty-five years of financial instability, you know?"

He reached out for her hand. "I know, *cher*. Okay, well, we've got appointments to see two more houses this week, and then that's it. For now, anyway."

"Maybe one of those will be better, and— *Wait! Stop!*"

Chase slammed on the brakes. "What? What's the matter?"

"There's a house!"

"*Cher*, there's houses everywhere. Oh—that one over there?"

He spotted the graceful, decaying mansion set back on a wide sweep of patchy lawn with a small, hand-lettered sign out front: FOR SALE BY OWNER. OPEN HOUSE TODAY. 9–5.

His heart sank. They'd entered an area of older homes near the park, and this place, in particular, needed a ton of work. Work that he didn't have the time or inclination to do or even to hire out.

"*Cher*—"

Phoebe glanced at her watch. "It's not five o'clock yet. Let's check it out. What do you think?"

He'd been hoping to finish some work and then catch the game tonight. But this shouldn't take long. They'd have plenty of time to fly through the place and get on with their day.

"The house isn't in good shape, but I'm game to look at it if you are." He parked and they got out of the car and walked up the uneven brick approach.

The house was set on a gentle slope, and the front yard was terraced in cracked and broken stonework. Two chipped stone urns that flanked the covered front porch were filled with old dirt, dead plants, and dried leaves. The driveway leading to a double garage was a cracked expanse of asphalt through which a vigorous growth of weeds had made remarkable headway.

The house itself was undeniably beautiful, with gracious lines that hadn't been built since the 1920s. Although it was obviously large, the building was a home, not an architectural wet dream. No turrets here anywhere. All brick, it had a deeply recessed front door with cement detail around the portico. Decorative stonework enhanced the mullioned windows. The craftsmanship was outstanding. They sure didn't make them like this anymore.

However, the brick needed tuck pointing, including the brick on the six chimneys that stuck up from a roof that had to be twenty years old. The windows needed caulking and the trim needed painting. The ivy needed trimming. The grass needed mowing or, even better, replacing.

Who knew what the house would need inside.

"Place feels empty," he said. "I wonder if anybody's home?"

"Let's find out." Phoebe pressed the doorbell, and a two-tone chime rang deep in the home's interior. "Sounds nice."

They waited. Phoebe rang again.

"We should go," Chase said just as someone inside fumbled with the lock.

The door swung open and revealed a short, wizened, elderly man. He seemed too small for the suit he wore, which hung off his shoulders and sagged away from his body, but he stood tall, his eyes were bright, and his smile was welcoming.

"Hello, hello!" he said. "You're here to see the house."

"We are," Phoebe said. "I'm Phoebe Renfrew, and this is my fiancé, Chase Bonaventure."

"I'm Amos Glenwethering," the man said. "The owner, along with my wife, Sophie. Come in, come in. Let me show you around."

As they entered the house, Chase watched Phoebe to see how she'd react. She took one glance and her face lit up. She spun around slowly, gazing at every detail.

"Oh," she breathed. "It's *beautiful*."

Oh *no*. No, no, no. Not this one. Not the house that needed millions of hours and millions of dollars for repairs.

But he had to agree, the bones of the place were good. The entryway was generous, a room by itself. A stained glass window threw shimmering panes of jewel tones across the black-and-white tiled hall. Arched doorways on either side, framed by intricate woodwork, revealed two sitting rooms, each with an enormous tiled fireplace and crown molding. Sunlight poured through those beautiful mullioned windows across smooth, wide-planked oak floors, the tongue-and-groove still tight despite the home's age. One room was painted a soft yellow; one a sky blue. Phoebe's favorite colors.

Dammit. It was almost as though somebody had painted those rooms just for Phoebe. Just so she'd love the house. He was doomed, unless she found some other feature of the house that didn't appeal to her.

"Glad you like it," Amos Glenwethering said. "We've always been happy here. Let me show you around." He flipped the light switch and the sconces in the entryway came on, wavered, went out, and came on again. The light revealed some flaking plaster on the ceiling.

"Probably a loose bulb," Phoebe said as Amos led the way into the yellow sitting room.

Possible, but not likely if the general condition of the place was anything to go by. When Amos's back was turned, Chase twisted the bulb in the sconce. Tight as a Louisiana politician's purse strings. The wavering light was not about the bulb.

They went through the house, Phoebe looking happier by the minute. She admired the woodwork, exclaimed over the colorful paint choices, polished the windowpanes with her shirtsleeve, pulled open all the drapes, poked in every closet. He tested every window, turned on every faucet, flipped every switch, checked the basement and the attic. She dismissed as inconsequential the ancient kitchen, awkwardly built bathrooms, inadequate water heater, and outdated electrical system. The end of the tour brought them to the lime-green sunroom bathed in golden, late-afternoon light, where Phoebe stroked the fireplace mantel like it was some kind of pet before she sat down in an overstuffed love seat by the window and gazed at him in silent appeal.

Dammit.

Phoebe liked the house. *Loved* the house, if he could judge by the expression on her face. And she deserved to have a house she loved. Not to mention, he'd told her she could pick the house she liked. He sat down next to her.

"I'm sorry we couldn't meet your wife today," he told Amos, who smiled and took the chair opposite.

"Sophie would have enjoyed your visit. But she's at home, resting. She's not doing too well these days."

"I'm sorry to hear that," Phoebe said.

"We both love this place," Amos said. "We raised four boys here, lived here for almost sixty-five years."

And haven't done a bit of maintenance on it for at least twenty-five, Chase thought.

"I love the history you have in this house," Phoebe said. "I can feel it. All the stories it could tell."

"Quite a few, that's for sure," Amos said. "But it's too big a place for people winding down. We got a place on the other side of the park that's a lot smaller but big enough for the two of us and the nurses who come in. And we're still in the old neighborhood, so it's easy for our old friends to drop by."

"Are you sure you're ready to sell this place?" Chase asked.

"Oh yes. Aside from everything else—the expenses on this place and the maintenance it needs—I need the money for Sophie. We're ready to sell."

"*Cher*, what do you think?" Chase turned to Phoebe, certain that he knew what her answer would be. "Do you like the house?"

"I *love* the house," Phoebe said, longing etched deep on her face. "Can we afford it?"

"What are you asking for it?" Chase asked Amos. He almost couldn't believe they were going to make an offer on this place. He didn't want to do the work it needed. But it did have six bedrooms. And Phoebe—Phoebe loved it. It *was* a beautiful old place. And he'd love it, too, once they had it fixed up.

Amos named a price much lower than that of the McMansion with the turrets. "There's an inspection report you'll want to see. The price reflects that."

"I'm not one to look a gift horse in the mouth," Chase said, "but my daddy would cuss me a blue streak if he thought I'd taken advantage of you." The old man was asking a lot less than he could get for his house, even as desperately in need of work as it was right now.

"Well, the thing is, I'm anxious to sell and—to tell you the truth—you're the only folks that came by today," Amos said. "And I like you. I'd like you to have it. If you can give me my asking price, we'll be set, and you'll have enough left over, I think, to make the changes to it that you'll want to make."

"What about your furniture?" Chase glanced at Phoebe, wondering if any of the stuff appealed to her. "Can you use it in your new place?"

"We've already taken out what we wanted," Amos said. "I was planning to donate the rest."

"What about it, Phoebe? We need furniture. We could buy everything Mr. Glenwethering doesn't want."

"What a great idea!" Phoebe beamed at Amos. "I love the furniture. And we'd save a *lot* of time not having to shop for other stuff."

And it would appeal to her budget-conscious self, so that was a plus, too.

Chase fiddled with calculations on his phone and then

tilted the screen to Phoebe before he showed it to Amos.

"What do you think about this number?" he asked the older man. "For the house and furniture? Does that work for you? I'm open to negotiate, if not."

Amos blinked a few times and nodded. "That's very generous."

"I hope it's a fair price for us both," Chase said. "And to tell you the truth, Phoebe and I have been house hunting for a while, and we were getting worried that we'd never find a place we liked. Let me write you a check for the down payment. I'll make arrangements with my bank tomorrow for the rest. Do you have paperwork prepared?"

He signed the sales contract, and they agreed to meet again for the legal filings.

"I'm willing to give you the key if you'd like to get in this week before we close and transfer the title," Amos said.

"Thank you," Chase said. "Getting a jump on the move would be very helpful."

They stood and shook hands all around.

"This house was right for our family at the time, but now it's the right time to sell," Amos said on the doorstep. He carefully locked the door behind them and handed Phoebe the key. "And you're the right people to move in, I can tell. You'll take care of this place the way it should be. And I hope you're as happy here as Sophie and I were."

"We will be," Phoebe said. "We're staying for sixty-five years, too."

Chase liked how that sounded. Phoebe might not want to get married right away, but as long as she was in for the long haul, he was okay with that. He could wait.

Amos smiled. "I called a cab for five o'clock, and here it is," he said. "I have to go. Sophie's waiting."

"We'll be in touch," Chase said.

They waved goodbye to the cab as it drove down the street.

"I saw what you did in there," Phoebe said, smiling up at him.

He smoothed a strand of hair back from her cheek.

"What I did? What did I do?"

"You paid too much for the house."

He hoped she wasn't worried about whether they could afford it. It was much less expensive than that monstrosity with the turrets, even considering all the renovations it needed.

Phoebe put her arms around him, burrowing against his chest. "That was the sweetest, kindest, best thing I have ever seen in my entire life," she said. "I love you. And I love the house. Thank you."

Well, okay then. He leaned down and kissed her.

"It's a beautiful old place," he said. "And it'll be even better when we've done some maintenance on it."

"I'm glad you love it, too."

That definitely was stretching it, but he wouldn't argue when she was so happy. She might sing a different tune when the lights went on the fritz or the sink backed up.

Maybe they should start thinking about fixing things up right away. "Now that we've got the key, do you want to go back in and—I don't know. Measure windows for curtains or something?"

"We're not getting new curtains," she said. "I love the old curtains." She beamed up at him with a smile that seemed to light up the skies. "I can't believe it! We bought my dream house, and I didn't even know I *had* a dream house. We can move right in! All our worries solved in an instant!"

"Don't tempt fate," Chase said. "We could be seeing a million repair guys for years to come. Who knows what nightmares lie ahead?"

Chapter 2

Yuri Severov ambled along the shady street in Washington, DC, trying to look like a tourist. Could he pass? Probably not. All the sunburned, plaid-shorts-wearing people he passed seemed to be gazing into their phones, not at the imposing buildings that lined the street.

However, strolling past the State Department would be normal for a scientist visiting from Russia who was attending a global conference about technical and scientific data sharing, which was exactly what he was. Everybody knew that visiting scientists were curious. They liked to know specific information, like where the US Department of State was located. Maybe even its hours of operation.

He needed to know these things because when the conference ended, instead of boarding a plane back to Moscow, he planned to head straight to the State Department and turn himself in.

He wanted to defect.

And he feared what his bosses back in the Kremlin might do to him if they learned of his plan.

They'd suspected him from the moment he'd asked for permission to go. At first they'd refused, then changed their minds at the last minute. Almost certainly they had spies scrutinizing his every step, making sure he did not approach the Americans. They would not hesitate to assassinate him if they realized he intended to switch sides.

Because he had information that the Americans would kill to get and the Russians would kill to keep secret.

Yuri had spent the best part of his career breaking into the servers, databases, and websites of political, economic, and cultural institutions of the West and stealing data and sometimes even cash for his bosses. He'd disrupted elections, power grids, manufacturing empires, and banking systems and improved the political standing, military power, and economic outcomes of his country. Very few Western secrets of any type were safe from prying Russian eyes, especially his.

And he'd done it all without any bonuses, rewards, or even gratitude from the apparatchiks up the food chain.

He was tired of working for an ungrateful Russia. The conference gave him a legitimate reason to come to America, and he'd heard that the Americans welcomed Russian defectors. He was ready to support an American government that knew how to reward scurrilous politicians, corrupt financiers, unscrupulous industrialists, and moral cowards of all kinds. He understood these people. They were his bosses, his colleagues. Even his friends.

America would welcome him with open arms, because for every secret he knew of theirs, he knew one of Russia's, too. America would pay handsomely for Russian secrets—and they'd pay even more to find out how to plug their own leaks.

He wouldn't just become rich, either. He'd be the man who single-handedly brought down the Russian oligarchs. The man who made America great again.

He was ready. He'd brought years of secrets with him, mostly smuggled out on thumb drives, microchips, and microdots that he'd carefully accumulated for this eventuality. He had passwords to documents stored in the cloud. He had codes. He had names. He had evidence. He had everything at his fingertips. And he'd give it all to the Americans. For a price.

All he had to do was get safely into the State Department

building, where he could talk to the diplomats. He wanted nothing to do with the FBI, CIA, Department of Justice, or Homeland Security. He didn't see how approaching a law enforcement agency could do him any good. He had no interest in winding up in some American gulag. Although the food would be better than in the Siberian work camps. And the weather would be better, too.

No. The State Department would give him asylum, a safe house, and money. His only worry was the Russian security forces. They were everywhere, and if they saw him go into the State Department, they would act swiftly and decisively. And then all his carefully laid plans would go with him to the grave.

Which was why he was planning his route, pretending that he was merely taking a pleasant walk on a lovely fall day. He wanted to know exactly where he was going. He wanted to get there safely and swiftly. He even had a plan for what he could do if things went wrong. If he saw a tail, he'd head down to the National Mall where the cabstands, bus stops, and metro stations converged. He'd get into a cab, make a loop, and come back by a different way.

He glanced around casually as he waited at the light to cross the street. So far he hadn't seen anyone remotely suspicious. For all intents and purposes, he was simply one more foreign scientist attending a conference, who would return home on time and on schedule.

When the conference ended on Saturday, he'd go to the State Department and tell the American diplomats what they wanted to know. And then he'd live in peace, prosperity, and comfort for the rest of his days.

What could possibly go wrong?

Phoebe knew that she was having a run of luck when she passed her driving test on Saturday. She'd started taking lessons back in Las Vegas, but what with moving some of Venture Automotive's functions to DC so Chase could work remotely and then house hunting, she hadn't practiced much lately. She was disappointed that Chase wasn't there to congratulate her on her triumph, but he'd been called back to Vegas on short notice for a problem that had cropped up at the plant. However, they could celebrate when he got back, and meanwhile, Sanjay Agarwal, her good friend from Vegas, had driven her to the examination, lent his taxi for the test, and now offered to take her to lunch.

"I passed the test!" She bounced a little on the taxi's passenger seat in her excitement. "And the examiner said I did a good job!"

She was still giddy from the thrill of it. Twenty-five years old and finally road legal.

"A most happy outcome!" Sanjay said. "Although I had every expectation that you would be successful in this endeavor. We have much to celebrate. Your driver's license, but also your new home."

"Yes!" Phoebe said. "Wait till you see it. I have to stick around there this afternoon because a contractor is coming to give us a quote for upgraded electrical and whatever. You want to join us?"

Sanjay shook his head. "Alas, I cannot. I am previously engaged with my classmate Jamal to do some self-defense practice this afternoon. Perhaps some other time."

"How about this, then? If you don't have plans, you could come over tonight and we can order out for something. Chase doesn't get back from Vegas until Monday, and it would be nice to have the company."

"The contractor is coming even though Chase can't walk him through?"

"Well, when we scheduled the guy, Chase was going to be here. And he wants to get the work started, so he didn't want to cancel. He's talked to the guy on the phone, and I've got a list to go over with him. It'll be fine. And frankly, the electrical can be a little scary. I'm glad it's getting taken care of."

"An unsteady electrical capacity is both disconcerting and conceivably also a serious fire hazard," Sanjay said. "And I would enjoy seeing your new place. Perhaps around five? Jamal and I will have completed our practice by then.

And now, what would you like for a celebratory lunch? I have discovered a most delicious barbecue establishment."

"That sounds great," Phoebe said. "Plus, I'm starving. I'm so glad you decided to take up protective driving and move to DC! How are things going?"

Sanjay had temporarily relocated to DC to take a protection and security driving course for the Fun Fares taxicab company for which he worked, in the expectation that celebrities, politicians, and the very wealthy would hire them.

"Very well indeed," he said, gliding to a stop at a red light near the Vietnam Veterans Memorial on the National Mall. "We have recently begun—"

A tall, flabby man wearing a stained and wrinkled gray suit yanked open the rear door to the taxi, flung himself into the back seat, and sprawled across the bench.

"Скорость перемотки!" he said hysterically. "Скорость перемотки!"

"I am so sorry," Sanjay said. "This taxi is currently out of service. You can find a convenient taxi stand—"

"Диск быстро!" The man curled up on the back seat, cowering.

From what, Phoebe couldn't tell. She surveyed the street and sidewalks around the cab, but nothing suggested trouble. It was just a normal, busy street in Washington, DC, full of tourists and government workers on a bright, early-fall day. Maybe this guy was deranged.

"Also, I am not understanding you," Sanjay said. "And your demeanor does not inspire confidence."

"He's speaking Russian," Phoebe said. "He wants you to go fast. Drive fast, he said."

"I had surmised as much," Sanjay said. "That desire is hardly surprising. Everyone wants to go fast. And why? What is to be gained? Certainly not time. Time is a fixed commodity, twenty-four hours of it every day. And you and I are going to lunch now. I'm not driving this man anywhere, fast or otherwise."

A muffled report cut off Phoebe's reply, and both the rear and front windows of Sanjay's cab exploded in a shower of glass.

"Диск быстро!" the man screamed.

"Go!" Phoebe yelled.

But Sanjay had already stamped on the accelerator. Tires screeched as he turned the corner too fast and too sharply, narrowly avoiding an oncoming truck. He peeled down the street, weaving in and out of traffic.

Phoebe whipped around, unbuckling her seat belt, and peered out the back window for any pursuers. She didn't see any, not that she knew what or whom she was looking for. The man in the back seat frantically brushed himself off.

"I think we're okay," she told Sanjay, on her knees in the seat but staying low. "I don't see anything suspicious. The shooter isn't following us. I *think*."

She settled back in her seat. The wind rushing through the open windshield cooled her face, a welcome relief from the adrenaline coursing through her veins. She held out her hand and saw it tremble. *Someone had shot at them.* Well, not at *them*. At the man in the back seat. But that had been *close.*

"Have you been injured?" Sanjay asked, his voice sharp. "Are you all right?"

"Scared," Phoebe said. "Not shot. You?"

"The same." Sanjay hunched over the wheel, gauging traffic. "This is the first time since I became a professional driver that I have regretted the Fun Fares taxicab marketing strategy. It is not a *retiring* design choice."

"No," Phoebe agreed. The Fun Fares taxis had an all-over paisley design in hallucinogenic shades of yellow, pink, and orange. And this particular Fun Fares taxi was the only one in DC. It would be easy to trace.

"If the traffic authorities don't stop us for driving an unsafe commercial vehicle with these broken windows, those reckless desperados will soon be spotting us."

Phoebe nodded. "Why don't you pull into that parking garage up there? We can get out of sight and find out what this guy's story is."

"And call the police," Sanjay said.

"No poleets!" the man in the back seat said. "No poleets!"

"He's got some English, anyway," Phoebe said. "That'll make things easier. Maybe."

Sanjay drove into the parking garage and went up a couple of floors, parking in a middle space away from the edges of the building.

Phoebe turned in her seat to inspect the Russian guy. "Let's start with your name," she said in Russian. "Who are you? And what was that shooting all about?"

"How do I know that you're not part of the conspiracy?" The Russian man poked his head up just far enough to peek over the back seat of the taxi and out into the parking lot.

"What conspiracy?" Phoebe asked. "And how could we be part of it? *You* jumped into *our* taxi. It's not like *we* were chasing *you*."

"It has been done," the man said. "The matter is simply one of planning. See? You speak Russian. That is enough."

"Oh, for Pete's sake." Phoebe turned to Sanjay. "He thinks we're part of a conspiracy with the people who shot at him. He won't tell me who he is."

Sanjay shrugged. "Then he should get out of the taxicab," he said. "The barbecue establishment does not stay open for lunch all day. And now I have broken windows to repair."

"Good point." Phoebe turned back to the Russian man, who was still anxiously peering out the damaged window.

"Okay," she said. "You don't trust us. Fair enough. You can get out now. We have things to do."

"I cannot get out!" the man shrieked. "They will kill me!"

"Not our problem," Phoebe said. "According to you, either *they'll* kill you or *we* will. Take your pick." She shook her head. *Russians*.

The man paused, furrowing his brow and pursing his lips. "I will take my chances with you," he said finally. "At least your driver succeeded in evading the assassin."

Well, *rats*. Now what?

"He wants to stay with us," Phoebe reported to Sanjay. "He was very complimentary of your driving." Phoebe turned back to the Russian. "Tell me your name."

"Yuri Severov."

"I'm Phoebe Renfrew, and this is Sanjay Agarwal. Sanjay's my friend, not my driver. Why did someone shoot at you?"

"I want to defect to the United States."

Great! Finally they were getting somewhere. They could turn this guy over to the men in black and go for lunch. Home run for freedom, barbecue, and apple pie!

"We'll take you to the State Department," she said. "They'll give you asylum. You'll be safe there."

"No! No! No! I *was* there! At the State Department. That's where the shots came from!"

"I don't think so," Phoebe said. "The State Department doesn't shoot visitors. At least, they never used to."

"No, no," Yuri said impatiently. "Not *inside* the building. *Outside*. I went to the State Department. I talked to an apparatchik, who said I should come back on Monday. That was bad! Very bad! How can I protect myself for two days? But I had no choice. So I left, and then there was a shot, a suppressed bullet. Yet I heard it because it flew right past my ear."

"That explains why Sanjay and I didn't hear a first shot."

Yuri nodded. "I know this man. I know what he is capable of. So I ran."

"You *saw* him? You *know* him?"

"Not his name. Of course, I did not see him. He was on a rooftop somewhere. But I know KGB when I see it. I know what they do."

"Yuri," Phoebe said. "I'm sorry. This is crazy talk. The KGB was disbanded more than twenty years ago."

"You think so?" He regarded her with contempt. "What about Alexander Litvinenko? *Ten* years ago."

Well, okay. Alexander Litvinenko was way before her time in the CIA, but everybody at the agency knew the story.

Litvinenko, an officer of a Russian secret security service, requested political asylum in the United Kingdom. He knew a lot about Russian assassinations, terrorism, and President Vladimir Putin. Russian spies murdered Litvinenko with radioactive polonium-210.

"What's he saying?" Sanjay asked.

"His name is Yuri Severov, and he wants asylum," Phoebe said. "He said he went to the State Department and a KGB shooter was waiting for him outside."

"*Some* kind of shooter was waiting outside," Sanjay agreed. "I have a broken windshield to prove it."

"He won't go back there, so State's out, even though I can't imagine the shooter would hang around, expecting him to return. But maybe we could take him to the CIA. Do you remember my friend Nattie, the woman I used to work with? Natasha Wilkinson. I'll call her. She'll take him or find somebody in the agency who will."

But when Phoebe reached her, Nattie couldn't take him.

"Phoebe, everybody's tied up," she said. "All the intake people are working the Chinese dissident group—you know, the scientists who were here for the climate change conference? Well, guess what? Those guys aren't going back to China. Although our record on climate change hasn't been that great, so you have to wonder. But the Chinese scientists couldn't do anything in China, so here they are."

"Tell me where to take this guy, then. I want him out of my hair. Well, out of Sanjay's taxi, at least."

"Why is he in Sanjay's taxi? Wait, never mind. I don't want to know. Take him to the FBI. Geographically, that's clear across town, away from State, so your guy should be happy about that, and maybe he's got something they can use. What can he tell them?"

"I have no idea. Hold on." She turned to the back seat. "Yuri. What do you know that you could tell the FBI? What kind of intel can you provide?"

"Everything! Where the bones are buried!"

"Specifics, Yuri. I need specifics."

"Communications," Yuri said, scratching his stomach.

"Hacking protocols into Western data organizations. Election tampering. Disruptions of the power grids. Media manipulation. Like that. I'm hungry. Shouldn't we be getting lunch?"

"*Crap.*" Phoebe went back to her phone. "Nattie, did you hear that?"

"I did. I don't know *what* you should be doing about lunch."

"*Nattie.*"

Natasha Wilkinson laughed. "And Phoebs? I can't wait for you to come back to work. I have a lot to catch you up on. The new group is going to be awesome. Let's get together beforehand, if you have time. Only not with the Russian."

"I'll call you," Phoebe said and disconnected. "Nattie said to take him to the FBI," she told Sanjay. "The CIA is all tied up this week with Chinese climate change defectors."

Sanjay frowned. "Why is it that everybody needs to be defecting *this* week? Somebody couldn't wait until *next* week? However, I wish the Chinese climate change scientists the best of luck with their efforts. They would appear to be jumping from the frying pan into the fire."

"I'm not worried about the Chinese defectors," Phoebe said. "I'm worried about this Russian guy."

"I am worried about driving him anywhere in this taxicab," Sanjay said. "It is entirely possible that none of us would survive the journey. And we have no specific assurances that the FBI will take him, either, correct?"

"I'll call and find out." But when she rang the agency, she got stuck in the automated message tree. After fifteen minutes of listening to prerecorded announcements from law enforcement, she hung up.

"There could be a bank robbery in progress!" she fumed. "What is the matter with these people?"

"They must be most desirous of reducing serious crime across all jurisdictions and municipalities," Sanjay said. "I am sure that such a regrettable disregard for customer service is due solely to unanticipated budget cuts. And don't forget, it's Saturday."

"Saturday," Phoebe said, disgusted. "Like crime ever

sleeps."

"I'm hungry," Yuri whined from the back seat.

"We're all hungry!" Phoebe snapped in Russian. "I'm doing the best I can."

"I know those FBI guys in Vegas," she said. "I'd hoped never to have to see them again, but I've got their direct numbers. I'll call them. Maybe one of them is working today and can get me some traction here in DC."

"Aren't those the persons who assumed momentarily that you were in league with terrorists?" Sanjay asked. "I'm not sure that is the best avenue for us to take."

"I don't know what else to do, Sanjay."

"There are two of us. Surely between us, we can push this fellow out of the cab and drive away."

"But what if the bad guys come looking for us?"

"They'll look for us whether we ditch Mr. Severov or deliver him to the FBI."

That was a thought calculated to instill fear, but Sanjay was right. Yuri had escaped in Sanjay's taxi, and if the person who'd shot at him was still searching for him, whoever was in the taxi was a logical target. Dumping Yuri and driving away had a distinct appeal, but it wouldn't get them off the hook with the shooter. And anyway, she couldn't expose a potential defector to danger.

"I wish I could leave him." She sighed. "But I can't."

She scrolled through her phone until she found the entry for the three FBI agents who'd interrogated her in Vegas. She pressed the first number, checking her watch. One thirty in DC, ten thirty in Vegas. Now she'd find out if the FBI in Vegas worked on Saturdays.

"Aaron Picone," said a voice. The nemesis was in.

"Hi, Aaron," she said. "This is Phoebe Renfrew. Remember me? Swedish-Korean terrorists?"

"How could I forget," Picone said.

"I need some help."

"On a Saturday?"

"You're working, right?" She explained her situation.

"And now you have a Russian defector in the back seat

of your taxicab," Picone said when Phoebe had finished.

"Yes, and I want to give him to the FBI, but I can't get through to anybody," Phoebe said. "Can you give me a real person? Somebody who can take this guy? A direct line to *anybody*?"

Picone put her on hold, and Phoebe listened to the Muzak on the other end, hoping that he could help her. But why wouldn't he? She'd been the injured party in their last encounter.

"Try this guy," Picone said when he came back. "Kevin Toth." He rattled off a number.

"Got it, thanks."

"You owe me one."

"No, I don't," Phoebe said. "I appreciate your help here, but we're not even *even* yet." She disconnected before Picone could start an argument and punched in the number he'd given her.

"Kevin Toth," a gravelly voice said.

"Mr. Toth." Thank heaven he was in and answering his phone. She gave him Aaron Picone's name, told him what had happened and what Yuri had said he could reveal about Russian snooping.

"Okay," Toth said. "Bring him in Monday. Three o'clock. By then I can line up the people we'll need."

"*Monday?*" Phoebe said. "I want to deliver him *today*. Like, *right now*. Somebody *shot* at him. He wants to *defect*. You know I can translate, right?"

"It's Saturday," Toth said. "Even if you translate, we still need interrogators and experts. Who works on the weekend?"

"You do," Phoebe said. "Aaron Picone's working. Me, too. My friend Sanjay Agarwal, sitting right here. Lots of people."

"Day after tomorrow," Toth said. "Bring your guy in Monday at three o'clock."

"You have to be kidding me. What am I supposed to do with him until then?"

"Maybe he plays chess," Toth said and disconnected.

"*Damn.*" Phoebe stashed her phone in her messenger bag. "Sometimes I just totally hate the FBI." She turned to the back seat.

"Hey, Yuri, do you play chess?"

"Of course, I play chess," Yuri said. "What does it matter?"

"No reason."

"Your conversation with the Vegas division of the FBI sounded remarkably cordial, given your history," Sanjay said. "What did they say?

"We—*I*—bring him in Monday at three," Phoebe said gloomily. "Not a minute before. And if I don't eat lunch soon, I won't be responsible for what happens. How are we getting out of here?"

"Fearing the failure of our government agencies to provide the assistance which we, as taxpayers, have every right to expect, I gave it some thought while you were busy chatting up the FBI," Sanjay said. "I do not wish to leave this parking garage in my taxi. However, Jamal Moscos, with whom I was engaged to practice physical maneuvers this afternoon, is already working for a company that leases armored cars and trained drivers. We could call him, and he could drive us safely out of here and wherever we wish to go. I assume home."

"But first to the barbecue establishment?" Phoebe asked.

"If you are feeling it is safe enough," Sanjay said. "They do have a drive-through window."

"Make the call," Phoebe said.

Sanjay took out his phone and made the call.

"He's coming," Phoebe announced when he disconnected. It had been impossible not to hear Sanjay's end of the conversation.

Sanjay nodded. "He expects that he can arrive here in about fifteen minutes."

"It's nice of him to drop everything to come to our rescue."

"He's happy to do it. He says the driving jobs he's had

so far in his part-time capacity at the protective services agency have not presented any danger to himself or his passengers, and he's looking forward to the challenge. He will be on his mettle."

While they waited, Phoebe filled Yuri in.

"*Day after tomorrow?*" Yuri said, echoing Phoebe's thoughts exactly. "That is the same as at the State Department! It is unacceptable! What will I do? Where will I stay? I cannot go back to my hotel. And it is imperative that I retrieve my belongings. That is *crucial.*"

"We'll take you to another hotel," Phoebe said. "You can cancel your room at the old one. I'll go in to get your stuff."

"I can't go to another hotel!" Yuri said. "They will find me! They will kill me!"

"Maybe not," Phoebe said, thinking that they probably would.

"You know this is a lie," Yuri said, shaking his head at Phoebe's willful denial of facts.

Phoebe sighed. "We'll figure something out. First, let's think about lunch."

"Lunch!" Yuri said. "It's about time. I am very hungry. But if I go somewhere to eat, they will kill me!"

Killing Yuri was starting to have some appeal.

"Sanjay's friend is coming in an armored car," she said. "We're getting barbecue from a place that has a drive-through window. You'll be safe. No one will kill you."

"And then what?" Yuri asked.

That's the million-dollar question, Phoebe thought.

Chapter 3

When a small, black SUV with tinted windows crawled down the aisle of the parking garage, Yuri threw himself down on the back seat of the Fun Fares taxi, quivering in fear. Sanjay rolled his eyes and got out of the cab, slamming the door and waving at the driver. The SUV glided to a halt, and the driver-side window rolled down. Sanjay leaned in, and seconds later a tall, thin man with cropped dark hair got out. He glanced around the parking structure, looking exactly as she imagined a bodyguard or protection specialist—*whatever*—would look, which was hugely reassuring.

"Our ride's here," Phoebe told Yuri, getting out of the taxi.

She introduced herself to Jamal and shook hands.

"Thanks for coming," she said. "We're in a bit of a pickle, as Sanjay told you."

"Where's your guy?" Jamal eyed the brightly painted Fun Fares taxi with its two gaping windows, his face inscrutable.

"Still hiding in the taxi." She raised her voice and called out in Russian. "Yuri, get out here. We gotta go!"

Jamal nodded. "Sanjay says you want to stop for barbecue?"

"If you have time to make a side trip, we're all hungry,"

Phoebe said. "And if we spot anyone following us, drive straight to the p-o-l-i-c-e station, no matter what—"

"Why did you spell out *police*?" Jamal asked.

"No poleets!" Yuri yelled from the back seat. "*No poleets!*"

"No poleets!" Phoebe yelled, whipping around. "We heard you already!"

She turned back to a startled Jamal. "Yuri's got a thing about cops. I don't know why. Don't say the *P* word. So anyway, Sanjay says the barbecue has a takeout window. You're more than welcome to join us. It's on me."

"Thank you," Jamal said. "I'll take you up on that. I don't expect any trouble, though. The shooter's probably long gone by now."

Yuri stuck his head out of the Fun Fares taxi and darted sharp glances around the garage. "Are we ready?" he asked Phoebe in Russian.

"Yes," Phoebe said. "A long time ago already."

Yuri planted one foot on the ground and stared at Jamal. "How do you know this man can be trusted?"

"I don't, not really," Phoebe said. "But he's a friend of Sanjay, and if you go around thinking everyone you see wants to kill you, we won't ever get out of this garage. Decide now: Go with us and go with the program, or stay here on your own. It doesn't matter to us."

"I'm picking up that he doesn't trust me," Jamal said.

"He doesn't trust anybody," Phoebe said. "Us, either. Yuri thinks everybody wants to kill him. *Russians.*"

Jamal shrugged. "Just because he's paranoid doesn't mean they're not out to get him."

"What are you all saying?" Yuri asked Phoebe. "You don't have to threaten me. I'm *going*, all right?"

"Fine," Phoebe said. "*Get in the car.*"

She held the door to the back seat for Yuri, who jumped out of the Fun Fares taxi, ran over to the black SUV, and leaped into the back seat. Phoebe slammed the door shut behind him.

"At least he's got good survival instincts," Jamal said.

Phoebe snorted.

"Thank you for driving us," Sanjay said. "I'm afraid that our situation is taking up a good portion of your weekend."

Jamal grinned. "Having fun so far. And I'm getting lunch out of it."

They drove to the barbecue joint without incident, picked up four orders through the takeout window, and then considered where to go to eat it. Phoebe was fiercely hungry, and the fragrant containers of barbecue were making her almost faint.

"Let's go to my place," she decided. "That should be safe. Jamal, Sanjay—have you seen anyone following us? I don't want to lead a shooter to our house. We just bought it a couple of weeks ago, and it's beautiful. Wait till you see the windows! I don't want those damaged. Or anything else, for that matter. Like us, for example."

Jamal shrugged. "I haven't seen anyone."

"We are *trained* to spot surveillance, but we lack real-world experience," Sanjay, riding shotgun, said. "We know what to look for, and we of course have practiced evasion techniques many times, but the actual spotting in a real-world situation—this has not been part of our experience as yet. Or I should say, it's not been part of *my* experience. Jamal has actually provided protection for actual customers."

"I'm the company newbie," Jamal said. "And so far, nobody's followed anybody while I've been on duty."

"Let's keep our eyes open, then," Phoebe said. "First sign of trouble, we go straight to you-know-where. I'm not saying the *P* word, because that sets Yuri off."

"In full accord with you there," Jamal said.

The drive home was uneventful, but Phoebe got nervous as they approached the house.

"Just to be on the safe side, why don't I move Chase's car over in the garage so you can pull in?" she said. "We can get into the house from there, and nobody will see Yuri. Or you guys, either. Or your car. If anybody's watching."

Jamal nodded. "Never hurts to play it safe."

"I saw no one following us," Sanjay said. "But I agree. Let us proceed with all caution."

Jamal pulled into the driveway, and Phoebe hopped out of the armored SUV and let herself in through the front door. Trouble, their dog, rushed to greet her with all the delight of a valued member of the family who'd been cruelly abandoned for an entire morning. Phoebe bent down to scratch his ears.

"We've got company," she said. "Sanjay and two new friends to pet you."

Trouble gave an approving woof. Phoebe laughed and sped through the light, airy foyer into the kitchen, grabbing the spare car keys on her way, and went out to the garage. She opened the garage door and got into Chase's yellow Venture Automotive electric vehicle, adjusted the seat to accommodate her shorter legs, and edged out onto the driveway, carefully avoiding Jamal's pristine SUV. Her first legal solo drive!

Then she pulled back into the garage, angling the vehicle to one side, and got out, waving Jamal forward into the garage and closing the garage door behind him.

"We're home," she said in Russian, opening the car door for Yuri.

"This is quite the place you have," Sanjay said. "Beautiful."

"If you like the outside, wait till you see the inside," Phoebe said. "I love it."

She turned to Yuri. "I have a dog," she said, pushing open the door to the kitchen. "His name is Trouble, but he's very friendly. He won't bite. Don't let him out."

Trouble danced around them, emitting happy yips as they entered.

"The house suits you, although you seem to be missing a table in here," Sanjay said as he inspected the bright, rambling kitchen with its old, colorful tile and cherrywood cabinets.

"Yeah, the former owner kept the kitchen table and some other stuff. We're coping until we can get replacements. The place needs work, too. I don't mind, but Chase isn't thrilled about that. But he appreciates the craftsmanship, and once it's fixed up, he'll be happy. It's got the six bedrooms he wants, and there's room for a gym in the basement—he likes that. Jamal, if you take the barbecue through that doorway into the dining room, I'll grab silverware and paper towels."

"You said a contractor was scheduled today," Sanjay said, grabbing the glassware Phoebe directed him to. "I had thought when we were driving up that the exterior window framing could benefit from a coat of paint. And other work."

"Six bedrooms?" Jamal said.

"The old place had fifteen, so they've downsized," Sanjay said.

Jamal whistled.

"The old place is a hotel now," Phoebe said. "Long story, not important. Let's eat."

They went into the dining room. Jamal set the takeout cartons on the long, polished table. Phoebe put the paper towel roll in the center of the table and handed out silverware. Sanjay poured the water. Yuri took a seat, and Jamal handed him his meal. Trouble followed them in, looking hopeful.

For the next few minutes, silence reigned while they dug into the food.

"It's delicious," Phoebe said around a mouthful of chicken. "Good find, Sanjay."

Sanjay nodded, tearing off a small piece of his chicken and handing it down to Trouble, who licked it off his fingers. "It is my new favorite place. So what are our plans for this Russian defector?"

"I don't know," Phoebe said. "We were so busy dodging bullets and then calling for help and getting lunch, I haven't formulated a plan."

Sanjay nodded. "Perhaps it would be prudent to call Chase and find out what he thinks. Since a target of international assassination is eating lunch in your beautiful dining room at this very moment."

"Chase doesn't get back from Vegas until Monday," Phoebe said. "I hate to interrupt him when he's busy at the plant. I'll call him tonight and tell him. In the meantime, where can we stash this guy?"

Everyone gazed at Yuri, who had pushed back his take-out carton and was now lolling back in the chair, picking his teeth. He noticed their observation.

"Какие?" he said.

"We're thinking about what to do," Phoebe said to him. "If you have any ideas, let me know."

"I want to get my things from the hotel," he said. "I can't stay there now that the KGB assassins have found me. But I have important documents there, and retrieving them will be dangerous. We shouldn't lose any more time."

She turned back to Jamal and Sanjay. "He wants to get his stuff from his hotel room. But it'll be risky to go back there."

"And then we take him to a different hotel?" Jamal asked.

"He doesn't want to go, and I have to agree that he'd be easy to find. I mean, finding him would be *time-consuming*, but it wouldn't be *complicated*."

"The police?" Sanjay asked.

Yuri glanced up sharply from sucking his finger. "*No poleets!*"

"Makes you wonder if he's done something illegal," Jamal said.

"It sure does," Phoebe said.

"Perhaps he has had an unpleasant experience with the Russian po— members of the constabulary," Sanjay said. "And then consequently he trusts no, ah, law enforcement body of any kind."

Phoebe and Jamal nodded. The three of them finished their meals in silence. Then Sanjay got up and took his and Jamal's empty cartons into the kitchen, returning with the trash bin. Phoebe realized with a sinking heart that she really had only one option for Yuri.

"I guess he can stay here," she said, smashing her own

takeout carton into the bin. "It's only two nights. The basement is finished, there's a bathroom down there, and the windows are small and high up, so he should feel safe enough."

When she straightened, Jamal and Sanjay were watching her. Sanjay's eyes were troubled.

"What?" she said. "I don't have any better ideas."

"I cannot like it," Sanjay said, shaking his head. "You are alone, exposed here, in your beautiful home, to a potential assassination attempt."

"I don't much like it either," Phoebe said. "Questions of safety aside, Yuri's not that much fun. But no one followed us, right? Nobody knows where we are. We're probably safe as long as Yuri doesn't go outside."

"Do you have a weapon in the house?" Jamal asked.

"There's a baseball bat in the cupboard with the sports equipment," Phoebe said. "And Trouble will bark if anybody tries to break in."

"I do not like it that you would be alone with Yuri and only your dog and a bat for protection," Sanjay said. "What do we know about Yuri, after all? He might himself have criminal connections or even disreputable aspirations. The security training that Jamal and I currently are undertaking has instilled in us the ethos that we must do everything we judicially can to protect those who have asked for assistance. I realize that you have not asked for such help. But I am thinking, it might be best if I slept here tonight, as an added layer of safety. If you have room. If you don't mind."

Phoebe had to admit, she didn't like the idea of a trained assassin shooting at her through her living room window, as remote a possibility as she knew that would be. And she didn't relish the thought of staying alone with the Russian defector. Sanjay was kind to offer to stay with her, but she didn't want to inconvenience him. Especially when she knew she'd be fine.

"Thank you, Sanjay, I appreciate that offer," she said. "But it's not necessary. The shooter didn't follow us. And maybe that person wasn't even shooting at Yuri. Maybe somebody was simply expressing a general dissatisfaction of the federal government. With, you know. A firearm."

Sanjay shook his head. "Please do not be making light of this situation. No. Here is my idea. I was planning to be home this evening because there is a televised football game on prime time that should be most interesting, and—"

"Yes!" Jamal said. "The Cowboys play Washington tonight. I've been a Washington fan since I was a kid. My dad has season tickets."

Sanjay nodded. "I was always having season tickets to the Rattlesnakes when I lived in Las Vegas, but Chase isn't there anymore, and now that I have made the move to DC, I feel that I must adopt the home team."

Right. If she needed help tonight, either with Yuri or the international assassins out to murder him, evidently she'd have to place the call during the half.

"So my idea is, we could watch the game here," Sanjay said, more to Jamal than to her. "I will sleep here if Phoebe does not object. And if we experience the slightest feeling of fear or worry in the middle of the night, we call the po— appropriate law enforcement agency."

"*No poleets!*" Yuri said.

"Yeah, yeah," Phoebe said to Yuri in English. "No poleets."

She turned to Sanjay. "You'd think he'd stop listening by now, since he doesn't understand us. But yeah, if you guys want to watch the game here, Chase has a great media setup. You're more than welcome to hang."

"Then I'm in, too," Jamal said. "And if Sanjay stays, I'll stay. If you have room and don't mind, that is."

"Six bedrooms, I think I mentioned," Phoebe said. "There's plenty of room. I can't imagine we'll have any problems, but actually, I would feel better if you both stayed."

"We are decided, then," Sanjay said. "And now, Yuri's hotel. We should be picking up his things."

"I'll go," Jamal said. "You stay here with Phoebe."

"What if they're watching the hotel?" Phoebe asked. "What if they shoot at you? I don't want you to get hurt."

Jamal shrugged. "Why would they shoot me? It's Yuri they want. I think the worst I can expect is kidnapping. And I have to tell you—if I find a bunch of secret documents and some Russian dude puts a gun to my head and tells me to hand them over, I'm handing them over. The feds will just have to figure out the Russian spy network or whatever it is without them."

"Okay," Phoebe said. "That makes sense. But be careful."

She explained the plan to Yuri, and he handed over his room key to Jamal.

"I don't expect any problems," Jamal said at the garage door. "I'll go in, pack up everything I see, and leave the key. No worries."

He backed the armored car out of the garage, and Phoebe and Sanjay watched him drive down the street, then turn the corner and disappear from view.

"So far, so good," Sanjay said.

Vladimir Golubkin, longtime sharpshooter and go-to foot soldier for the Russian security agencies—KGB (former) and FSB, FSO, and SVR (current)—presently on assignment in Washington, DC, glanced up and down the corridor of the modestly priced hotel that housed the attendees of the global conference on technical and scientific data sharing. He saw no one. Surveillance cameras were not in evidence.

He strode down the hall and let himself into Yuri Severov's room. He'd missed killing the would-be defector by a hair's breadth, so the dirtbag was probably off somewhere, drinking his troubles away, as any reasonable Russian would do. He had time.

Getting Severov's room key had been a simple matter—the young weekend clerk had handed him a new one without glancing up from whatever screen was momentarily engaging his attention. It was a miracle that the hotel still had any of its furniture or that any of its guests actually paid for their accommodation. The place had more leaks—security and otherwise—than the *Titanic*.

Inside the room, Vlad slipped on a pair of gloves and closed the drapes. He tossed Severov's suitcase on the unmade bed and scooped up all his clothes—two clean dress shirts; a pair of jeans and two gray T-shirts; underwear, worn and clean; socks and running shoes—and dumped them into it.

When he was done with the clothes, Vlad went into the bathroom and stuffed Severov's toiletries into his shaving kit—his gear and all his lotions and creams as well as the tiny bottles the hotel provided. Then he jammed the shaving kit in the suitcase.

Severov had a couple of books for recreational reading—a thriller and a biography, both in Russian—as well as some scientific magazines and papers and folders he'd picked up from the conference. Vlad put those in the suitcase.

Then he gazed around the room. He turned slowly, wanting to make sure he'd gotten everything. The place was clean. No object that Yuri Severov had owned, used, borrowed, bought, or stolen was still lying out.

But Vlad liked to be thorough. He went to the window ventilation unit, unscrewed the top, checked inside. Nothing. He inspected inside the toilet tank cover and the fan in the bathroom ceiling. He took off the vent cover in the wall over the bed. He unscrewed the switch plates and the outlet covers. He pulled out all the dresser drawers and checked their backs and bottoms. He felt inside the easy chair and underneath the mattress.

Finally satisfied that he'd left nothing behind, Vlad closed the suitcase, dropped the plastic card key on the dresser, and left the room, turning aside as a hotel guest walked by. The whole operation had taken less than fifteen minutes.

The secrets that Severov had stolen were hidden somewhere in his belongings. Vlad did not need to find them. He was not a specialist in data recovery. He was the cleanup and removal man. He'd carry everything back to Moscow, and someone else would figure out what data Severov had stolen and how to make stealing it more difficult for the next potential traitor.

They wouldn't be able to recover all the information that Severov had taken out of the country. Whatever the aspiring defector carried in his head—his passwords, his organizational knowledge—those would stay with him.

That's why it was so important to find him. And kill him.

And that was the job that he still needed to finish.

"Они пришли убить меня!" Yuri screamed later that afternoon in response to pounding on the front door. He tore out of the blue parlor where they'd been sitting and flung himself down the stairs into the basement.

"No one's here to kill you," Phoebe called after him. "It's the contractor."

She went into the foyer, where she saw someone standing on their front porch. And the truck parked in the driveway had a logo that read MORALES CONSTRUCTION, so she was pretty sure they were on safe ground.

"Phoebe Renfrew?" the guy said when she opened the door. "I'm Mateo Morales, the contractor. Chase Bonaventure said you'd take me through the house?"

"Thank you for coming," Phoebe said, picking up the clipboard on the little table by the door. "I've got the checklist right here."

"I can tell you right off the bat that your doorbell isn't working," Mateo said. "I was out here ringing for a while before I realized that."

"It goes in and out," Phoebe said. "Mostly out. We think it's bad wiring. But I wonder why our dog didn't bark?"

Just then, Trouble came trotting downstairs and barked.

"Too late," Phoebe told the dog. "The time for barking was before." She turned to Mateo. "This is Trouble. I mean, that's the dog's name. But don't worry. He won't bite."

"He's very friendly," Mateo said, reaching down to pat Trouble, who squirmed in happiness at the attention. "So where would you like to start?"

"Well, there's something you need to know first," Phoebe said. "We have a Russian defector living temporarily in the basement, and there's an assassin out there somewhere trying to murder him. So, you know, we're all a little on edge."

"Excuse me? Say that again."

She explained the situation. As she'd talked, Sanjay and Jamal had wandered into the foyer, and the men shook hands.

"It sounds crazy, I know," Phoebe said. "We have an appointment Monday afternoon to deliver Yuri to the FBI, so we're hoping this situation will be cleared up by the time your crew starts work. But if not, then you'll have to introduce us and Yuri to each of your crew before they can come into the house. Otherwise, he'll be afraid that the one he doesn't recognize is the assassin out to kill him. Which might be correct. Oh, and he doesn't speak anything but Russian."

Mateo blinked. "Well, as far as that goes, one of my guys is Polish. So we might be able to communicate a little bit, anyway. Will my crew be in danger here from your Russian assassin? I can't take the job, if so."

"I can't say definitively, but we don't think so. We think the assassin wants only the defector. And we believe that he doesn't know that Yuri is here. We're just operating under an excess of caution. And Yuri will be out of here Monday at three."

"Okay, that'll work then," Mateo said. "I'll let the crew know. Chase offered us a bonus if we start on Monday, so maybe we should walk through the house and then you can introduce me to this guy?"

Phoebe beamed. "I can't tell you how much we appreciate this. Dealing with our defector, for one thing. And agreeing to work so quickly. I mean, I love the house the way it is, but there's no question that the electrical is wonky." She flipped the light switch in the foyer and pointed to the wavering light in the sconces. "See?"

"In a house this old, the wiring's got to be knob and tube," Mateo said. "And it's wearing out."

"Don't forget the slow drains," Sanjay said.

"We better get going then," Mateo said. "Lead on."

By the end of the tour, Phoebe's head swam with possibilities, limitations, and variations.

"Chase will be back by Monday, and he'll want to talk to you," she said. "But you can get materials and a crew here by then for the roof?"

Mateo nodded. "Not a problem. And we'll get the electrician lined up, too."

"Great. Let's wait to introduce you to Yuri until then, when your crew will be here."

"Sounds good. Say, maybe I'm off base here, but there's a Chase Bonaventure, he's retired now, the former quarterback for the Las Vegas Rattlesnakes. I'm wondering—"

"That's him," Phoebe said. "This is his house. *Our* house."

"I wondered," Mateo said. "I mean, that playoff game in his last season?"

"Against the Steelers." Phoebe nodded.

"The pass to Dan Freer," Sanjay said.

Mateo shook his head. "Unbelievable. I mean, I'm a Washington fan all the way, but I watch the playoff games."

Sanjay nodded. "Who does not? We were lucky to have had as many years of enjoyment watching him play as we did. The Snakes won't see his like anytime soon."

Mateo laughed. "*The* Chase Bonaventure," he said. "And a Russian defector in the basement with an assassin on his tail. If that don't beat all."

"Well, the defector is my fault," Phoebe said.

"It'll keep things interesting," Mateo said. "See you Monday."

After Mateo left, Phoebe and Sanjay went through the house, trying to make it more secure. They closed and locked all the windows and, later, drew all the curtains. But she worried that anyone walking through the entryway would be visible from the street, because the front door's clear glass panel and the entryway windows didn't have coverings. The leaded panel with its art deco design was beautiful, and if the assassin shot through the door and broke it, she'd be very upset. But of course, if anyone was hurt, that would be a lot worse.

To reduce visibility, Jamal and Sanjay pinned a sheet to the front door and entryway window frames, blocking the view to the inside. The look wasn't pretty, and when she went out to the yard at sunset to check their work, she saw that it also wasn't a perfect solution. When Yuri walked in front of the windows, you could see an indistinct image behind the makeshift curtain. If an assassin spotted her walking around, he might realize that she was too short to be Yuri, but when Chase came back—a wave of fear chilled Phoebe to the bone. Yuri was a few inches shorter than Chase and quite a bit heavier, but from a distance, through a decorative window, behind the sheet, that difference might not be obvious, even to a long-range shooter. *If the assassin shot Chase*—but she couldn't think along those lines.

She had to remember that no one knew where Yuri was. If he stayed indoors—if they all stayed indoors—they'd stay safe.

Jamal had returned from Yuri's hotel without Yuri's suitcase. The room, he reported, had not seen maid service, yet all of Yuri's clothing, toiletries, books, papers, and baggage had been removed. Everything was gone. The room, except for the rumpled sheets, used water glass, and damp towels, was as cold and empty as a Russian czar's still, dead heart.

"No, no, no," Yuri groaned when he heard this news. "Not *everything*. Say it isn't *everything*. Not the *toothpaste?*"

"Everything," Jamal confirmed after Phoebe translated. "Toothpaste, mouthwash, deodorant, shaving cream—everything." He demonstrated as he spoke, pretending to brush his teeth, rinse out his mouth, swab his underarms, lather his face.

Yuri moaned, clearly interpreting the pantomime correctly.

Phoebe sighed. The CIA could have given this Russian defector-in-training a few tips on how to hide data. *In the toiletries* was so last decade. Maybe last *century*.

"So now we are hiding a man who has expectations of defecting to the United States, but has no information to

50

reveal to the American authorities that would make him a valuable asset?" Sanjay asked. "I am not well versed in diplomatic statecraft, but this situation does not seem to be optimal. For any of us."

"It isn't," Phoebe agreed. "If somebody stole everything that Yuri meant to turn over to the FBI, how valuable is he? How much would they want him? But one thing for sure—*I* don't want him. Yuri can't stay here indefinitely. That is *out*."

"He's already missed his flight back to Moscow," Jamal said. "The hotel people told me that the conference is over and everybody went home. It's probably too late to send him back now without exposing him to danger on his return."

"Of course," Phoebe said. "It would be. Just my luck." She turned to Yuri. "Yuri, is *everything* gone? Every bit of intel?"

"Of course not," he said. "I have been thirty years in the spy business. Do I *look* like an idiot?"

Sort of, you do, Phoebe thought, eying the unkempt man in the cheap, wrinkled suit.

"So what *do* you still have?" she asked.

He dug into the torn pocket of his sagging pants and opened his bulging wallet. "I have a thumb drive," he said, pulling out a drive so tiny it could have been built for a Barbie doll computer. "It is small, but it holds more than you'd think. This is what I'd planned to take to the State Department to show them the quality of the data I can provide. And it is what I think the Americans would be most interested in. Communications protocols. Utility grids. Election tampering."

"That does sound like info we'd like to have," Phoebe said.

"Now it is the *only* information I have," he said. "Five years of intel instead of thirty. Plus what I remember." He tapped his head.

"Let's hope that's a lot," Phoebe said.

The situation could be a lot worse, she thought later as she set out towels and a new toothbrush in the basement bathroom for him. Yuri could have been killed or hurt by that shooter, or she could have, or Sanjay. And even though the KGB—or whoever wanted Yuri dead—had gotten into Yuri's room and stripped it, even though they had all the intel that he hadn't carried with him, that didn't mean that they knew where he was now. Obviously not, since no one had shot at them through the windows or sent them poisoned pizza. And no burly strangers had come to the front door under some pretext and tried to muscle their way in.

Meanwhile, Yuri could shower and sleep down here in the basement. There was a foldout couch and even a tiny bit of a kitchenette for snacks. She'd stocked the minifridge with cheese and sausage and beer and put some old sweats of Chase's in the closet for him to wear. Chase's clothes wouldn't fit Yuri that well, but they'd do for now—until Monday, when she could drop him off at the FBI. Then dressing him—and everything else—would become their problem.

She smiled, thinking of Kevin Toth's reaction when he found out that he'd have to go clothes shopping with their latest defector.

Phoebe had already shown Yuri the downstairs space, and he understood before she explained it to him why sleeping underground with no windows was a safer option than sleeping upstairs.

"Upstairs, too many windows," he said, helping her to pull out the sofa bed. "Too easy to shoot inside."

She didn't find that idea particularly reassuring, but at least the assassin didn't want her, Sanjay, or Jamal. He probably was totally focused on Yuri and would leave the rest of them alone. *She hoped.*

Just before sunset, she and Sanjay took Trouble out for a walk. When she and Chase had bought the house, its location directly across from the heavily wooded park had seemed like an ideal a location for exercising the dog. But those same trees would give an assassin a lot of cover. Another problem: park visitors often left their vehicles on the street when they entered the recreation area, so unfamiliar cars in the neighborhood were to be expected. As they walked on the edge of the park, Sanjay and Phoebe checked all the vehicles, looking for anyone who might be surveilling the neighborhood. They saw nothing suspicious. The area seemed clear. If they were lucky, the weekend would be super boring and on Monday they could drop Yuri off at the FBI with no drama.

When they got back from their walk, Phoebe dug into the freezer to see what they might be able to eat without going to the store or ordering a delivery.

"I know Sanjay doesn't eat beef," she said. "Jamal, what about you?"

"I don't eat pork," he said. "Otherwise, I'm good."

"Yuri?" she asked in Russian. "Anything you can't eat?"

"Green crap," he said, making a face.

"You mean like salads?"

"*Especially* salads. Also broccoli. Also anything else that is green."

So basically no matter what she made, somebody couldn't eat it.

"I'll make turkey burgers," she said. "And a salad. Yuri doesn't have to eat it."

When dinner was over and Jamal and Sanjay had cleaned up the kitchen, goading Yuri to help, it was time for the Washington-Cowboys game. Phoebe directed the men to the TV room—even Yuri was an American football fan—and she went upstairs to the master bedroom to call Chase. She was beyond tired. Well, it had been a big day, starting with getting her driver's license, then getting shot at, and now having three houseguests, one of whom was the target of an international assassin.

How much should she tell Chase now? It was a long story, and he'd be home Monday. She didn't want him to worry. Or worse, fly back immediately in a private jet. He'd do that if she asked him to, or even if he thought she needed him. But she wanted the move to DC to be successful for him, and it wouldn't be if he couldn't get his work done in Vegas when he was there.

Or if he paid for a lot of flights on private jets. He was wealthy, but he wasn't a billionaire.

His phone rang four times, and then his voice mail kicked in. Phoebe listened to him on the message, a sharp ache of longing swamping her. She missed him. They hadn't been engaged very long—not more than a few weeks—but already she couldn't imagine living without him. This week-long separation while he was in Vegas for meetings was their first time away from each other since they'd met.

"Hi," she said, doing her best to sound cheerful when the phone beeped at her. "Just checking in. I miss you. I hope everything is going okay back there. Let me know if I should pick you up at the airport, because guess what? Good news! I passed my driver's test."

She paused. Should she say anything more?

"Can't wait to see you," she said. "Love you." She disconnected.

He'd have a bit of a surprise when he met Yuri, but they'd overlap only for a few hours before she could take the Russian to the FBI. And then he'd be out of their lives forever.

Only forty-eight hours to go.

Chapter 4

At seven o'clock on Sunday morning, Chase let himself into his new house, dropped his roller bag, and yanked down the sheet that for some reason was pinned over the door and entryway windows. The handle of the suitcase tangled up in the sheet, knocking over the wooden baseball bat that had been propped up next to the door. Why had Phoebe hung a sheet over the door? And why wasn't this bat in the cupboard downstairs? Somebody could trip over it.

He was glad to be home. He'd missed Phoebe, and when his meetings in Vegas had ended earlier than he'd expected on Saturday, he'd changed his ticket to take the red-eye back to DC. When he landed and got Phoebe's message, he was doubly glad that he had. She'd sounded tired and stressed, not like herself at all. Something was up with her. And knowing her, that could be anything.

Trouble came charging out from the kitchen, wagging his tail and making happy woofy sounds, giving him the long-lost hero's welcome. Chase reached down and scratched his ears.

"Hey, you eating machine," he said. "How's everything here?"

Trouble nuzzled his hand and whined.

"Let's go see what's in the kitchen," he said. "And maybe you'd like to go out."

He took off his jacket, kicked off his shoes, and took the bat with him into the kitchen. Phoebe must have had a party last night—the trash bin was full of takeout containers, and several empty bottles had accumulated in the recycling bin—although he didn't know who she knew in DC other than Sanjay and Nattie Wilkinson, her friend at the CIA. Still, if she was lonely and worried about something, he was glad she'd invited people over. Usually she'd be up by now, so she must be sleeping in.

He felt buoyant. All his meetings back in Vegas had been productive—moving Venture's headquarters to DC was going to pay off big-time. And Phoebe had passed her driving test, too. He decided to surprise her with breakfast in bed. Maybe she'd like that.

He started a pot of coffee and checked the fridge—they had orange juice and eggs, cheese and bread and some cold cuts, so there was plenty. Maybe he could make them mimosas to celebrate. They had a bottle of champagne in the basement, a gift from Amos Glenwethering after they'd signed the sales agreement on the house. He took out the carton of juice and headed for the basement and the wine cellar, taking the bat with him. Might as well put it away while he was down there.

As he descended the stairs, he heard some faint clinking noises in the basement. *Weird.* What was that? They'd bought this old, ramshackle place against his better judgment because Phoebe's face had lit up when she'd walked through the front door. But if the house had mice, or worse—and Amos hadn't told him about that—he'd have something to say about it, no matter how much he liked the old guy.

He entered the open space and—to his shock and fury—saw a tall, disheveled man at the counter by the wet bar and minifridge on the far side of the room. His wispy hair stuck out all over, and even from the back, Chase could see that the man's belly hung over the waistband of what looked like *Chase's own* workout sweats. Had he been *sleeping* here? What *the hell* was this asshole doing in his basement, acting like he *belonged* here?

56

The man turned around. In his hand was a long, sharp knife.

Fear and rage surged through him. A *knife*. Was this guy the reason Phoebe was tired and afraid? Had this guy *hurt* her? Was she upstairs right now, unconscious or cut? Bleeding? *Worse?*

With a roar, Chase charged across the room, baseball bat held high.

"Who are you?" he bellowed. "*Where's Phoebe?*"

"Кто вы?" the man yelled. "Что вы хотите?"

Chase swung the bat but the man leaped away, brandishing the knife, putting the small kitchen island between them. The bat swished through empty air, and the man danced behind the island, keeping as much space between himself and Chase as he could.

"Отойдите от меня, вы убийцы КГБ!" he yelled.

The guy wasn't speaking English. What was he trying to say? Not that it mattered if he'd hurt Phoebe.

The man lunged across the kitchen island, sweeping the knife through the air, trying to slice him through. Chase leaped back. That was *close*. He needed to focus. He had to put this guy out of commission and find Phoebe, see what she needed. God, please not an ambulance. Although an ambulance would be better than an alternative that came to mind.

Chase came around the corner of the island, paying attention, wary now, determined to end this quickly. He held the baseball bat like a home run slugger, waggling it a bit, daring the creep to come for him.

"Try that again," he taunted the guy. "I dare you."

The man weaved back and forth, shifting his weight from one leg to the other. Chase caught the rhythm, feinted to the right when the man shifted left, and caught him off-balance. The guy reached out and stabbed the air with the knife, trying to keep him at bay.

But Chase had seen that coming. Without taking one step closer, he brought the bat down with all the force he could muster across the man's outstretched arm. The lowlife maggot screamed and clutched his arm, falling to the floor and dropping the knife.

Chase stepped up and kicked away the knife. Now what? The guy was hurt, but he wanted to tie him up, secure him for the cops. *Bungee cords in the cupboard with the sports equipment.* That's what he could use. Although the guy didn't seem to have any fight left in him. He just sat there, rocking and wailing, cradling his arm. Didn't seem like he was fixing to run.

Then he heard footsteps pounding down the stairs. And not only one set, either. Several people were coming. He jerked his head up, bringing up the bat again. Who knew how many guys this loser had brought with him?

Chase jumped behind the door, holding the bat high. Three against one, it sounded like. Not good odds. But he had the element of surprise on his side.

The first foot stepped onto the floor of the basement. Chase swung the bat down as hard as he could.

And deflected it just in time to avoid hitting Phoebe, who whirled at the movement and saw him standing there. Her sudden smile brightened the whole room and left him dizzy with relief.

"Chase! You're home!" she said, throwing herself at him. Chase dropped the bat and wrapped his arms around her. *Thank God she was alive.*

He held her a little too tightly as his heart rate slowed to that of, say, a runaway locomotive. Finally he leaned back to peer at her face.

"Are you all right?" he asked, running his hands down her arms and then her back, feeling for injuries, focusing on her responses. "What did this guy do to you?"

"Nothing," she said, burrowing into his chest. "I'm fine. It's all right. I can explain everything."

In the seconds that he realized Phoebe seemed to be in one piece, he became aware that others were standing in the basement. He glanced up.

Sanjay and a guy he didn't know. Looking rumpled. Like they'd slept in their clothes. And been woken abruptly.

"So, *cher*," he said, kissing the top of her head, feeling his adrenaline subside. "Have you been havin' a sleepover while I was gone?"

"Yes," Phoebe said, hugging him. "And you hurt Yuri."

"You *know* this bozo?" But even as he said it, he realized that of course Phoebe knew who the guy was. She'd given him his sweats to wear. Although why this clown was sleeping in the basement on a foldout couch when there were at least three nicer bedrooms upstairs, he had no clue.

"I don't exactly *know* him," Phoebe said. "Let's go upstairs and we'll tell you all about it."

Sanjay cleared his throat. "Chase," he said, sounding diffident. "Good to see you. I'm sure I don't have to tell you—"

"You've been helping Phoebe with whatever's going on around here." Chase nodded. "You and your friend."

"Jamal Moscos." Jamal reached around Phoebe to shake Chase's hand.

"Chase Bonaventure."

Jamal grinned. "Chase Bonaventure. That's a good one." Then the grin faded. "Wait. Chase Bonaventure. Not *the* Chase Bonaventure? The quarterback? Good grief. *Of course,* you're Chase Bonaventure. I mean, Sanjay and Phoebe said *Chase*, and you're from Vegas, but I never thought— I never connected— Oh, my God. *Chase Bonaventure.*"

Chase suppressed a sigh. *Not this again.*

Phoebe leaned back and grinned at him. "I thought you said this kind of thing wouldn't happen in DC."

"Oh, man, I'm sorry to embarrass you, but I'm your biggest fan," Jamal said. "That playoff game against the Steelers—that pass you threw to Dan Freer—I've never seen anything like it, and I've been a football fan—well, mainly a Washington fan—since I was a kid."

Chase laughed. "You've had a hard row to hoe, then."

Jamal grinned back. "No lie."

"Whatever this is all about, I appreciate your staying over, since it seems like you weren't prepared for it."

"No, although we were happy to do it," Sanjay said.

"The situation is rather complex, and I'm thinking that with this development, our problem has worsened, because now we have Yuri here lying on the floor with what I believe is a broken arm, which must be treated."

"Yuri," Chase said. "This guy's name is Yuri?"

"Yes," Phoebe said. "Yuri Severov."

Yuri glanced up and bared his teeth at them. "Ты пытался убить меня."

"Uh, hi." Chase lifted his hand in a wave. "Sorry about the arm."

"Yes, well, he doesn't understand a word you say," Phoebe said. "Except for the *P* word."

"Yeah, don't say that," Jamal said.

"Instead, say *law enforcement* or *constabulary*," Sanjay said. "Or something similar."

"What's the *P* word?" Chase had started to feel like he was trapped in a lunatic asylum. Nothing made sense.

"Think of what word would replace law enforcement or constabulary," Phoebe said.

"You mean *police*?"

"*No poleets!*" Yuri shrieked, staggering to his feet.

"Now you've done it," Phoebe said, turning to Yuri. "No poleets!"

"No poleets!" Sanjay and Jamal echoed, patting the air to reassure him.

Yuri sagged against the tiny kitchen island, moaning. "No poleets," he repeated, whimpering.

"See what we mean?" Phoebe said. "That gets tiresome after a while."

"Yes, and as I mentioned, what do we do now?" Sanjay said. "He needs medical attention."

"I'm missing something here, because otherwise we'd just take him to the hospital, right?" Chase asked. "Or somewhere. Without all this discussion. Is it about insurance?"

"No, although that's a good point," Phoebe said. "He's Russian, so he probably doesn't have insurance. They probably don't need it."

"It is highly doubtful that he would agree to go to a

hospital," Sanjay said. "Insurance or no."

"I wonder if the FBI would do it," Jamal said. "Set the arm, I mean."

"Does the FBI have medical personnel on staff?" Sanjay asked.

"I wouldn't think so," Phoebe said. "Although what do I know about the FBI? I could call Kevin Toth. Maybe he's working on a Sunday. He was working yesterday."

"The FBI?" Chase asked. "Why are we talking about the FBI? And who's Kevin Toth? Why can't we take him to the hospital?"

"Long story," Jamal said.

"Tell it to me," Chase said. "I'm tired, and I'm not following this."

"I'll ask Yuri about the hospital, see what he says," Phoebe said. "Maybe he'll go if the arm hurts bad enough."

She disengaged from his arms and walked over to Yuri, placing a gentle hand on his shoulder and started talking to him in Russian. The conversation got heated, so Chase figured she wasn't making much headway. He might not understand Russian, but he sure did understand body language. And volume.

After a few minutes, she sighed and returned to the little group by the stairs.

"He won't go," she said. "He says he won't be safe there. He wants a different plan. And he's sorry he attacked you with a knife, Chase. He thought you were the assassin."

"It is incomprehensible that he could make that kind of mistake," Sanjay said. "How would you have gained entrance to a secured house and known that he was in the basement?"

"Let's go up," Chase said. "I started coffee, and it should be done by now. I want the background here, and we'll think better after breakfast."

They all trooped upstairs, Yuri leaning against the wall for support.

"I'll get you something for the pain," Phoebe told him, translating for the others. "It won't be much, but it's all we have." She found the acetaminophen bottle and shook out the dosage for Yuri, who chomped the pills down without water.

"This medication is crap," he said. "Like candy. You don't have anything stronger?"

"No," Phoebe said.

"In Russia, every home has prescription pain killers. Percocet. Oxycodone. Good stuff."

"You're not in Russia now." Phoebe put the bottle in the kitchen cabinet. "If you want more, I'm putting it here. Don't take more than twelve pills a day."

"Twelve, twenty, forty." Yuri shrugged. "The outcome is the same. The arm will still hurt."

"Not if we take you to the hospital and get it set."

Yuri shrugged again, and Phoebe turned to the other men in the room, rolling her eyes.

"We can use that as an argument to take him to the hospital." Chase took eggs out of the fridge and broke them into a bowl. "Are you going to tell me what's going on here?"

"Let's get breakfast on the table," Phoebe said as she poured coffee and orange juice. "But if we all stay here for much longer, we'll need to do a big grocery run."

"I could do that," Jamal said, taking silverware out of the drawer while Sanjay sliced bread and put it in the toaster. "I could go in the armored car."

"*Armored car?*" Chase said, his arm halted in midair as he poured the beaten eggs into the hot pan. And why would they all have to stay in his house for much longer? "It's past time you filled me in." He glanced over at Yuri, who stood at the counter and was trying to butter his toast with one hand, moaning the whole time. This guy was Russian, huh? No wonder they lost the Cold War. Guy was a wimp.

"Okay," Phoebe said, reaching over to butter Yuri's toast for him. "Here's what happened."

Breakfast was over by the time she'd finished telling the story, and Chase sat back, horrified by what she'd said. *Someone had shot at them in Sanjay's cab.* Phoebe and San-jay—*Phoebe*—could have been *killed*. Because of this stupid Russian. The sooner they got rid of him, the better. The sooner they called the cops, the better.

"We're taking him to the hospital," he said, pushing back his chair. "They'll take care of him. And then we'll see if they'll keep him overnight. If not, he can go to the po—*local law enforcement* people and spend the night in the cells. And then tomorrow he can take a cab to the FBI. He got himself to the State Department without any trouble."

"He doesn't want to go to the hospital," Phoebe said. "He doesn't feel safe."

"I don't care what he wants. *I* want him out of our house. He makes us a target if anyone's still looking for him, and we don't have the resources or the training to protect ourselves or him. And we can't keep him here with a broken arm."

"It is possible that we are not the target," Sanjay said. "Nothing has happened to us since Jamal picked us up in the parking garage. Perhaps we have lost his pursuers."

"And there might not have been any pursuers," Jamal said. "We're *assuming* somebody was out to kill him. It might have been a random shot. This is DC, after all."

"Well, his stuff *did* disappear from his hotel room," Phoebe said. "*Somebody* was keeping an eye on him. Unless we think a hotel employee ripped him off."

"I'm not worrying about hypotheticals or eventualities," Chase said. "Fixing his arm is our responsibility—or my responsibility, anyway. We're taking him to the hospital, and then we're done. If he refuses to go, there's four of us and one of him. We can *force* him to go."

"He does need to get that arm set." Phoebe started talking to Yuri, probably trying to persuade him to their line of thinking, as Sanjay and Jamal cleared the table.

Chase wanted to shower and change, and he wanted some time to think about what they were up against and what he could do about it. He excused himself to go upstairs, and by the time he came down again a half hour later, Yuri had agreed to go to the hospital.

"I made some calls while the water heated up in the shower," Chase said. "There's an emergency twenty-four-hour alarm place that will be here in fifteen minutes. By the time we get back from the hospital, we'll have alarms on all the doors and windows."

Phoebe's head jerked up. "Are we letting them work in here alone while we take Yuri to the hospital?"

"No. Amos Glenwethering is coming over to babysit the house. He said he'd be here in ten." As he spoke, the doorbell rang. "And I bet that's him now."

They went out to the entryway to answer the bell.

"Happy to help out," Amos said as they ushered him into the foyer. "The nurse is with Sophie, and she's napping anyway. So I was as free as a bird to come over."

He glanced around as Jamal, Sanjay, and Yuri, holding his broken arm across his chest, came into the entryway from the kitchen.

"My," he said, beaming at Phoebe. "You have interesting houseguests already. But I would have expected nothing less."

Chase blinked. What did the old guy mean?

Phoebe had no idea what Amos was talking about. "Excuse me?"

"Well, you *are* Phoebe Renfrew," Amos asked. "If I'm not mistaken, *the* Phoebe Renfrew."

Phoebe felt a surge of—*fear* was not too strong a word—at Amos's statement. What could he possibly know about her?

"I'm *a* Phoebe Renfrew," she said cautiously.

"Of, I think, the CIA," Amos said.

Phoebe gulped. She knew she was too quick to identify herself to others as a CIA officer. The agency frowned on that sort of thing, because employees made good targets for kidnappers, blackmailers, even murderers. But for the most part, Phoebe had found that announcing her employment status worked to her advantage in sticky situations, of which lately she'd had a few. But she'd never told Amos she worked for the agency, and she didn't like it that somehow he knew about it. How did that happen?

"Um," she said.

"CIA." Amos smiled. "I thought so."

"This is an unexpected switch," Chase said.

"Unexpected and unnerving," Phoebe said. "How did you know?"

"Well, I made some assumptions and put it together," Amos said, almost apologetically. "Your name's been in the newspapers, and for so many intriguing things. Only a month or two ago you saved the Secretary of State from a kidnapping attempt."

"It wasn't only me," Phoebe said. "A lot of people helped. Chase especially."

"I remember there was a sports connection." Amos nodded. "I'd wondered about that. And then after that there was something about a data-theft ring. So I got to wondering why a CIA officer would be in Las Vegas."

"Things happened." Phoebe was *not* telling Amos about what had landed her in Vegas. That had not been her finest hour.

"Things tend to do that," Amos said. "And the only reason I could figure for a CIA officer to be in Vegas was that either you were on some top secret, illegal mission, or you were in disgrace."

Phoebe gulped. "Ah."

"I went for disgrace because of that whole Empire State Building thing."

Phoebe felt cold. *How could he know about the Empire State Building fiasco?*

"Jesus," Chase said. "You got that nailed. Who *are* you?"

Amos beamed at them both. "I'm—"

"What's happening? What are you saying?" Yuri whined. "I thought we were going to the hospital. Are we just going to stand around all day? My arm hurts."

"Yuri—" Phoebe started, but Amos had turned and sized up the Russian defector with eyes that were as cold as the Siberian steppes in January.

"You are asking to join a civilized nation," he said in

perfect Russian. "It's time you started acting the part. Respect these kind people, or they will turn you over to the police. Or the American black-ops team. And if they don't, I will. You remember Litvinenko? We can do that, too."

Yuri turned pale and Phoebe felt faint. Amos had seemed like such a nice old guy, but that speech of his scared the living daylights out of her. How *on earth* had he figured out that Yuri was a defector? Other than that he spoke Russian. Yuri was too freaked even to go into his "no poleets" routine.

"I don't even want to know what you said," Chase said, glancing from Phoebe to Yuri.

"Who am I, I think you asked." Amos nodded to Chase. "CIA field officer, Russian division, retired, at your service." Then he smiled at Phoebe. "Hello. From an old spook to a young one. Sorry to scare you."

"It's clear I have a lot to learn," Phoebe said. "American black-ops team?"

"Most of that was bluff," Amos said. "But I'm sorry to say that it might be too late for you to become a field officer. Too many people already know you're CIA."

"I never thought I had the chops for fieldwork."

"I think you're wrong about that, not that I'll be sorry if or when you give up chasing bad guys who carry guns," Chase said. "Thanks for coming, Amos. Now that you're here, let's get this guy to the hospital. We're not expecting trouble, but evidently somebody is after Yuri. And of course, we'd like someone here while the security system is set up to keep an eye on things."

"It's no trouble at all," Amos said.

It took them a couple minutes to fill Amos in about what had happened so far and who everyone was.

"The good news is that if the hospital doesn't keep Yuri overnight, I can take him to the FBI tomorrow," Phoebe said. "So it's only one more day of this, and then it'll be over. He'll be safe and out of our hair."

"The danger will not be over tomorrow," Amos said, "unless this shooter manages to eliminate his target."

Phoebe sighed. "Yeah, I'm kind of hoping that doesn't happen on my watch. I've had enough trouble."

"I entirely see your point," Amos said. "Well. Things are under control here. I have your baseball bat. No unauthorized persons will gain entry to the house. I'm prepared for a four-person team from the security company. I will make sure everything works as advertised before they leave. And now, you better get this... this *defector* to the hospital."

Chase nodded. "I'll feel a lot better when we get rid of this guy."

They said goodbye to Amos and headed out to the garage, where they all poured into the armored car. Jamal got into the driver's seat, and Sanjay rode shotgun again. Phoebe offered to sit in the middle of the back seat because she was the shortest, which meant Chase was smashed up against the door. This SUV wasn't very big. Evidently the manufacturers of armored cars didn't feel the necessity of building for the big-and-tall crowd.

"I'm sorry about everything," Phoebe said softly, leaning into Chase and speaking into his ear. "This isn't the greatest way to move in together. You and me and Yuri, I mean."

"Don't forget Sanjay and Jamal," Chase whispered, smiling briefly. "I've always liked a house party, but I can't say I welcome the danger."

Her pulse kicked up at his smile. She hadn't seen Chase in almost a week, and they hadn't had a private moment since he'd been back. This wasn't exactly how she'd pictured his homecoming.

Her phone trilled from her bag, and she leaned into him to pull out the device. "This better be Kevin Toth telling me he can take Yuri today." She checked the phone's display and then sighed. "But no. It's Mom."

"Better answer," Chase said. "She'll keep calling."

"Don't I know it. Death by a thousand wedding plans. Hi, Mom!"

"Hi, sweetie!" Brenda said. "How are you? Listen, did you get the magazine I sent?"

The latest magazine seemed so long ago now, and she'd

barely looked at it. And she remembered none of it, not that it mattered.

"I got it," Phoebe said, rolling her eyes at Chase. "The one with all the pink sticky notes."

"Well, what did you think? I know you said you're not ready to set a date yet, but it's never too soon to think about what you want. You know that the best venues can book up as much as two or even more years in advance? It can't hurt to make plans now. You can always cancel."

"Not without incurring fees," Phoebe said.

"So I was checking out this place in Mexico," Brenda said. "It's right on the beach. It's a beautiful resort with a—"

"I don't think Mexico, Mom."

"Okay, that's good to know. We can eliminate that one. You never know about Mexico anyway, right? A hurricane might blow in and wreck all the decorations. The photos would be *ruined*. We'd have to take shelter in the tiki bar."

"Aren't the tiki bars in Polynesia?" Phoebe said. "Anyway, I don't want to plan wedding venues right now. I'm kind of busy, and anyway, it's too soon. We don't even have a date yet."

"I know—that's what I'm saying. You can't wait. You want your special day to be *perfect*. And that means *planning*. All right. Here's a beautiful place in Kentucky. It's modeled after a castle, and if we get started now, we could all go to the Kentucky Derby while we're there. Hats! Mint juleps!"

"No," Phoebe said. *Castle?* Her mother wanted a *castle*? Would she never be able to escape the turrets? "No castle in Kentucky for the Derby. Absolutely not. We could all be killed by runaway racehorses. Mom, *I don't want to plan a wedding*."

"I wouldn't mind planning a wedding," Chase said.

"*Do not* gang up on me with my mother," Phoebe hissed.

"Was that Chase?" Brenda asked. "What did he say?"

"Nothing. So listen, Mom, when we get married, which might not be for *years* because I am *not ready yet*, we'll get married in DC. Or maybe Louisiana, where Chase's family lives. There's a lot of them, and it makes sense not to ask them all to travel. So no exotic locations."

"Now we're talking!" Brenda said. "Thank you for the guidelines. I'll start working on those places. Claire will want to help, I know. She's been thinking about colors for the bridesmaids. How does yellow sound?"

"Oh, look!" Phoebe said. "We're almost to the prison. Gotta go. Love you, Mom. Bye!" She disconnected.

"Prison?" Chase asked.

"I thought maybe I could scare her into backing off a little."

"It is my opinion that your mother is not the type of person who would be frightened by the mere mention of an incarceration facility," Sanjay said. "Your mother has great initiative and a willingness to take on the world headfirst."

"Yes, and that's why she's had so many concussions," Phoebe said. "I'm not letting her plan a wedding. With Claire or anyone else."

"Too bad," Chase said. "Would save us a lot of work if all we had to do was show up."

"Don't *start* with me," Phoebe said.

Jamal slowed down and made a right-hand turn. "There's the hospital. We're here."

Chapter 5

Vlad sat in the vinyl-clad, mustard-colored booth of the chain restaurant early on Sunday morning and gazed at the breakfast special he'd ordered, now cooling before him. The food was delicious here, but he was too upset to eat.

First he'd called the airline to change his ticket back to Moscow, a frustrating and time-consuming task, plus he incurred a ton of fees. Then he'd called the Moscow number that automatically encrypted all telecommunications and reported that he'd need more time to complete his mission. The Boss had not taken it well. In fact, the Boss had just about had a hemorrhage because the bullet intended for Yuri Severov had not eliminated him—and as far as Vlad could tell, had not even nicked him. Vlad did not explain that Severov had disappeared, because revealing that key fact served no purpose. As far as the Boss knew, the tracking device that had been secured inside Yuri Severov's jacket before he left Moscow was still in place, revealing his every movement.

Except that it wasn't. And Vlad had no idea where the traitor was.

But Vlad revealed none of that. Instead, he explained only that the target had a bodyguard disguised as a taxicab driver—a bodyguard trained in evasive maneuvers. This bodyguard had a partner, a woman, no doubt also highly trained, so eliminating Severov would be more difficult than other jobs. Further, to maintain mission integrity, both this driver and the partner might also have to be eliminated.

At this point, it was too soon to tell.

The Boss had asked many pointed and insulting questions about Vlad's age, manhood, skills, and devotion to Mother Russia. That worried Vlad, because the repercussions for failure in his line of work were severe. Especially if Severov had already managed to defect. Especially if he'd managed to defect with any data that he'd taken with him.

Vlad had retrieved all of Severov's belongings from his hotel room, so if the stolen data was stored on chips hidden, say, in the toothpaste tube or shaving cream can—a cliché at least from the 1950s but still effective—then all was not lost. At least he'd recovered the data, if not the traitor. The situation was a mess, although not a *total* mess.

But Vlad's confidence had taken a terrible beating. He'd missed his target. *Missed!* The first time ever that he'd failed to execute as ordered. Severov had made a clean getaway.

How could that possibly have happened? Was he losing his touch? Had the winds shifted, sending the bullet slightly off course? Were his eyes failing him? Were his hands not as steady?

Should he think about retiring after this job? He'd been around for a long time. What exactly happened to the old warhorses of the security services when they weren't needed any longer? He realized that he hadn't seen Alyosha Andreyev or Kolya Dedov—former cleaners for the KGB—in months. What had happened to them?

Maybe he knew too much. Maybe they all knew too much.

Vlad shook off that unprofitable line of thought. When he'd pulled the trigger outside the State Department, Severov should have dropped like a felled ox. But somehow, unbelievably, for whatever reason—a shift in the wind, a flaw in the weapon, an itch, Severov's desire to smell the roses—his first shot had gone wide. Upon hearing the soft crack of the suppressed shot, knowing what it meant, Severov had run down the street, braying like a panicked donkey before flinging himself into that damn taxicab and getting clean away. Missing the second shot—missing Severov but not the vehicle—was not as surprising, because it was unplanned and his angle wasn't good. Still.

Plan A had been simple: follow the tracker that was placed in Severov's jacket, and if—*when*—the IT engineer headed into the US State Department, take the shot. If plan A failed, Vlad would go immediately to plan B if there had been a plan B. Which there wasn't, because they had never before needed one.

But Vlad would have a second chance. If Severov wanted asylum, he would have to return to the State Department on Monday. And when that happened, Vlad would not miss again.

Or else.

Staring at his breakfast, Vlad felt the stirrings of resentment. It was true, he had never failed on an assignment before, and missing a target could not be considered one's best work. Still, sometimes things did not go exactly according to plan. Being forced to alter the plan did not mean that the plan was bad or unachievable. In the end, he would succeed, because Yuri Severov could not stay away from the State Department. Monday would work just as well for killing traitors.

A chilling thought occurred to him. What if the State Department had taken steps to protect against random gunfire? Brought in extra security, set up barriers, who knows what? He could not risk failure. His own life depended on it.

He couldn't wait until Monday to kill Severov. He had to act sooner, *immediately*. He must find Severov today and eliminate him wherever he was.

The key was *initiative*.

Cheered by the decision, he regarded his meal with new interest. The breakfast special—the bright sunny-side-up eggs, crisp bacon, golden-brown toast, and endless coffee, all for only four dollars and ninety-nine cents—was a wonderful experience at a rock-bottom price. One that he would never again enjoy if he did not kill Yuri Severov on the next try. He would be in the gulag, eating moldy bread and breaking up rocks. Or worse. He shuddered thinking about it.

The middle-aged waitress, wearing a ruffled, turquoise-checked apron and sensible shoes, stopped by with the coffeepot, looking concerned.

"You all right, hon?" she asked. "Everything okay with your food?"

"Iz good," Vlad said. The breakfast had made him rethink his entire life and occupational choices, but nothing was wrong with the cooking.

She seemed relieved. "More coffee?"

He nodded. The dark brew flowed into his cup, rich and strong. He loved the flavor and the effect this coffee had on him, energizing him both morning and evening. The Americans never charged you for a second cup—or even a third or fourth cup. How could capitalist enterprises afford to give coffee away? He had never understood this business model.

"Let me know if you need anything else." The waitress hustled off to her next customer.

He drank some of the scalding beverage and channeled his thoughts. What kind of professional security organization used such distinctive and poorly built vehicles as that brightly colored taxi? The cab's paint job was attention grabbing, and its windows had blown out from a single shot. Unless perhaps this taxi was some kind of elaborate double-blind trickery that so far had eluded the Russian security analysts back home. He would have to inquire.

The bigger question was: How could he find the traitor? Severov had been wearing the jacket when he leaped into the taxicab, and the needle on the tracker hadn't moved since. Maybe Severov left the jacket in the taxi, or maybe the tracker simply fell out during the defector's escape and was still lodged somewhere in the taxi's upholstery. No matter. When Vlad found the cab, he could discover the name of the driver. And then the driver would tell him where he'd taken Severov.

Even if Severov had discovered the tracker and dropped

it into a sewer, for example, where it now moldered in the murky depths below the street, the brightly colored Fun Fares taxi would be registered through the local taxicab commission. He could always find the driver that way. He had to smile, thinking of how local laws and regulations would deliver his target to him for assassination. That was irony for you.

Either way, the taxi would lead him to Yuri Severov. And this time when he fired his weapon, the bullet would find its mark.

Back in his hotel room, Vlad powered up the electronic tablet that held the monitoring software for Severov's tracking device. It was still throbbing, and it was still in the same place. It hadn't moved now in almost twenty-four hours.

It was time to put the *tracking* into tracking device. He picked up the tablet, grabbed his wallet, phone, and room key, and hefted the sturdy nylon carry-on duffel that held a long-range rifle, semiautomatic handgun, and other tools of his trade. Then he left his room and headed for the lobby.

Today he would find the traitor.

Today the traitor would die.

Phoebe scowled at Chase as they drove back from the hospital. "I can't believe the local constabulary wouldn't take Yuri. They didn't even take *you* seriously, and you're *famous*. What do we pay our taxes for?"

"Not to cramp your argument," Chase said, "but technically we haven't paid *any* taxes here yet."

Phoebe rolled her eyes. "Well, if you want to get all narrow and legalistic about it," she said as Chase grinned.

"The, ah, law officers did seem to have a most cavalier disregard for our safety," Sanjay said. "Their promising to send a patrol car around in the evening, even if such an event actually occurs and was not merely an empty assurance to belay our concerns, is insufficient to suppress criminal activity. And we do have solid evidence that some criminal force is after Yuri."

"Good thing there's us, then," Jamal said. "At least we

have an armored car. I have to call my boss about that, by the way. They let me have it for the weekend, but it's supposed to go back to them tomorrow."

"Can we rent it for a day or two?" Phoebe asked. "And you, too, of course, if that's how it works. I'd like to drive Yuri in this car when we drop him off at the FBI tomorrow afternoon."

"Shouldn't be a problem." Jamal nodded.

The atmosphere in the car was gloomy. Even Yuri's bright pink cast ("Clean break," the doctor had told Chase. "You haven't lost any strength in your passing arm.") failed to lighten the mood.

"I can't believe the cops," Phoebe said, still annoyed. "Did you hear what that one guy said? *We're not a hotel.* As if that's what we wanted!"

"That is basically what we wanted, though," Chase said.

"I am understanding the hospital's reluctance to keep him overnight, however," Sanjay said. "Yuri's diagnosis isn't one of illness. And his injury, while unfortunate, isn't severe enough to require hospitalization."

"No, that's true," Phoebe said. "I get that they want the beds for people who truly need them."

"Damn them," Chase said.

Phoebe laughed. She couldn't help it. "Despite everything, I have to say that I'm enjoying our house party," she said. "It's like one of those British movies, you know? Where the unwelcome guest comes and then doesn't go home."

"I can't believe I'm suggesting that we do a favor for the unwelcome houseguest, but maybe we should stop someplace and get Yuri some clothes," Chase said. "His current options are that wrinkled old suit of his and my old sweats, which don't fit him. And after he's done with them, they won't fit me, either, so I'm in the market for new sweats."

Phoebe grinned. "You're worried that he'll look so disreputable that the FBI won't take him, and we'll be stuck with him forever."

"I'm not worried. I'm terror-stricken. And a discount store is coming up."

Phoebe glanced at Yuri, who had his hand up his shirt again. Did the man have *fleas*? He seemed to have a perpetual itch. She hoped that it was just dry skin. He was without his toiletries, after all.

"Yuri," she said in Russian. "Chase thinks you'd be more comfortable if we got you some clothes that fit you better. Some jeans and a T-shirt or two? What do you think? You can wait in the car with Jamal, so you'll be safe. And maybe while we're in there, we could get you some toiletries you prefer."

"Thank you," Yuri said. "I thought you would never ask. Yes, I will stay in the car."

"We're on," Phoebe said to the group.

An hour later, as they turned into their street, the storage area of the armored car stuffed with shopping bags, Phoebe's phone trilled. *Not her mother again.* Honestly, she could just about—

She checked the display. *Kristin.*

"Hey, girlfriend!" she said, picking up. "How are you? What's up?"

"Phoebe! I'm at your house, and there's an old guy inside who won't let me in!"

"At my house? Really? I had no idea. Sorry about that! The guy is Amos. But—wait for it—we're home."

Jamal pulled into their driveway and Phoebe disconnected. Off to the side, huge stacks of plywood and roofing tiles leaned against the house. And in the front yard, a forlorn-looking Kristin perched on the stoop, a suitcase beside her.

"It's an assassin!" Yuri shrieked.

"It's Kristin!" Phoebe said in Russian.

"In all the excitement, I forgot to tell you," Chase said. "She's moving out here to be VP of operations. At least I hope so. I told her she could stay with us while she checked things out."

"Great!" Phoebe unbuckled her seat belt, climbed over Chase, and hopped out of the car. She ran up the front walk as Jamal drove into the garage, lowering the door behind them.

"Kristin! So glad to see you!" Phoebe said, hugging her friend. "Come into the house right away before anyone shoots us."

"*Shoots* us?" Kristin pulled back, turning her head sharply to inspect the street.

"I'm probably exaggerating," Phoebe said, digging her key out of her messenger bag. "But we're taking precautions."

"Phoebs, what are you talking about? Is it safe to be here? Who are all those people in your car? And a roofing company said they were supposed to drop that stuff off. I signed for it. I hope that was okay."

Phoebe stuck her key into the front door lock. "Oh, thank you," she said, pushing open the door. "Yeah, things have been jumping. We're starting maintenance work on the house. I'm sorry I didn't know you were coming today, or I'd have warned Amos. That's Amos Glenwethering. Former CIA, old school. Don't cross him. He is one tough dude."

"You don't have to tell me. I *know*."

"The driver of the car is Jamal. He's trained to thwart assassins. Totally sweet guy. We were bringing Yuri back from the hospital. Yuri's the assassin's target. He's trying to defect, but it hasn't been easy. Sanjay's here, too. And that's everybody. We're having sort of a weird house party, so you're just in time. Come in! Wait till I show you around! It's a great house."

"*Assassin's target?*" Kristin said, stuck on the critical essentials. "There's an *assassin*?"

"Yeah, but nobody's shot at us for a while now. Come in!"

Kristin hauled her roller bag up the step, and Trouble raced to greet them in the entryway, woofing happily. Kristin reached down to rub his ears.

"At least some things never change," she said. "Hi, Trouble, sweetie. Are you the watchdog?"

"Leave your stuff here for the moment," Phoebe said. "We'll get you settled in a bit. Are you hungry or thirsty? Would you like some lunch?"

An alarm screeched, wailing an earsplitting scream that made speech impossible and hurt Phoebe's eardrums. Trouble howled.

"I guess the alarm's installed," Phoebe said over the noise, shutting the door. "So that's one thing that's going well."

Amos rounded the corner from the sunroom, holding a book, and Chase tore into the entryway.

"Alarms are set," Amos said almost apologetically. He punched in six numbers, and the alarm's horrible shrieking abruptly stopped. "It's on a twenty-second delay; I hope that's not too long. The alarm company said you might also be interested in motion-detection lights or cameras and a video doorbell. They left some literature."

"Good idea," Chase said. "We definitely want that. Kristin, good to see you. Amos, Kristin is my assistant and, I hope, my future vice president of operations."

"I'm sorry about not letting you in, young lady," Amos said. "You can't be too careful with Russian assassins."

"Phoebe said something about assassins," Kristin said, her voice faint. "She left out the part about the Russians."

"Yeah," Chase said. "We've had a little excitement here."

"So I understand," Kristin said. "What with trying to nab the Russian assassins and all."

"We're not trying to *nab* them as much as we're trying to *avoid* them," Phoebe said.

Sanjay and Jamal rushed in from the kitchen.

"Is everything all right?" Sanjay said. "We were momentarily otherwise occupied with unloading the medical supplies and clothing purchases. Kristin! It is most good to see you. This is Jamal."

"Hi, Jamal," Kristin said, shaking hands. "Hi, Sanjay. It's nice to see you, too."

"Chase tells us that you are contemplating or have accepted a promotion at Venture Automotive and are relocating to DC in the near future?" Sanjay asked.

"We have to talk about that," Kristin said to Chase. "I want to get a feel of what you want your vice president of operations to do, but I thought at least I could help you organize the new headquarters. You know, multitask."

"Great," Chase said. "We can start Tuesday on the office. Tomorrow we have to— And here he comes now. The target of rogue Russian assassins and the reason for everything."

Yuri shambled into the entryway, scratching himself. "What's going on out here?" he asked. "I nearly went deaf with that alarm."

"That alarm is installed for your protection," Phoebe said in Russian.

"This is Yuri," she told Kristin. "Our potential defector. He doesn't speak or understand English. An assassin is after him and, by extension, us. We *think*, although we haven't heard from the assassin since yesterday, knock wood. Tomorrow I take Yuri to the FBI for his first debrief. At which point we're done, and he becomes the FBI's problem."

"We're counting on it," Chase said. "Because somebody shot at him yesterday when he jumped in Sanjay's cab with Phoebe after she passed her driving test. Missed by inches."

Kristin's eyes went wide as she glanced around the circle. "Seriously, I think my head is about to explode. Phoebs, you're all right?"

Phoebe nodded. "The only damage is to Sanjay's taxi. Did you catch the part where I got my drivers license?"

"I think I did," Kristin said. "Congratulations!"

"Thank you," Phoebe said. "We'll have to celebrate later."

"It's a lot to unpack," Jamal said. "We have an armored car now, that's where I come in. It'll be an asset if the shooter tries that again."

Kristin glanced at Yuri, who was digging his finger inside his bright pink cast, scratching his arm. His stomach was exposed by Chase's sweatshirt and sweatpants not meeting across his middle.

"It's kind of hard to imagine that the FBI wants this guy," she said.

Phoebe nodded. "My feelings exactly. But then again, it's the FBI. Who knows what they're thinking half the time."

"What happened to his arm?"

"It got broken," Phoebe said. "Mainly because Chase hit him with a baseball bat. It was an accident."

"Okaaaay," Kristin said. "I think the less I know about that, the better. So, the Russian assassin. Did you guys call the police?"

"*No poleets!*" Yuri shouted.

Startled, Kristin jumped back, tripping over her suitcase.

Jamal reached out a hand to steady her. "Just what we don't need: another injury."

"No poleets!" Sanjay told Yuri. "It is completely unnecessary to raise your voice to such tremendous volume every time you hear a syllable that sounds like your greatest nightmare."

"He didn't understand a word of that, you know." Phoebe turned to the defector and switched to Russian. "Yuri, stop acting like an idiot."

"Sorry about that," Jamal said to Kristin. "Yuri has a thing about the *P* word—don't say it—but we forgot to warn you. Are you hurt?"

Kristin rolled her shoulders. "Just surprised is all. What's the *P* word?"

"P-o-l-i-c-e," Jamal said. "Don't say it. Say *constabulary* or *law enforcement*. Something like that."

"Seriously?"

Jamal grinned. "You heard him. Seriously."

"That's just weird," Kristin said.

"Yuri seems to be hyperaware of the possibilities for danger," Sanjay said. "That can only benefit us in our efforts to stay safe until we can deliver him to the FBI as promised."

"There's that," Kristin said. "Listen, guys, I hate to be the party pooper here, but that red-eye was a killer, and now I've walked into an assassin's target zone. Phoebe, can you show me where I'm supposed to sleep? I need a nap, but I'd like to catch you up on some stuff first. You too, Coach.

Maybe a little later?"

Chase nodded. "I need to catch a few z's too. I didn't sleep on my red-eye, either. That seems like centuries ago, and it was only last night. *Cher*, before you go, could you tell this Russian numbskull that he's got no reason to bellow *no poleets* every two seconds? The only people we're worried about around here are the *assassins*. If the po— constabulary want to come, that's fine."

"I'd be happy to do that," Amos said, looking cheery.

"Have at it," Chase said. "Be forceful. Use threats. Spare nothing."

"No worries on that front," Amos said.

"Well, then," Sanjay said. "While Phoebe and Kristin talk, Amos terrorizes Yuri, and Chase rests, everyone should be assured that Jamal and I will be keeping our eyes open for the aforementioned Russian assassins."

"And making sandwiches," Jamal said. "Because it's lunchtime."

Vlad flagged down a cab outside his hotel. He disliked leaving paper trails of his movements, but the location of the Fun Fare taxi was too far to walk, he didn't have a car, and he didn't want to waste time figuring out the bus system. And leaving a paper trail was not a problem, because he wouldn't get caught.

"Where to?" the driver asked.

Vlad consulted the tablet for street names. The blue button still throbbed on the map, illuminating the neighborhood.

"Georgetown." He asked the cabbie to drop him a couple of blocks from where the blue dot had settled. That turned out to be a big parking garage, but despite the structure's size, he found the shattered cab easily. The vehicle was a mess. Both windows were blown out, and glass was everywhere on the seats. Vlad didn't see any blood. So that answered one question.

The cab driver's photo, taxi identification, and registration number were laminated to the visor. *Sanjay Agarwal*. This was a real break, the first bit of luck he'd had since he'd arrived in DC.

He ripped out the ID and checked the glove box. Maybe there'd be some kind of identification or other information for the accomplice, the woman passenger. But there his luck ran out. The glove box was empty.

He typed "Sanjay Agarwal, DC cab driver" into the tablet's search engine, and in a split second he got dozens of results. As he scrolled through the information, most of it usclcss, hc saw that thc namc Sanjay Agarwal was occasionally linked to a woman, Phoebe Renfrew, although this pairing occurred in news stories about events that had happened in Las Vegas. Maybe they were a crack security team carrying out secret assignments around the country for the US government. Or they might be ex-military specialists working freelance.

Whoever they were, this pair—Sanjay Agarwal and his assistant, Phoebe Renfrew—were the people he wanted.

Now all he had to do was track them down. Unfortunately, many Americans—especially those in the financial, military, or data storage services industries—held unreasonable prejudices against Russian accents. He doubted that anyone at the cab registry would reveal Agarwal's home or even business address, no matter how convincing a reason he presented.

So he relied on email.

Before he left Moscow, Russian IT engineers had created email account aliases for him that looked remarkably like American FBI email addresses. These accounts could be very helpful. People tended to cooperate with the FBI. Not always, of course. But often enough.

He emailed the Washington, DC, taxicab commission from his fake FBI account, asking for Sanjay Agarwal's home address. While he waited for a response, he searched the online white and yellow pages, business license and gun permit applications, and real estate records. Nothing for Sanjay Agarwal, but in a remarkably short time, he had an answer from the commission.

We are always happy to cooperate with federal law

enforcement agencies, they wrote, attaching the information he needed.

Vlad shook his head as he searched a Google map for the address. *Idiots.* No one should ever release that kind of information without better verification. Or perhaps a search warrant? He was unclear on the finer points of American jurisprudence. He'd never had to pay any attention to that kind of thing.

Google's street view showed that Sanjay Agarwal lived in an unassuming four-unit apartment building not far from the National Mall. Time to find out where Yuri Severov had gone—and what exactly Sanjay Agarwal and Phoebe Renfrew knew.

Chapter 6

Phoebe thought Kristin was holding up well given her exhaustion, but she was looking drained. Well, she'd had a long flight and then a lot to process.

"Let's go up, Kristin," she said. "You have accommodations to choose."

Chase hoisted Kristin's suitcase and led the way up the stairs. Phoebe followed, turning her head to talk.

"Sanjay and Jamal each have a room, but Yuri's in the basement, so there are three bedrooms left up here that you can have," she said. "This first one's smaller, but it has a little private parlor that's nice, and the bathroom is adjoining. Come see."

"It's perfect," Kristin said, stopping at the bright, airy room at the top of the stairs. "I'll take it."

Chase set Kristin's suitcase next to the dresser. "I'll leave you guys to it. Get some rest, Kristin. We'll talk later."

"Thanks, Coach."

"We'd been house hunting for what felt like forever, checking out all these awful places," Phoebe said as she took towels from the linen closet and carried them into Kristin's bath. "And then we found this one by accident. It needs some work, but I love it. So what's up? How are you really?"

Kristin's shoulders sagged as she dropped her purse on the chair by the door and slumped onto the bed.

"Everything's a mess, and I don't know what to do."

Phoebe closed the door to the hallway and gave Kristin a hug. "Come into your parlor and tell me all about it."

The small parlor was just big enough for two comfortable chairs, a side table, and a strong reading lamp. The longest wall had a small fireplace, beautifully tiled in a deep green with copper trim.

"Oh!" Kristin said. "My own fireplace! Phoebe, this house is wonderful."

"Thank you," Phoebe said. "I could not be happier about it. Now tell me."

"It's Nick." Kristin sank into one of the chairs and drew up her knees. "He won't— He doesn't—" She stopped to sniff. "*Dammit*. I swore I wouldn't cry."

"You can cry. What did he do? Do I have to kill him? Remember, I work for the CIA. I can arrange it. Hold on a sec. I think there's tissues in the bathroom." Phoebe jumped up and zipped into the bathroom as Kristin snorted through her tears.

"Now tell me what the rat bastard did," Phoebe said when she returned, putting the box near Kristin's elbow.

"Thanks." Kristin ripped a couple of tissues from the box. "How much do you already know? Does Coach tell you stuff about the factory?"

Everyone at Venture Automotive's manufacturing plant in Las Vegas called Chase Coach because of his football career with the Rattlesnakes. Most of the employees had been fans of the team—and its quarterback—long before Chase invested in the nearly defunct factory.

"He tells me some things," Phoebe said. "Not a lot."

"Well, when he decided to move the company headquarters out here to DC, he offered big promotions to all his department heads back in Vegas. Me too, even though I'm not a department head, unless you called my department 'Chase Bonaventure.'"

"You've always been way more than Chase's admin," Phoebe said. "You've kept the whole place on track since you started there. So now you'll be vice president of operations? I think that's what he said."

Kristin nodded. "That's what he offered me. It's way more than I expected. It's a tremendous opportunity with a huge increase in salary." She looked bleak.

"So what's wrong? Don't tell me you don't feel up to the challenge. Because I know you are."

"I'm not even sure what a vice president of operations *does*, so I am a little nervous about it. But I want that job, and I'd work superhard because I don't want to let Coach down."

"I'm not seeing what the problem is, then. Nick's still Venture Automotive's main data security guy, right? Didn't Chase offer him a promotion, too?"

"Yes. But Nick declined it."

"He *declined* it?"

Kristin nodded. "Yeah. Coach wants the VP of data security to be located here in DC, but Nick wants to stay in Vegas. He's got a lot of family back there, and he rides dune buggies and stuff like that in the desert on weekends with his brothers. So he won't move east."

"Seriously? He won't accept a huge promotion because he wants to ride *dune buggies*?"

Kristin nodded. "Basically, I think he doesn't want the responsibility of being VP. He doesn't want to be a manager."

"Okay, so he'd be in Vegas doing his thing, and you'd be here in DC being VP of operations. Did you guys talk about trying a long-distance relationship? At least until you figure something else out?" Phoebe wasn't blind to the problems of that. The logistical nightmare of managing a cross-country relationship was exactly why Venture Automotive's headquarters were now located in DC, while the manufacturing plant was still in Vegas. Phoebe's CIA job required her to work in DC; Chase had moved the company headquarters here so they didn't have to be separated.

"That's the thing!" Kristin said, leaning forward. "It doesn't have to be long-distance! Coach said I could be VP of operations from *Vegas*."

Phoebe blinked. "I *really* don't understand, then. If

you're both in Vegas, what's the problem?"

"Income disparity, for one thing, if you can believe that." Kristin thunked her head back against her chair. "I told Nick how much I'd be making and what I thought we should do with the money. You know—increase savings, buy a house, like that. And I'd *really* like to take a nice vacation, maybe to a place where I need a passport. I thought that trip could be a honeymoon. I love him, and he loves me. It feels like the right time to get married. So I said that."

Phoebe was happy to hear that when the right time came to get married, a person would know it. At the moment, she herself had no clue about when was a good time to tie the knot. "What was his reaction?"

"Not good." Kristin turned her head to face Phoebe. "He doesn't want to think about it, and he certainly doesn't want to talk about it. Not a long vacation, not marriage, not my promotion, not his promotion, not what to do with the extra money. *None* of it."

Phoebe frowned. "Why not? You'll have the job, you'll have the money, you have to decide what to do with it."

Kristin sighed. "Nick's a modern guy, you know? He thinks men and women should be paid the same for the same work."

"Of course."

"But deep down he's got a thing about earning less money than I do. Which would happen if I accept this promotion, since he declined his. Isn't that stupid? Wives have been earning less than husbands for *centuries*, and you don't see *us* bitching about it, do you?"

"Well, yeah, sort of, you do."

Kristin brushed her hand through the air impatiently, dismissing Phoebe's objections as mere trifles. "What if something happened and I couldn't work? Then he'd be the primary earner again. That's the give and take of marriage. I love *him*, not his *job*, not his *income*. And I thought he loved me, too, for *me*, and not in part because I earn less than he does. I can't believe that he's still living in the freaking *Dark Ages*."

She finished by thumping her fist on the arm of the chair. Her voice had risen while she talked, too, and now she looked like a warrior. A heartbroken warrior, but still.

"I'm so sorry that—"

"I'm in a lose-lose situation," Kristin said. "If I *don't* take the promotion so as to… to allay Nick's fears about what the job change could do to our relationship, I could keep my job as Coach's assistant. But then I'd *have* to move to DC, because Coach needs an assistant where he is. And if I'm here and Nick's there, where does that leave us in relationship land?"

"Been there, bought the T-shirt."

"If I *do* take the promotion, I could stay in Vegas," Kristin said. "But Nick doesn't want me to take the promotion. So that's not a better option."

"I don't see a good solution." Phoebe frowned. "Except to find another job."

"*I want that promotion.* I want the challenge. And I want to keep working for Coach. He's a great boss."

"He wants you to stay, too."

"I love Nick," Kristin said. "But here's something else I didn't know until this week: If somebody says, *I sort of want to get married*, and the other person says, *I sort of don't*, then you really can't go on the way you have been, can you? The line's been drawn. You might as well break up and get it over with." Kristin's warrior pose deserted her and she slumped in the chair, looking sad again.

Phoebe leaned forward and squeezed her hand. "I hope it doesn't come to that," she said. "But if it does, I guess the thing to know is that he isn't the right guy for you. Or he was the right guy two years ago, but he's not the right guy for you now."

Kristin blew her nose. "And he won't talk about it. It's up to me, he says. What kind of partnership is that? So that's what's going on with me."

A knock sounded on the door, and Phoebe got up and went through the bedroom to answer it.

"Room service," Jamal said, handing her a tray of

sandwiches and a bottle of wine. He glanced behind her to Kristin, who'd followed Phoebe to the door.

Kristin took the wine from the tray.

"Dump the creep," he told her.

"You were *listening*?" Phoebe said, horrified.

"No," Jamal said. "I have no idea what you were talking about. But I have sisters. My mother tells them, whenever a woman weeps, it's always about a man. Usually a worthless man. Actually, she tells me that, too."

Kristin glanced up from uncorking the wine. "I'd like to meet your mother."

Jamal nodded. "That can be arranged."

After lunch with Kristin, Phoebe went down to the bedroom she shared with Chase. He'd been back for more than half a day, and so far, they hadn't had a minute to themselves.

Chase was asleep on the bed, his back to her. He was beautiful, strong and lithe, even with his bad knee. She almost couldn't believe how he'd muscled his way into her heart, a place that, until she met him, she'd thought was closed for business. And now, here she was. Engaged. Living with him in this beautiful house.

She kicked off her shoes and pulled off her T-shirt and jeans. Then she slid under the sheet with him and eased up against his back, careful not to wake him, reveling in his warmth and closeness, feeling secure.

But either Chase hadn't been asleep or she'd woken him after all. Without turning around, he reached behind and took her hand, tugging her arm around him and snugging it against his chest.

"There you are." His voice was as warm and thick as honey, slow and full of burrs, a sleepy sound. "I was waiting for you."

She bumped her forehead gently against his shoulder. "I missed you. Go back to sleep."

"Why would I want to do that? Now that you're here, I've got other ideas."

He rolled over, tangling his legs with hers, keeping her

arm around him. Then he smiled a lazy, sleepy smile and kissed her.

She sighed in pleasure against his mouth, feeling the hum that started low in her belly and ran down to her toes and out through her arms. The energy made her feel light and strong, supple. She brushed her lips softly against his, relaxing into the strength of his body, tasting the mintiness of his breath. His kisses were like butterflies, a series of soft, light touches, brushing her lips and the edges of her mouth and warming her through.

Time stood still while she reconnected and recharged, absorbing his touch, his energy, feeling their bonds strengthen and her spirit renew. This was not a day that they could spend only with each other, but she could focus on this moment, this instant, when he was all hers and she was all his, and everything they wanted to say and everything they meant to each other could be communicated by the touch of their lips and fingers, by their soft breath and exploring hands.

"This is a nice wake-up call," Chase said, nibbling her ear.

"I didn't mean to wake you." She ran her hands down his back, enjoying the feel of coiled strength. For a guy as big and strong as Chase, his skin was incredibly soft. Well, his chin was a little bristly now, but that was fun, too. His tastes and textures made time slow down and her heart speed up.

"I'm glad you did." He trailed a hot row of kisses down her neck to her collarbone, then edged aside the shoulder strap of her bra to continue down the smooth skin of her arm. The slight rasp of that chin sent little shivers down her spine. "This is better than sleeping anyway. And I wasn't feeling all that restful."

"I'm not feeling all that restful *now*."

Chase laughed and unhooked Phoebe's bra, shoving it to the floor. "Rest is overrated."

An hour or two later, Chase lay on his back, legs tangled in the sheet, feeling sleepy again. Phoebe was dozing, her head was cradled on his shoulder, and she'd thrown her arm across his chest. The bright sun, dappled through the lace curtains, illuminated dust motes floating lazily in the warm air. He felt in tune with the dust motes—lazy, relaxed, drifting. Life didn't get any better than this.

Unless it included a HEPA filter on the HVAC unit. He'd have to check into it now that Mateo Morales was ready to start work tomorrow.

"Mmmm?" Phoebe said, not moving.

He kissed her. "This is nice. It's good to be home."

"Mmmm."

He thought that was agreement.

It was weird. At this time not that long ago, he'd have been suited up for a game, working at the only job he'd ever known. He'd have talked to the guys in the locker room, met with the coaches, and warmed up before going out onto the field and playing his best, like he'd done every Sunday in the fall for more than a decade. But then he'd taken that hit in the Super Bowl, and he was finished with football. *Boom*. One bad tackle, just like that, and it was all over.

Did he miss football? Absolutely. He missed his teammates. The camaraderie of the locker room. The strategy sessions with the coaches. The roar of the crowd after a successful play. The euphoria after a hard-fought win. The determination after a bitter loss. And the money had been ridiculous.

But that hit had brought home to him how suddenly and unexpectedly life could change. He appreciated things more now. He was better at rolling with the punches.

And life after football had brought him nothing but good things. His new business, for one thing. Turning a failing electric-car company into a successful operation was a daily challenge, the kind of challenge he enjoyed. And now Venture Automotive, still a young organization with plenty of room for growth, was doing great. Back in Vegas, good people were taking on more responsibilities. And moving the headquarters to the East Coast had opened up all kinds of business opportunities.

The move was due entirely to Phoebe, who'd needed to relocate to DC. He loved her—her stubbornness and independence, her humor, her courage, her energy, and her brains—even though she drove him crazy sometimes. But they were solid, despite not having been together that long. He *knew* they were meant for each other. And he thought she felt that, too.

He wouldn't give up his current life for all the Super Bowl rings in the world.

That reminded him of what he'd wanted to ask her. "My mom called a while ago. Did Brenda say anything to you about, I don't know, anything? Anything wedding related that I should know about?"

Beside him, Phoebe tensed and lifted her head from his shoulder like a hunting retriever on high alert. Damn, he shouldn't have brought that up now. He just wanted to marry Phoebe and get on with things. Phoebe, he knew, wasn't on the same page. He couldn't blame her. They'd known each other only a few months, and he'd married his first wife after an acquaintance so brief the ink had barely dried on the prenup. And then they'd divorced nearly as fast. So Phoebe wanted to wait to be sure that their—*his*—feelings would last.

And she didn't want to repeat the mistakes of her mother—a woman who'd loved too often, too briefly, and not well enough, behavior that had damaged her prospects for building a better life for herself and her daughter and put Phoebe at risk growing up. Brenda had often disappeared for months at a time with whatever new guy caught her fancy, farming Phoebe out since her infancy to the immigrant families in their Brooklyn apartment building for long-term babysitting. Maybe if those families had had less fear of the authorities, they'd have called Child Protective Services. Instead, they took care of Phoebe as well as their own children. And she learned their native languages as well and as quickly as she absorbed English, making her a great language analyst at the CIA.

Chase would have had a much harder time forgiving

Brenda for her lousy parenting had Phoebe not emerged from the experience strong and confident, if overly cautious about making a legal commitment to him on top of the emotional one. But he believed that Phoebe loved him as much as he loved her, so he was fine to give her all the time she wanted if that's what it took to get her to the altar eventually. But the constant buzz of well-intentioned wedding plans from both their mothers made her angry.

He'd had plenty of experience fighting off three-hundred-pound linebackers on the playing field, so he thought he could hold off his mom and a slightly wacko future mother-in-law until Phoebe settled into the idea. Especially if it meant that when Phoebe did finally walk down the aisle, she'd be enthusiastic about it. Right now, she wasn't.

"I haven't talked to Mom since this morning, and you were there for it," she said, frowning. "What did Claire say? What should have happened?"

He laid his hand against the side of her head and gently urged her back to his shoulder. "I don't know. Mom got cut off. Something about Brenda and traveling. I'm sure it's nothing."

"You heard me tell Mom this morning that the wedding has to be in DC or Louisiana," Phoebe said, fuming. "I hate the way our moms—well, *my* mom—is pressuring us. Pressuring *me*. Because you'd said I could have all the time I needed, and—"

"Relax, okay? It's our wedding; we can do what we like. Including never having it, if that's what you want."

Phoebe reared up, propping herself on one arm, and leaned into his face. "*Wait*. Are you having second thoughts?"

He only had to tip his chin up a little bit to kiss her, so he did.

"Nope, never, I'm in two hundred percent," he said, settling back. "I'll be at the altar whenever you give me the go sign. But it's been a long week, and Kristin is a bit of a wreck, which is a first, and I got home and found out that we're engulfed in international intrigue *and* a house party, so I'm feeling a little disoriented."

"I'm with you there." Phoebe flopped back against the pillow. "So let's keep the wedding date elusive. And speaking of elusive, what's the budget for sheets and towels?"

"We're going from wedding plans to sheets and towels?"

"Yes, because I don't want to talk about wedding plans, and Kristin's got the last set of sheets and towels. So if anybody else comes to stay, they'll be wrapping up in sleeping bags. If we had sleeping bags."

Chase laughed. "There's not really a budget. Let's set up a housekeeping account, and then we can buy what we need when we need it."

"Okay, but we have to have a serious talk about money, too, because I don't know how much we have earmarked for anything, and I don't want to go over budget when we're just starting out."

"*Cher*, you don't have to worry about going over budget. Not for sheets and towels, anyway."

"Don't you think we need to know where the money goes? Officially, I mean. Now that there's two of us. I don't want to be in the dark. What if a hacker steals it when we're not paying attention? A rogue Steelers fan, say. Somebody with banker's credentials."

"I don't think there are any rogue Steelers fans with banking credentials who are out to hack our bank accounts."

"What if you want to fund a charity? Or you decide to abandon everything to live on a tropical island and eat pineapple? We need to know what's in the retirement account."

He laughed. "Not gonna happen, *cher*. Pineapple gives me a rash."

She scowled. "But *we need a budget*. Even if we change it, we should start out with financial goals and parameters. Did you know that the single biggest reason people get divorced is disagreements about money? And we are *not* getting divorced because of money. That's *stupid*."

"We're not even married yet, and already you're planning the divorce?"

"I'm *not* planning it," Phoebe said, huffing in indignation. "I'm not *ever* divorcing you—that's my *point*. Unless you take up with a pack of cheap floozies, then all bets are off. That's why I want to wait to get *married*. To get stuff figured out ahead of time. *Like the money*."

Chase laughed and reached out for her hand. Really, sometimes she was too easy to tease. "I'm just messin' with you now. We're not gettin' divorced over money, *cher*, or any other reason, especially not cheap floozies. Although I would think that if we were going the floozy route, you'd appreciate a cheap one."

Phoebe gazed at him, he thought, a bit like an exasperated farmer might look at a nonproducing cow. Give the beast another week to show some interest, or send it to the glue factory? Which should it be? Argue some more, or take him at his word?

He grinned at her. "We'll set up a budget as soon as you get your first paycheck, okay? You're getting a raise. When we know for sure exactly what that is, we'll figure out who puts how much where. How's that?"

"Okay. That's better. But I hope you're taking our budgeting seriously. I need it, even if you think you don't. Or even if you actually don't. But of course, I think otherwise."

"I know." And he did, even though he enjoyed giving her a hard time about it. Budgeting every dollar tighter than a size-two corset on a size-twelve church lady was the only reason she and her mom had stayed solvent in her childhood. However, those days were over, and he was determined to show her that.

She did a happy little squiggle next to him. That felt pretty good, so he took a few minutes to appreciate it. Even so, and as happy as he was to be home and see her, that red-eye had taken its toll on his sleep rhythms. He couldn't prevent a yawn escaping.

"Go back to sleep," she said, getting up and pulling the sheet over him. "I'll check on things downstairs. I'll wake you if anything happens."

That would give him about ten minutes of shut-eye, then. He'd take it.

Because with Phoebe, things happened.

Chapter 7

Vlad stood on the sidewalk across the street from the small, unassuming apartment building where Sanjay Agarwal lived, looking around. Since he'd arrived ten minutes ago, no one had entered or left the building by the front door, which had no obvious security. No locked gates, no doorman, no lobby, no exterior cameras.

He didn't want to linger out here any longer, making himself noticeable. He shouldered the black duffel bag of weaponry, crossed the shady thoroughfare, and checked out the mailboxes. Agarwal's was apartment number three.

The front door, a sheet of heavy glass framed in solid oak, was locked. He went around to the alley and checked the back door. Also locked.

A few people wandered around back here in the alley, but people who roamed alleys were less likely to question surreptitious activity that didn't concern them, so he unzipped the duffel, took out his lockpick set, and started to work. The lock was sturdy but not particularly complex, and he had it open in less than a minute. He entered the building and went up.

He didn't hear anything as he climbed the stairs: no music, crying kids, vacuums, or any other sounds of occupation. The tenants must all be at work. That simplified matters.

"Zuper," he called out, knocking on the door of apartment three. Apartments always had some kind of problem that needed fixing. If Agarwal was home, he'd open the door.

No one responded, and Vlad was inside in a matter of seconds.

The tidy apartment was sparsely furnished with unmatched thrift store pieces. A big television, the most expensive item in the room, filled one wall. A scarred maple desk had pride of place in front of the picture window, and on it rested a sleek laptop. That was where he'd be most likely to find an address book, files, records—something that would reveal the relationship that Sanjay Agarwal had with Yuri Severov. Because Severov had not leaped into Agarwal's cab by coincidence. Severov had planned this escape and must have hired Agarwal on the basis of his training in protective driving. So Agarwal might have a record of *something*—where Severov was, planned to go, or needed to be. Something that Vlad could use to find the traitor.

He opened the laptop and turned it on. At the password prompt, he dug out the taxi registration and ID he'd found in the Fun Fares cab and wasted a few minutes trying combinations of letters and numbers, but nothing unlocked the computer.

He had to let it go. He wasn't a computer expert. To get this thing open, he'd need a lot of time and help from the specialists back in Moscow, and in this operation, time was a scarce commodity. Today was Sunday. Tomorrow Severov would return to the State Department to request asylum. Vlad wanted to kill the defector today, when Severov would least expect it. That's what the Boss would expect. That's what he *required*.

Vlad turned off the computer and sifted through a small heap of paper stacked next to the machine. Hope flared when he found an envelope with a local address and the name "Phoebe" written on the back. Surely this was the Phoebe Renfrew who was linked to Agarwal in the newspaper articles. How many people named Phoebe could one cab driver know?

This was the address of the accomplice. Work or home,

he didn't know, but either way, he would find her, and she would lead him to Severov. Because clearly Agarwal and Renfrew were hiding the defector somewhere. He'd checked out of his hotel, and according to the IT support staff in Moscow, he hadn't checked in anywhere else.

But even if Moscow didn't know where the traitor was, Agarwal and Renfrew would.

Nothing else in the desk pointed to his quarry. Vlad searched Agarwal's bedroom, too, turning out the pockets of his clothes and checking the dresser and nightstand. Nothing.

Vlad left the apartment, locking the door behind him, and typed Renfrew's address into his tablet. Within seconds, a blue dot throbbed on the map. The place wasn't very far: only about five miles from where he stood.

He hadn't rented a car when he'd arrived in the States because paperwork, even falsified paperwork, made identification or capture more likely. Now, however, he wished he had better transportation options, because five miles was a long way to walk in dress shoes on a hot, humid afternoon with a heavy, awkward bag of high-powered weaponry. But he felt edgy about leaving a paper trail of his movements with registered private drivers. No more cabs for him. No Uber. No Lyft. He'd already been in DC too long, and he needed to remain as invisible as possible. Trips in hired cars—especially trips that ended in assassinations—could be traced too easily.

He hoisted the weighty nylon bag of guns and tools and walked down the street to the bus stop. Buses were full of commuters as well as the lost and forlorn. No one would pay him any attention. And he'd be at Renfrew's place in a matter of minutes.

After that, finding Severov would be child's play.

"Jamal and I have been discussing some contingencies," Sanjay said to Phoebe when she got down to the kitchen.

The two men leaned against the kitchen counter, holding steaming mugs. The rich aroma of Jamal's coffee mingled with the scent of cardamom from Sanjay's favorite tea, which he liked sweet and milky.

"Contingencies? Such as?" She poured herself a cup of coffee. She'd had wine with Kristin, but she didn't want to get too relaxed. Not with a Russian assassin lurking out there somewhere.

"I must at some point soon rescue my taxi from the parking garage where we abandoned it," Sanjay said. "It has been sitting there for more than twenty-four hours. The weekend offers considerable rate reductions, but tomorrow the daily fee increases substantially. And I must get it repaired before it is tagged as derelict."

Phoebe's heart sank. Of course, Sanjay had to rescue his cab. But if Sanjay and Jamal both departed for the parking garage, that left Chase sleeping upstairs; Kristin, also sleeping or possibly weeping upstairs; and Yuri, nursing his broken arm in the basement. Not exactly an army in fighting trim. Still, Chase usually woke fairly quickly, just in case the assassin should arrive and try something. And Jamal and Sanjay might need each other's expertise to get themselves out of danger if the shooter was waiting for them at the parking garage. An unlikely scenario, probably, but you never knew with Russian assassins.

"What's your plan?" she asked.

"We have been discussing the likelihood that we threw off the assassin with our evasive maneuvers," Sanjay said, finishing his tea. "We have not seen or heard or even suspected any danger in the past thirty hours. We have considered the possibility that all these events are the result of a random shooting."

"I doubt that," Phoebe said.

Sanjay nodded. "I also, and we are not committed to this line of thinking. However, given that we have perceived no danger since we picked up our defector, Jamal and I are speculating that the house would be safe enough during the short time period that we would need to return to the parking garage and get the window repaired. And then, if all goes well, we could possibly do some grocery shopping while we're out."

"Grocery shopping would be fantastic," Phoebe said. "We're almost out of everything. And then what? Could you stay here through tomorrow? Until we take Yuri to the FBI. If you don't have other obligations. I'd feel better if you guys were around, and not just because you have the armored car, Jamal."

Jamal grinned. "I'm happy to help. I mean, I got to meet Chase Bonaventure. You can't say that every day."

Phoebe laughed. "Yeah, really, you can say that only once. After that, you have to switch to how you *know* Chase Bonaventure. How long do you think you'll be gone?"

"Perhaps an hour or two," Sanjay said. "The emergency glass installers are remarkably swift."

"Go," Phoebe said. "We'll be fine."

Sanjay pulled out his phone to the call the glass installers, and Jamal finished off his coffee and rinsed the cup in the sink.

"I'll reimburse you for all your expenses and lost income," she said when Sanjay got off the phone. "I can't thank you enough for staying here last night."

"There is no need for reimbursement; it is my pleasure to do this," Sanjay said. "Moreover, the experience has been excellent practice for my future career as a protective services provider and, furthermore, is a strong indicator of what future assignments might entail. In addition, Jamal and I are thinking that we might earn extra credit in class, should we write a report that is sufficiently detailed to satisfy our instructors."

Phoebe blinked. "Really?"

"Maybe," Jamal said. "Be careful while we're gone. Don't open the door to anyone you don't know."

Phoebe nodded. "Never do. You be careful, too."

They went out to the garage and, seconds later, Phoebe watched as they drove down the street. With everyone else in their rooms, the house now felt eerily quiet. Maybe this would be a good time to order the sheets and towels they needed.

She had no idea what to buy. Her skill sets were weird:

she could speak eight languages fluently—thanks to the immigrant families her mom had left her with growing up—but she didn't know Spanish from Swahili when it came to purchasing power. Brenda had always been broke, and paying the bills had always been a challenge. Everything they'd ever owned had been bought at a thrift store. She'd never bought anything new.

Her life had been a lot different than Chase's. Chase's folks were middle class, and then he'd become wealthy beyond anyone's dreams while he played football. He could afford to buy the best. She'd have to figure out what that meant for sheets and towels, because she wanted to get value for their money, not overpay for something because it had a fancy label.

She'd left her laptop in the sunroom, so she went in there, stretched out on the chaise, and powered up her machine. Trouble followed her in and flopped down on the rug. The lime-green walls were bright with buttery sunshine, and the warm floral prints of the upholstery fabrics lifted her spirits. This room had a fireplace, too, tiled in a golden amber color. She took a moment to absorb the bright color, the warm light, the craftsmanship of the mantel. She loved this house. She wanted to live here forever.

Sheets and towels. Where to go for nice sheets and towels? And maybe matching bath mats while she was at it.

She was lost in research when Trouble barked. Someone was knocking on the front door. Pounding, more like it. Maybe it was Mateo Morales coming to talk about the roof. The slate had been delivered earlier.

Trouble scrambled to his feet and charged out into the entryway, barking his head off. Phoebe sighed, following him into the foyer. They put the sheet up over the glass only at night, so she could see a figure through the clear leaded glass—a wiry man of medium height. Not Mateo.

The guy held up a big cardboard carton so she could see it through the glass. "Delivery," he said. "Zignature."

She didn't know anything about an imminent package arrival, but Chase had been ordering stuff like crazy. Still, you couldn't be too careful. Misplaced trust got a lot of people in trouble.

She picked up the baseball bat and opened the door a few inches, pushing Trouble away from the opening and poking her head around the edge. She was careful to keep her body behind the heavy panel.

"Veebe Renvrew?" The man looked hot and disheveled, and he had a terrible skin condition. Red welts covered his face, and some were bleeding. He seemed to have some kind of weird acne. Or bleeding chicken pox.

"Y— What?" Phoebe said as alarms went off in her head. If he was a delivery guy, why was he asking for her by name? She hadn't ordered anything—not that Chase couldn't have bought something for her and put her name on the shipping label. But she didn't see a delivery truck.

"Zignature." The man forced the door open a few inches and thrust the box at her.

She tried to slam the door shut, but her hands were full pushing against the carton and holding the baseball bat, and Trouble jostled against her legs, trying to get out. She struggled to push the box away, shut the door, and corral Trouble, and in doing so, dropped the bat.

"No—"

The man reached across the box and leveled a Taser at her. Thrusting the weapon against her shoulder, he pulled the trigger.

Phoebe cried out and crumpled to the floor.

Vlad hadn't wanted to shoot anyone who wasn't Yuri Severov, but he hadn't counted on having such a lousy afternoon. The damn bus had never come. He'd waited forty-five minutes, stewing in the unbearable heat and humidity, but he couldn't wait forever. It would be *dark* before it showed up. This kind of service is what made America great? Americans were *losers*.

So he walked to Phoebe Renfrew's address—five miles in stiff leather shoes that gave him blisters, on sidewalks that were too hot, carrying a heavy and slippery nylon duffel bag full of expensive guns and other items he needed. After five miles, every part of his body ached, and he thought that even if he set up his long-range rifle, his arms would tremble so much from the strain that he would miss his target again. And he didn't want to think what the Boss would say about *that*.

Then, ninety minutes and five long, hot, sweaty, tiring, painful miles later, just before he'd arrived at the address that Sanjay Agarwal had written down—the address labeled PHOEBE—the bus, nearly empty, had whooshed past.

He hadn't realized he could be so furious at a bus.

And now he had serious questions about this location, a big house on a quiet street that faced an enormous park. The house looked like crap. It had been nice once, but now it was run-down. Would a successful protection unit work from a place like this? Or was the house a front for something else?

One thing: they had chosen the address for maximum privacy. All the houses on the block were quiet. No one stirred, not even cleaning or security services. Only the occasional car drove by. Packages sat unattended on front porches, indicating no one was at home.

He'd been pleased to see the heavily wooded park across the street. The trees would provide shade and coolness, and the dense cover would shield him from observation, so he could safely watch the house and discover who and how many besides Agarwal and Renfrew lived or worked there and by what schedule. He could determine the best way in. And if he was very lucky, Yuri Severov would be inside, and then he could take care of business and be on his way back to Moscow.

But he had not expected the ferociousness of the park's mosquitoes, which had swarmed him the second he stepped into the shrubbery. They flew into his eyes, his nose, and his ears, and even his mouth when he yawned. They bit ferociously, raising welts on his face, neck, and hands. He slapped and scratched for what seemed like hours, becoming increasingly miserable, frustrated, and angry as he watched the house. His arms and shoulders ached, his feet and knees throbbed, his back hurt, and there was nowhere to sit. Everything itched or bled, or both. He couldn't even hold up the rifle with any degree of certainty that he could hit his target, should he appear, because his fingers were swollen and seemed to have lost all sensitivity.

Eventually the garage door opened and a black SUV—probably an armored SUV—drove out. So Agarwal had a fleet of vehicles—this car as well as the taxicab, at least. The armored car backed out of the driveway and headed down the street. Vlad thought he caught a shadow of a person—a man—in the passenger seat. So two people in the car, and one of them was possibly Sanjay Agarwal. If so, that left Phoebe Renfrew unaccounted for.

Was she inside the house? And who else might be there? He could detect no movement through the windows, but curtains covered some of the glass. If she was there, now would be a good time to question her, with Agarwal and a second operative out of the way. The house would probably never be emptier than it was right now.

A mosquito bit him on the ear, and he slapped viciously. He dropped the rifle, which did not go off, thank all the Bolshevik martyrs, and when he looked at his hand, blood smeared the palm. *His* blood. From the mosquito. Which had bitten him.

Enough. He shoved the rifle back in the duffel bag and pulled out his Taser. A Taser would be sufficient for his plans. He didn't want to lug that bag of weapons any farther than he had to, and he didn't want to shoot this Phoebe Renfrew in any event. He could leave the guns behind until he was finished with Renfrew.

What did he have for a disguise? Nothing. But he could use one of the packages from a neighbor's porch and pretend he was delivering it.

He zipped the duffel and shoved it under a bush. No one would find it there. No one had passed by him in this godforsaken park for good reason, and no one with any sense ever would. Between the bugs and the heat, it was like hell.

Then, fury and frustration overcoming his better judgment, he'd marched across the street, lifted a carton from the next-door neighbor's porch, and rung the bell of the big, run-down house of Agarwal's protection group.

And now he was seeing the results.

He gazed down at the woman who'd said she wasn't Phoebe Renfrew. What to do with her? He wished he'd thought this through a little more. She was fairly well-hidden from the street because the front door was recessed in this small porch, but he couldn't leave her here for long. For one thing, he wanted the information she had. For another, she'd screamed, so someone might have heard her and called the police.

Not to mention, her asinine dog was barking loud enough to wake the dead. If his Taser had had another charge, he'd have shot the dog, too, to make him shut up. Instead, the stupid mutt barked and pranced and snarled at him.

They did not pay him enough for this kind of aggravation.

He felt his impotent rage and frustration recede and resignation and regret take over. He shouldn't have tased the woman, even if she was Phoebe Renfrew. He knew better than to operate from an emotional place. The facts of the matter were that he was tired and hungry, he was hot and miserable, and he hurt everywhere. So his frustrations had bubbled over. He hadn't meant to shoot her, just threaten her. Too late now.

First, get rid of the dog.

He tried shoving the animal back in the house, but the dog was a good size, maybe forty pounds or even more, agile, and surprisingly strong. The creature didn't want to be pushed, and when Vlad prodded him, the dog growled and snapped at his hand, drawing blood. Vlad yanked his arm back and wiped the blood off on his pants. What if the beast had rabies? Why had he left his guns in the park? *Stupid.* Well, he couldn't shoot it, and he couldn't shut it up, either.

Forget about the dog.

Vlad glanced around, taking stock of his surroundings, which he should have done when he arrived. Was there a garden shed? He might find a wheelbarrow inside. He could haul her away in a wheelbarrow.

But there wasn't a garden shed. Just the garage, with the door firmly closed. He ran over to test it. Locked.

An earsplitting alarm rent the air. The brain-melting shriek came from the front door, now open only by an inch or two. But enough to set off the alarm, which might alert the cops and certainly would alert anyone left in the house.

If he wanted to talk to her in private, he'd have to carry her.

He bent down. She wasn't a big woman, but she was dead weight, and he wasn't as young as he used to be. He tried hoisting her up by putting one of her arms around his neck and his other arm around her waist, but she flopped back to the concrete step. He tried scooping her up with one hand under her back and one under her knees. But he couldn't get the leverage to bring her up.

Пиздец!

He needed to talk to her, interrogate her, and he needed to do that away from the house and her other soldiers and this dumb dog. He was out of time and out of options.

He grabbed her wrists and, the dog barking and snapping at his heels, dragged her across the lawn toward the street and the park.

Chapter 8

C hase woke from a sound sleep without knowing what had roused him. He'd been dreaming. Or maybe something was wrong. He'd heard something. A noise. Maybe a shout? Or a cry?

He might not have worried if they didn't have Yuri in the house. Old houses made funny noises, after all. But they did have Yuri in the house. Uneasy, he sat up and listened.

Trouble was barking. And then the alarm went off, a screaming wave of sound.

That shouldn't be. They all had the alarm code. Even Yuri. Did someone forget to turn it off for some reason?

Had someone broken in?

He got up and strode naked to the window, twitching aside the curtain to peer out.

And saw a man straining to drag an inert Phoebe over the lawn toward the street. Trouble was barking and snapping at the man's legs.

The shooter was kidnapping Phoebe. Who was unconscious, at best. Fear and fury surged through him. In seconds he'd pulled on his jeans and, still barefoot, charged down the stairs.

"Sanjay! Jamal!" He ran through the foyer, grabbing the baseball bat lying on the floor, flung open the front door, and tore out of the house. "Stop! *Stop right there!*"

The man dragging Phoebe dropped her arms. For a split second, he appeared uncertain. Then, as Trouble snapped at his leg, he took off running down the street.

"*Cher!*" Chase dropped to the ground beside Phoebe and felt for a pulse. It was rapid but steady. She was breathing. With a wave of rage that momentarily clouded his vision, he saw the two Taser prongs sticking out of her shoulder.

"*Cher*, sweetheart, can you hear me?"

Her eyelids fluttered, and then she opened her eyes. Thank God. At least she hadn't been hit with a bullet.

"Hey," she said, swallowing. Her voice was raspy, but she didn't seem to be in any immediate danger. "Assassin, I think. Just a Taser. Get him!"

Chase glanced down the street at the would-be kidnapper, who had a decent head start but wasn't much of a runner. Two choices. He could catch him. Or he could help Phoebe.

She understood the dilemma.

"Go," she said, more clearly. "I'm fine. *Be careful.*"

She wasn't fine, but she'd be all right for a few minutes. He jumped up, still holding the baseball bat, and sprinted after the guy. He was tired of waiting for the other shoe to drop with this shooter. If he could catch him and turn him over to the cops, they'd all sleep better tonight. And presumably the country would be better off if he could get a Russian assassin off the street.

Phoebe's assailant was ahead by about a block, and Chase was almost as fit as when he'd played football. But running barefoot on a hot sidewalk definitely curtailed his speed. The loose stones, twigs, and sometimes glass that he stepped on hurt and threw him off his pace, and his knee, still not fully rehabbed, reminded him at every stride that running on cement without footgear was not advised. He wished he had the four legs and footpads that Trouble did, who ran ahead, barking and jumping at the assailant. Phoebe would never forgive him if the guy shot her dog. He must not have a weapon other than a Taser, which was confusing. What kind of Russian assassin went out with only a Taser?

Chase ran on, gaining ground. The guy was limping, too, and slowing considerably. By now he was less than a half block ahead, well within striking distance, and Chase had started to think about how he could restrain him once he had him. He didn't have handcuffs or twine or anything else that he could use to secure the guy—not even his phone to call the cops.

Traffic picked up as they approached a major artery, and the shooter turned his head and squinted over his shoulder. Chase wondered if the guy was looking for someone and felt a cold stab of worry: Did the assassin have an accomplice? Would it be two against one now?

He turned his head to ascertain the new danger and saw a bus lumber up behind them.

No! *Dammit!* He couldn't let the guy get on the bus.

He doubled down and ran faster, sweat pouring down his back and chest, feeling a hard jolt every time his bare foot hit the ground and sent a shock wave up to his bad knee. But he needed only another minute—just a few more seconds— and he'd have him.

The bus whooshed by and pulled up to the stop at the corner. The shooter put on a burst of speed and, running hard, waved like a madman. The doors opened and the guy fell inside. Trouble, only a step or two behind, barked and put his paws on the lowest step. Would the dog jump on the bus? Trouble wasn't vicious, but Chase didn't want to think what the driver and the shooter, between them, could do to the animal.

Surely the bus would wait. Surely the driver would think that Chase was also running to catch it. He ran faster, waving his arm.

"Stop!" he yelled. "Wait!"

But the bus didn't wait. With another whoosh, the doors closed, pushing Trouble to the curb. Then, gears grinding, the bus pulled away and trundled down the street.

Chase dashed after it for another half block, but he couldn't catch it. The bus made no more stops. And then it turned a corner for the express route downtown.

Too late.

Dammit to *hell*.

He leaned against the tree, feeling the heat and humidity blanket him. Had no one seen them dashing down the street? Had no one called the cops? He gazed around at all the big houses, their windows staring blankly back at him. Maybe everybody was at work. Or maybe somebody had called and the cops simply weren't coming. That would fit with everything else they'd experienced so far with this guy.

And—another possibility—maybe if anyone saw them, they thought that the younger, bigger, faster guy with a dog and a baseball bat was out to mug an older, less athletic guy. No one would have seen the Taser in the guy's hand. He hadn't seen it, and he was looking for it.

A frantic Trouble trotted up to him, whining, and jumped against his leg.

"Good try, boy," Chase said, reaching down to pat him. "You did your best. It wasn't your fault that he got away."

Trouble barked, one short, sharp exclamation.

"I know, I'm upset about it, too," Chase said, straightening. "But now it's time to get back. Phoebe needs us. Let's go."

He was worried. If Sanjay and Jamal had been home, they'd have come out when the alarm went off. So Phoebe was alone and injured on the sidewalk, and who knew if this guy was simply a decoy to get people out of the house. He might have accomplices who followed up and did worse things.

The thought terrified him as he ran back. But when he got there, Phoebe was slumped on the concrete bench by the front door. Kristin sat next to her, patting her hand. And a stranger stood off to the side, thumbing his phone.

Where was Yuri? He tried not to hope that a second Russian assassin had kidnapped him. If it had been up to him, he'd have left the Russian defector out on the curb and let him find his own way to the FBI or the State Department or wherever he needed to go. But it wasn't up to him. Or not only him. And this kind of stuff was Phoebe's life.

He knelt down beside her. "Phoebe, *cher*, sweetheart, how are you feeling?"

"I'm fine." Phoebe sagged against him.

"She isn't fine," Kristin said.

"I think she needs a hospital," the stranger said. "I've been looking for the closest one. I think Memorial's your best bet."

Chase nodded and then saw the pickup truck with the logo on the street. "Memorial *is* the closest, I have reason to know. You must be Mateo Morales. The contractor." He stood to shake hands.

"Mateo just got here," Phoebe said unnecessarily.

"The shooter got away, I guess," Kristin said. "Since I don't see him."

"No," Chase said. "Bastard got on a bus and the driver took off without me."

Phoebe snorted. "Figures. DC always did have lousy bus service." She sucked in a breath as she moved, and he saw the Taser darts still stuck in her shoulder through her thin top. Those had to hurt like a bitch.

"We have to go to the ER," he said. "Somebody has to take those barbs out of your shoulder. Somebody with training. What else hurts?"

"I'm not sure. Do we really need a hospital? Can't you take the darts out? We've got antiseptic cream. I'll be fine."

"*Cher*, you've been tased. You might need stitches or antibiotics. Maybe they'll want to run tests."

She would have hit her head on that concrete step when she fell, and even though she was wearing jeans, she was probably scraped up, too. She might be hurt worse than she realized.

"But Mateo dropped by to talk about the schedule."

"Mainly I wanted to be sure that it's okay if we start with the roofers rather than with the electrician," Mateo said. "That way my guys won't have to come inside for a couple of days, and your, ah, houseguest might not be so freaked out by the strangers. He just about screamed when I showed up."

Kristin grinned. "Yeah, Mateo scared Yuri half out of his wits. I hope he's not having a heart attack down there in the basement as we speak."

"Our domestic situation is sort of complicated right now," Chase said to Mateo. "Phoebe probably told you."

"She did. And even if she hadn't, that Taser attack was a pretty big clue. One thing, though—I can't put my crew in danger. Now that your assassin is hurting people besides his target, I'm a lot happier knowing that your defector's leaving tomorrow."

"Couldn't agree more," Chase said.

"Okay, I'll take off, then." Mateo nodded. "The roofers will be here by eight. They're bringing a big pulley to hoist the plywood up to the roof. I hope that won't be a problem."

"The lawn's a mess," Chase said. "Have at it. *Cher*, sit tight. I'll just put some shoes on and get the car."

Upstairs, he yanked a T-shirt over his head, stuffed his feet into his sneakers, and picked up his wallet and keys, then charged downstairs again and into the garage, grabbing Phoebe's messenger bag along the way. Their yellow Venture Automotive SUV made them a conspicuous target, but for right now it was the only vehicle they had. It would have to do.

When he got outside, Kristin helped him get Phoebe to the car.

"I'm supposed to be your VP of operations, and I wasn't ready," she said. "From now on, I'm keeping shoes by the bedroom door. We have to be able to respond to emergencies more quickly."

"That's the truth." Chase shook his head. "I wasn't prepared, either."

"All my fault," Phoebe said. "I wasn't careful enough."

"None of it was anybody's fault except Vlad's. Kristin, take care while we're gone. Don't forget to reset the alarm. You've got my cell number if you need me. Phoebe, I've got your bag, you need anything else?"

She shook her head.

"Then let's go." He waved to Kristin, put the car in gear,

and headed for the hospital.

He wasn't happy that he already knew the way.

Even though the barbs in her shoulder hurt more than she'd thought possible, Phoebe thought that—if her previous ER experiences were anything to go by—the trip to the hospital would be mostly a waste of time.

"What will the emergency room do for me that you can't?" Phoebe asked as they drove. "I mean, yank out the barbs—that's it, right? You can do that."

"*I'm not yanking out the barbs.*" Chase's voice was steely.

Yeah, she should have phrased that better, but she just felt so *muzzy*.

"They're in pretty deep. They should be removed by a professional so you don't get infected. And they might give you a prescription. They might give you an MRI. They'll check you out. *Because you got hurt.* You got *tased.*"

Well, when he put it like that.

"I'm worried about everybody in the house," she said. "What if the shooter comes back? With reinforcements?"

He reached out and took her hand. "*Cher*, sweetheart. He won't. But if he does, they'll call 911. They'll be fine."

She frowned. "You know what? You're right. I'm not thinking straight. The shooter doesn't have reinforcements, does he? What assassin works in a group? No. He's working alone. And you said he got on the bus. Maybe he doesn't even have his own transportation."

"And he got on the nonstop express bus. So even if he wants to come back, it'll take some time to make the return trip."

"Even if he thinks that's the best plan, which it clearly isn't, because he's lost the element of surprise."

Chase nodded. "Maybe he'll lie low for the rest of the day and work out something else. Who knows what, though."

"Yes, and you know what? He looked sick. His face was a mess of bleeding pockmarks. He might need a doctor, too."

"That might make him easy for the cops to find, then.

We'll call them when we get to the ER."

The emergency room was crowded when they got there, almost every chair occupied by someone who looked miserable. Well, that was understandable. She probably looked miserable, too. She certainly *felt* miserable. The Taser barbs really did hurt.

They checked in at the registration window, and then Phoebe sat down while Chase went outside to call the cops and report the attack. On his way back, he ambled over to the magazine rack and picked out a couple of periodicals. Who could read at a time like this? And what magazines would the hospital provide? Some kind of medical journal probably. Not exactly page-turning excitement.

"There wasn't much over there," he said, sitting next to her. "I skipped the home-decorating and wedding magazines, because you *know* Brenda will be sending you the latest issues of those any day now."

Phoebe nodded. "I hope you brought *X-Ray Technology Today*. I'm behind on my reading with that one."

He grinned. "That ten-year-old girl over there wearing the glasses got the last copy ahead of me."

"Pity. So, do you think I'm concussed? Is that why you were talking about hospital tests and MRIs?"

"The thought had crossed my mind. You were dragged, too, you know, so best to be on the safe side. How are you now? Do you feel anything else?"

Anything *else*? Did there have to be something *else*? But she did feel a little woozy and sick to her stomach.

"Not really," she said. "Not too bad."

He held up three fingers. "How many fingers am I holding up?"

"Three. I can *see*, you know. *And* count. It's my *brain* I'm wondering about."

"It's just a little layman's neurological test while we're waiting," Chase said. "Let me see your eyes. Sometimes with a concussion, your pupils are dilated."

She tilted her head up, and he leaned down to peer into her eyes.

"Still the beautiful pools of light I fell in love with."

She laughed. "I bet you told that to all the concussed football players, too."

"Only Dan Freer."

"Seriously, though. What happens if I have a concussion?"

He put his arm around her and tucked her against his chest. She recognized that look on his face, calm and determined, like there wasn't anything he couldn't do. She liked that face.

"I'm no neurologist, but I played football a long time." His voice rumbled in his chest like a distant thunderstorm. It was incredibly soothing. "Hits can scramble you. Afterward, all the docs say to rest. Don't do anything big physically. Mentally, either. Don't fret. Think gentle, happy thoughts. Like *cupcakes*. Think cupcakes. Doesn't that sound good? Mmmmm. Meanwhile, I have a plan."

He had a *plan*?

"*Cupcakes?*" Phoebe lifted her head. "Cupcakes are your plan?"

Chase laughed and released her. "Not exactly," he said, taking his phone out of his pocket and thumbing the device. "Although that's not a bad idea. There's not much we can do while we wait, so let's order some towels."

"Towels. I've got barbs burning into my shoulder and I'm threatened with a life-altering brain injury, and you want to talk about *towels*?"

"What better time? Do you think we should get all one color, like maybe white, so everything matches with everything else? Or do you think we should get towel sets to match the colors of the bathrooms? Although those might change when we paint."

"Towels. *Now* you want to talk about towels."

"Sure. Why not? We're not doing anything else. And then we should order some sheets."

Phoebe gazed into Chase's calm face, his eyes now lit with amusement.

She shook her head, cheered in spite of herself. She

loved this guy. "Towels it is," she said. "And maybe some bath mats to match."

Chase was relieved when the ER doctor ruled out concussion, as he thought she might. And then she removed Phoebe's Taser barbs in a brief, anesthetic-free procedure that appeared surprisingly painful. Phoebe sucked in her breath with a hiss as the sharp prongs were taken out, and she was as tough as they came. Then the nurse cleaned and bandaged the little wounds and gooped up her abrasions with some kind of antiseptic cream.

"How does that feel?" the nurse asked.

"A lot better," Phoebe said, still clutching his hand from the barb removal.

Good thing he didn't have to throw a football anymore. By the time this ER visit was over, Phoebe might have permanently displaced some of the bones in his hand. Not that he minded. He was happy to sacrifice his bone placement if Phoebe needed it.

That said, the ER experience had been about as much fun as gator wrestling.

And then the cops showed up, which made the experience about as much fun as gator wrestling with a live chicken strapped to your head.

"You were assaulted?" the older cop asked Phoebe, taking a small notebook from his pocket.

"Yes." She sat down again on the narrow bed of the ER. She looked wrung out, as well she might.

"By a guy with a Taser," Chase said. If the district cops could catch the Russian assassin, so much the better. Leave it to the experts. He wondered why the cops had shown up at the ER instead of their house, unless the ER doctor had to report anything weapons-related.

The cop glanced his way before returning to Phoebe. "What did he look like?"

"Average," Phoebe said. "Five-ten or eleven, maybe 165, 170. Brown hair. Bloody welts on his face."

"Did he enter the house?" The cop scribbled away. "Take

anything?"

"No." She seemed to be losing steam by the minute. Her eyes were closed now, and as much as Chase would like the district cops to apprehend this guy, he wanted nothing more than to get Phoebe home and comfortable. And secure.

"It wasn't a robbery attempt," he said. "Her assailant is a Russian assassin who tried to kill our houseguest a couple of days ago."

"*What?*" The cop's voice went up a notch.

"On Saturday," Chase confirmed. "The assailant shot at our houseguest, who was in a car with Phoebe at the time."

"Did you report this incident?"

"I wasn't there, but Phoebe did not, no, because the target is a Russian national trying to defect. Phoebe's scheduled to deliver him to the FBI tomorrow afternoon."

"I'm with the CIA," Phoebe said.

"Oh, so it's *federal*." The cop, looking bored now, closed his notebook and shoved his pen back into his pocket.

"Wait, *what?*" Chase said, startled by this sudden change in attitude. "So what if it's federal? You won't try to catch him?" What was *with* these guys?

"Not our jurisdiction." The cop shrugged. "The feds handle their own. Say, don't I know you from somewhere?"

"No." Chase flagged down an orderly who was passing with a wheelchair. "Come on, *cher*. Let's get out of here."

"Hold on!" The cop slapped his notebook against his leg. "I got it! You're on TV, right? One of those reality shows?"

"Absolutely not," Chase said.

"You mean, you don't *know?*" Phoebe said, unbelieving.

"Hush, now, sweetheart, don't get upset." He helped her up, and the orderly eased her into the chair and pushed her out of the room toward the exit.

"What a dope," Phoebe said as they headed down the hall. "He doesn't know who you *are*? Where's he been living? Even *I* know who you are!"

Chase grinned, taking her hand. "Very reassuring."

Phoebe woke from the little nap she'd had in the car as

Chase pulled into the garage. Her chest and back felt like she'd been kicked by a mule. Not that she'd ever actually been kicked by a mule, but she thought this was what it would feel like if it happened.

"We're home," Chase said.

"I'm hungry," Phoebe said, surprising herself.

"No wonder. It's past dinnertime. And whatever you want, if we don't have it, we'll get it." Chase came around the car and put his arm around her, easing her out of the vehicle.

"Sanjay and Jamal said they'd go to the store, so we should have plenty. I didn't give them a list. But then I didn't know I'd be getting tased, or I might have been more specific." Phoebe grabbed his arm as the floor of the garage heaved and tried to wrestle her to the ground.

"Steady a bit," he said, holding her securely. "Let's go in."

He pushed open the door to the kitchen and nearly hit Trouble with it, who woofed, prancing at their feet. As they entered, everyone clapped.

Phoebe grinned as a rush of affection swamped her. Even Yuri was doing a one-handed clap against the counter.

"Phoebe, how are you?" Kristin, her forehead creased with worry, hugged her. "Come in! Sit down! We've been so worried!"

Sanjay smiled. "It is most reassuring to see you ambulatory. We have been extremely anxious about the seriousness and extent of your injuries. You must tell us what the doctors said."

"Good to see you're okay," Jamal said.

"Thank you, everybody," she said. "I appreciate the welcome. I'm sore, but that's it. I'm super glad to be home. *And* I think I'm going to have to lie down soon."

"What do we have to eat for someone who's sustained a Taser attack?" Chase asked.

"There's chicken noodle soup," Jamal said.

"That sounds really good," Phoebe said.

"Jamal and I were unsure of personal favorites or food requirements or restrictions at the grocery, so we made a very comprehensive run through the aisles," Sanjay said. "We have an extensive selection of prepared foods and ready-to-eat snacks, as well as the basics. Also we acquired a couple bottles of a lovely Beaujolais, which, we were reliably informed, has a beautiful bouquet and a floral nose. Also, the chicken noodle soup. In a can, but it's the gourmet variety."

Phoebe smiled. "That's what I want. Is there ice cream? Or cupcakes? I've been thinking about cupcakes."

"Ice cream, yes," Sanjay said. "No cupcakes, but a family-sized, double-chocolate layer cake with raspberry filling."

"I'll have that, too."

"Maybe start with the soup," Chase said.

Sanjay opened the can and poured it into a bowl that he put in the microwave. "Done."

"I made kibbe for the rest of us, if you'd like to try it," Jamal said. "It's a savory pie with lamb and cracked wheat. My mom's recipe."

"Sounds good," Kristin said. "I like your mom."

"Same goes," Chase said.

"Could we all watch something on TV together?" Phoebe wanted to lie down, but she didn't want to be alone. "I'd like that."

The microwave dinged and Sanjay took the soup out. "We could eat in front of the television," he said, putting Phoebe's soup on a tray. "You could lie down, and we could all have a quiet night, which would be most welcome after such a trying day."

"The Snakes are playing tonight," Kristin said, grabbing an assortment of drinks from the fridge.

Phoebe didn't understand much about football, but she didn't care what was on. "Sure."

"We should watch something that we don't holler at the TV for." Chase stacked plates and cutlery on the tray with the soup. "*Cher*, take my arm, okay?"

"I'm not helpless, you know," Phoebe said, but she tucked her hand inside his arm, and they headed toward the TV room.

"We won't be cheering much if the Snakes play that rookie at QB," Kristin said, following them. "He won't have the chops to beat the Lions."

"ESPN says that the Snakes offense has been completely reworked." Jamal carried the steaming kibbe into the TV room.

"It would have to be." Kristin put down the drinks as Sanjay brought in the salad. "Everybody set?"

Phoebe sat next to Chase on the sectional sofa and leaned against him, tucking her feet underneath her and protecting her bowl of soup as Trouble jumped up and sprawled across her feet. Kristin sat next to her, and Yuri stretched out on the L on the other side. Sanjay took the end, and Jamal took the footstool. This was nice. She was happier already.

Chase thumbed the remote, turning on the TV as everyone dug into the food. "Let's see what we've got."

Phoebe tasted her soup. It was delicious, just what she needed. And everybody was together, and everybody was safe. Things were finally looking up.

But she couldn't be entirely easy. Somewhere out there was a crazy Russian assassin who had tased her.

And the next time he went after somebody in this house, he might use real ammunition.

Chapter 9

By the time Phoebe woke early the next morning, the pain relievers, antiseptic creams, and chicken noodle soup had worked their magic. No question she was feeling a lot better.

The air was cool, and a gray, early-morning light peeked through the lace curtains. She turned over and stretched to discover that the other side of the bed was empty. Then she heard something across the room and saw Chase crouching before the cobalt-blue-tiled fireplace, poking a small flame into life. The fire crackled in the grate, licking against the kindling and wood, sending out a flicker of heat.

He was naked. Which sent out a different wave of heat.

His skin gleamed golden in the fire's reflection, glowing in the pearly light. His dark hair, always unruly, stuck out everywhere, looking like he'd combed it with a Weedwacker. His scarred knee added enough tough reality that he couldn't be taken for a mirage. Or a swimsuit model. The muscles in his back flexed every time he reached to poke the fire, which was just plain beauty in motion.

Now *that* was a sight a woman never got tired of.

"Hey," she said.

He turned his head and smiled at her. And for a second, she felt her heart stop and her breath catch, amazed as always by how he could focus on her like that and how much she loved him. And then she breathed again and her heart picked up speed, beating a little faster, making up for the time it had lost when he'd stopped her breath.

"Morning, *cher*. How are you feeling today?"

"A lot better. Are you coming back to bed?"

He stood, putting away the fireplace tools. And there was the utterly delicious full backside view.

"Heck, yeah. It's way too early to get up yet." He came back to the bed, showing her the full monty.

Holy crap. Give a woman a heart attack, why didn't he?

"The fireplaces will be a pain to clean, but I like a fire," he said as he slid under the covers and wrapped his arms around her. "Feel the air? Cool weather's coming."

She nodded, liking the friction of her head against his warm, hard chest. "Mmm. The fire's nice. And the tile work is all so beautiful."

He kissed the top of her head. "Big day today."

Phoebe nodded again. Today at three they could turn Yuri over to the FBI. And then she could get her regular life back, together with Chase, in their beautiful new house.

Of course, Mateo Morales and his crew would be coming to start the rehabbing, so it would be busy for a while with workers and dust. But *then* she'd get her regular life back.

"I had a dream about my shooter last night," she said. "Or maybe it was a thought, I'm not sure. I was so tired yesterday."

She felt his arm tighten.

"What did you dream?" His voice sounded calm, but she knew that voice. A controlled calm.

She didn't blame him. She got tense thinking about the shooter, too.

"It's about the timing," she said. "He came to the house pretty soon after Jamal and Sanjay—the two guys who are trained in protection—took off to get Sanjay's taxi fixed. Either the shooter's timing was beautifully coincidental, or—"

"He watched them go."

"Right." Phoebe was pleased that it made sense to him,

too. She propped herself up on one elbow so she could see his eyes and gauge his reaction. "He doesn't have a car, right? Because he jumped on a bus. If he'd had a car, he'd have driven away. Much more reliable."

"Much. I wonder if he *came* on the bus."

"He might have. I didn't hear one go by before the doorbell rang, but I wasn't paying much attention to anything outside. I was researching towels. Fat lot of good *that* did." She flopped back on the bed in exasperation. "I should have been researching books like *A Beginner's Guide to Disarming Russian Assassins.* That would have been a lot more helpful."

Chase grinned. "Amos knows something about that. Maybe he could give you a tutorial. Or all of us."

Phoebe snorted. "And then I'd have a skill to fall back on when the agency turfs me out again."

"They'll never turf you out again. Anyway, all your towel research paid off with multiple purchases, so it all worked out in the end."

"Unfortunately, the shooter's still out there somewhere," Phoebe said. "Where, though?"

"He's been here a few days, so he must have a hotel room. Too bad we don't know which hotel."

"Yeah. I wonder—if he was watching our house, he must have been hiding in the park. Those woods are pretty thick. The welts I saw on that guy's face could be bug bites. I bet there are lots of mosquitoes in the park."

"Maybe he left something behind, something the cops could use for evidence," Chase said. "After breakfast I'll go over there and see if I can find anything. I'm still pissed they wouldn't make an effort to find him."

"I'm coming, too." If anybody was going to nail that guy, she wanted to be in on it.

"You should take it easy. You had a tough day yesterday, and you still have to go into the FBI this afternoon."

"The search shouldn't take that long, right? The area we're interested in can't be that big."

"I'd say so." Chase smiled at her, that heat-inducing, toes-curling smile that made her forget her name. "So now we have a plan, and it's a while until breakfast. I wonder what we could do to fill the time?"

"I have an idea." Phoebe rolled to her side. "Maybe you could put more of that antiseptic cream on my back."

By the time breakfast was ready, Mateo Morales had arrived with the roofing crew. He came to the door, and Phoebe introduced him to Yuri, who regarded the contractor with suspicion.

"You'll be safe," Phoebe told the defector. "Chase lined him up before we ever met you, and with so many people outside working, the assassin won't dare come up to the house. You'll stay inside, just in case, and this afternoon you'll go to the FBI and all your troubles will be over."

"сомневаюсь."

Of course Yuri had his doubts. What Russian didn't? But for all their sakes, Phoebe hoped that Yuri was wrong.

Mateo cleared his throat. "Приятно встретить тебя," he said, shaking Yuri's hand.

Phoebe blinked in surprise. The contractor's accent was off, but you could understand what he said. It was nice of him to learn the phrase "nice to meet you," although "nice" was maybe a stretch. But the sentiment was good and might help to put Yuri at ease.

Mateo left the porch and went to check on the crew. A couple of men pushed a giant trash dumpster into the yard and others lugged some kind of pulley machinery closer to the house.

"How long to do the roof?" Phoebe asked Chase.

"A couple of days. See that gizmo? They can hoist the plywood up to the roof with that mechanized pulley. It goes like greased lightning. What will add a little time is the sky-light for the purple bathroom."

The small bathroom under the eaves was so low that Chase—and any person taller than a child—couldn't stand upright at the sink. A skylight would fix that problem.

"Does that bathroom have to stay purple? It's such a dark color. And that bathroom is so small."

"Any color you like. That's why the construction guys are here. We could get some paint chips and start thinking about it."

Phoebe beamed. "That'll be fun. I've never picked out paint colors before."

"I think this house will offer an array of firsts for all of us."

After breakfast, everyone but Yuri trekked across the street to the park. Phoebe left her phone with him to dial 911 if the assassin showed up or anything else bad happened.

"Or just yell," she said. "We'll be right across the street."

"I will be alone and unprotected!" Yuri said. "He could kill me!"

"You're not alone. See all the construction workers? They'll keep the assassin away. Focus on happy things. Like going to the FBI this afternoon." That would be a happy thing and not just for Yuri. Everybody in the house would be glad to see him go.

"And I don't understand your American television!"

"Maybe there's a football game on," Phoebe said. "Or some other sports thing. Don't worry. We won't be gone long."

After that, it was almost a relief to get out in the hot, humid, mosquito-laden air to search for assassin trash.

"What are we looking for?" Kristin slapped at a gnat as they stepped into the trees. Based on Phoebe's description of the shooter's bleeding welts, Chase had passed out bug repellant before they headed out. It didn't seem to be effective enough.

"Anything that suggests a guy hid somewhere in front of our house," Chase said. "Maybe a pile of cigarette butts or the remains of a lunch. A discarded hat. I don't know."

"How far afield should we go?" Jamal asked.

"When you can't see our garage door, you've gone too far. Phoebe, stick with me, okay? In case you get woozy out here."

"I won't get woozy."

"Okay, then in case *I* get woozy, all right?"

Phoebe grinned. "That's more like it."

Chase shook his head, but he laughed as they started down a path. Everyone fanned out, taking different routes into the park.

Examining the trail was slow going. They scrutinized both sides of the path, pushing back bushes and lifting soggy plant debris. It was hot, buggy, itchy work, and Phoebe wondered if it was pointless, too. What kind of assassin would leave trace evidence behind? Before long she was wishing that she could fake wooziness just to get back to the coolness of the house.

And then Sanjay gave a shout.

They turned back and found him standing next to an enormous chestnut oak that was surrounded by a dense group of saplings and thick, thorny bushes. Clouds of gnats and mosquitoes rose from the underbrush.

"Ugh!" Phoebe said as she approached, slapping her arms. "What did you find, Sanjay?"

"This." He pointed to a black nylon duffel.

"Good work!" Chase said. "Is anything in it?"

"Indeed, yes. Thinking of furthering our investigation, I opened it without sufficiently considering the consequences, and I touched both the handle and zipper. Given the bag's contents, I am not wishing to touch it further for fear that fingerprint analysis might point any law enforcement personnel in my direction."

"Guns?" Chase said.

Sanjay nodded. "And other items that a lawbreaker might find helpful. It is most alarming that it has been outside here, exposed to the public for more than twelve hours. Anyone could have stolen the contents or the bag in its entirety."

"What should we do with it?" Jamal asked.

"Let's take it back to the house." Chase slapped his arm. "The mosquitoes are too miserable out here for us to stand over it while we wait for the cops. *If* the cops decided to come."

"I don't know if we have to worry about fingerprints,

but I have a tissue," Kristin said. She fished in her pocket and handed a clean, if crumpled, tissue to Chase.

He shrugged but palmed it to spread the opening wider so they could all see.

Inside lay at least a half dozen guns of various lengths, boxes of shells, high-powered binoculars, and other field glasses that he thought might be night vision goggles. There was a heavy baton, a couple of handguns, and a weird-looking handgun—probably a Taser—and other stuff too far down to identify.

"Holy smokes," Kristin said, startled. "It's an arsenal. All that was to kill Yuri?"

"I'd say, yeah, probably," Chase said. "We definitely can't leave this stuff out here. In fact, I'm surprised the shooter hasn't come back for it by now. If it is the shooter's."

"It is manifestly disappointing that we did not also uncover other items that might reveal DNA," Sanjay said. "A soft drink container, or some such thing, would go far to tie the weapons cache to our Russian assassin."

"I guess that was too much to hope for." Chase hoisted the heavy bag over his shoulder.

"We can turn it over to the FBI this afternoon," Phoebe said. "I bet it's part of this case. They'll have a better lab than the local police, too. And then it's out of our hair."

"Here's an encouraging thought," Jamal said, scratching his cheek. "If this is the assassin's sole weapons cache, we're all a lot safer. At least for now."

That was true, if they'd found all the shooter's guns. Had they? They couldn't be sure. They couldn't even be sure that these guns belonged to the assassin who'd tried to kill Yuri. Phoebe hoped so.

But they couldn't count on it.

Vlad woke on Monday morning tired, angry, and hungover. *Never* had one of his targets given him as much grief and aggravation as Yuri Severov. If he didn't have orders to kill the traitor on sight, he'd like to torture him slowly until his every bone was broken, he bled from his hair follicles, and mushrooms grew on the moldering graves of his ancestors. Vlad was following orders, just trying to do his job the best he could. And Severov, that no-good, money-grubbing, imperialist running-dog *turncoat*, was out there making life miserable for all concerned. It wasn't *right*.

Vlad had wasted all of Sunday chasing after the traitor, and he had *nothing* to show for it. He'd been eaten alive by bugs. He'd abandoned his weapons, tased one of Sanjay Agarwal's lieutenants without achieving any results, engaged in dangerous, attention-grabbing evasion maneuvers, and been accosted by the authorities of the metropolitan transportation system. All that aggravation when he just wanted to finish the job early and get home smoothly and without detection.

And had he been able to do that?

No, he had not. Because Yuri Severov was a worthless, despicable rat, pointless excrement discharged from the bowels of Mother Russia.

Vlad shook his head, trying to clear it. After all his best efforts, he'd been outmaneuvered by that wretched traitor and the protection unit that helped him.

He was angry, and he had every right to be. But now he had to *think*. So—what did he know and how should he best proceed? Yesterday, everything had gone wrong, starting with his tasing of the woman he'd thought was Phoebe Renfrew. Except maybe it wasn't. When that big man had come charging out of the house, he'd distinctly yelled a different name—Cher. Was she a new operative? Another member of the protection group?

Could be. So although he had Sanjay Agarwal's address for "Phoebe," the woman he'd tased was named Cher. Phoebe Renfrew was still out there somewhere.

And who was that big guy who'd chased him? He must work for Sanjay Agarwal and Phoebe Renfrew, probably as the muscle, because he could run fast, even on bare feet. Vlad had been lucky to escape.

He'd been hugely relieved that the bus had come by, but his relief had been short-lived. When he'd tried to give the driver money for the fare, the driver had engaged him in vigorous and incomprehensible debate before eventually waving him away. He'd taken a seat, thinking that a complimentary ride was a courtesy for international visitors, until two burly men in uniform got on board and yanked him off. In front of all the other passengers! Like he was a common criminal!

They'd taken him to an office, where he learned—after a few hours—that they thought he was a fare cheat. Him! Vladimir Golubkin, a fare cheat! As if he would risk his reputation—not to mention, the entire *operation*—on something so insignificant, so pointless, as avoiding a bus fare. It was beyond contemptible.

Not that he could tell those bureaucratic robots why he was here. They might call a higher authority if they learned that his major crime was *not* ripping off the Metropolitan Transportation Authority of a two-dollar fare, but assassinating a Russian defector.

Using many gestures and with his limited grasp of English, plus the benefits of an online translator, he'd learned that the simplest way to pay the fare was with a special card that you bought in advance. Paying cash on the bus required exact change. Who knew? No wonder the bus driver hadn't wanted to accept the twenty-dollar bill he'd offered.

Eventually he'd paid an extortionate fee and fine for the card, but at least he'd avoided greater trouble. And now he could ride the bus all he wanted for a week.

Like he'd need the fare card for a week.

But transportation was a secondary problem. His primary problem was still the elimination of Yuri Severov—only now it wasn't just Severov he had to contend with. Severov's security detail—Sanjay Agarwal, Phoebe Renfrew, and now Cher and the Running Man—had to be overcome, as well. His task would be monumentally more difficult. But the bosses never thought of *that*, did they?

By the time Vlad had limped back to his hotel, he'd wanted nothing more than an ice-cold vodka to wash away the pain, aggravation, and humiliation—as well as the dust and dirt—of the day. One vodka in the hotel bar had turned into two, had turned into—he wasn't sure how many.

He rolled over and sat up gently, feeling the pain in his head, the cotton in his mouth, and the roiling in his stomach. The light that edged past the drapes over the window was blinding, like a knife stabbing his eyes.

He might be getting old. Past it.

The phone rang, a shrill clangor that almost split his skull.

It could only be the Boss, reminding him of his assignment today. As though he needed reminding.

He got up slowly, using the bed's headboard for support, and walked carefully across the room to where his phone sat on the console recharging. He sighed and picked up.

"Я не забыл," he said. "Я готов."

Of course, he hadn't forgotten. Of course, he wasn't ready, either, despite his assurances. And maybe the Boss picked up on his misgiving, because he started a long, hot diatribe about Vlad's responsibilities. His obligations. His duty.

As though he could possibly forget.

He had to pee, and he didn't want to listen. If he didn't get the Boss off the phone, he'd never be ready.

So he hung up. The hell with him.

He shuffled into the bathroom and peed. Then he tossed a half dozen pain relievers into his mouth and swallowed some cold water, which made his stomach pitch. He kept the pills down, though, and shuffled back to the bed, where he sat down gingerly on the edge of the mattress.

The phone rang again. This time he ignored it.

Today Yuri Severov would return to the State Department to defect. Therefore, retrieving the weapons that Vlad had stashed so carefully in the woods before he tased Cher was of paramount importance. He needed his weapons to kill the traitor. The State Department opened at nine, and Severov probably would make his move soon after. Vlad had to be in position, armed and ready, when the traitor got there.

Could he do it? Could he hold a rifle steady and hit his target?

Vlad stood up, using the wall for support, and held his arms in a shooting position. They were steady. Well, mostly steady. Of course, he wasn't holding a gun. The added weight of a weapon would increase the difficulty of hitting his target. He picked up the bedside lamp and held it with an outstretched arm to see how that felt. His arm trembled and sagged.

So, not perfect. But the actual shooting wouldn't happen for at least another couple of hours, and by then, he'd feel better. He was pretty sure he could hit *something* if he had enough time to focus.

Feeling optimistic, Vlad checked the airline for direct flights to Moscow and scheduled the earliest available that afternoon, paying the change fees again. This time, though, he didn't care. Anything to get home as soon as possible. Then he dragged himself back into the bathroom, showered under water so hot it almost burned his skin, dressed, and drank all the coffee that the hotel's complimentary hospitality service provided. Two small pots of bitter brew later, six more pain relievers down his gullet, and another quart or so of water to dilute the vodka still running through his veins, and he was ready to go. Or as ready as he'd ever be. He hoped that he'd stop sweating by the time he got to the State Department. A slippery finger on the trigger would never do.

He took the elevator to the lobby and hailed a cab. He couldn't worry about paper trails now. He needed his weapons immediately, and he'd never be able to retrieve them and get to the State Department by walking. Or riding the bus.

He'd be done here in an hour or two and on a plane back to Moscow. In that small window of time, the American authorities wouldn't find him, not even with a neon sign pointing the way.

The cab driver was a man of few words, for which Vlad was thankful. He leaned back and closed his eyes as they drove out to Agarwal and Renfrew's address. When they got there, his head still pounding and his stomach still roiling, the house swarmed with activity. Men climbed up ladders to the roof, no doubt establishing their positions, while others hoisted heavy wooden slabs up there to provide cover for the snipers.

That wasn't good.

He'd want to make a quick getaway before anyone spotted him. He asked the driver to wait.

Once inside the trees, he paused for a second to gaze back at the house. How big was Severov's protection detail, anyway? Getting to him would be monumentally more difficult now. He counted five more men on the ground and the roof of the place, pretending to work. Who knew how many more were inside.

As if he'd fall for that subterfuge! Five snipers on the roof, that's what they had there. He'd have to take extraordinary care now. Be wilier than ever.

It was time to get on with it.

He walked into the park, directly to the thick undergrowth where he'd hidden the duffel.

It wasn't there.

He couldn't believe it. He picked up a stick lying nearby and swacked the shrubbery, sending clouds of tiny black gnats into the air. They choked him, and he waved his arms wildly, trying to clear a space in front of his eyes. A mosquito chomped on his neck and he swatted it, hating the park and this job and that lousy, stinking traitor Yuri Severov, who refused to be put down like the worthless capitalist lackey that he was.

Hoping desperately that one bush was much like another and that he'd merely been mistaken about the duffel's location, Vlad cast his eyes farther, searching nearby, then in ever-increasing circles. Panic rose as he scuffled through undergrowth and pushed back vegetation. Flying insects swarmed him, stinging and biting, increasing his misery. He became warm and then too warm from the exertion and the humidity. And all the while as he bent and lifted and searched and found nothing, he cursed the name Yuri Severov. Sanjay Agarwal. Phoebe Renfrew. Cher. Running Man. Vicious

Attack Dog. And everyone else who had thwarted him on this evil venture.

After half an hour, he had to admit defeat. The duffel wasn't here.

They had stolen it. The security detail! How had they managed it? How did they *know?*

His weapons! All of them, gone.

What could he do now? How could he tell the Boss? *What* could he tell the Boss?

And how in the name of Mother Russia could he kill Yuri Severov?

Chapter 10

When they got back from their trip to the park, every-one went to their rooms to shower and change. Phoebe stepped into their bathroom first, and after she dried off, she applied some medicated lotion to her face and arms. Already the insect bites she'd received were itching a lot less. Then, refreshed, she left Chase to his own shower and went down to the kitchen to think about lunch. Feeding a crew was a big responsibility, and everyone would be hungry after their rummage through the park's underbrush.

Kristin was at the kitchen window, munching an apple and watching the roofing crew work. "That cab's been out there a long time," she said.

Phoebe plunked the cutting board on the counter and came over to stand with her friend at the window. "It's so weird to be suspicious of everything," she said. "And yet, I am."

"You've got good reason."

They watched for a couple of minutes. The cab was double-parked on the street, not moving. Eventually, Phoebe gave up and opened the refrigerator to see what she could turn into soup.

"Did I mention that Amos is coming for lunch?" she asked. "He's going to tell us—"

"Here comes the passenger," Kristin said, still at the

window. "He's coming straight out of the park."

Phoebe dropped some raw vegetables on the cutting board, wiping her hands as she came back to the window. "That's kind of weird. I wonder what— *Hey*! That's the shooter! That's the guy who tased me!"

She threw the towel into the sink and, dashing into the foyer, flung open the front door. She almost ran over Yuri, who had come up from the basement and was heading toward the kitchen.

The shooter had just slammed the door of the cab, and the cab was pulling away. It was yellow—A-1, it said on the side. Phoebe squinted at the license plate and got some of it before the cab turned a corner.

The cops could do something with that. The cops could do even more if she knew where to send them.

She charged back into the house.

"Это стрелок! Я пойду за ним!" she yelled to Yuri as she ran into the kitchen and grabbed her messenger bag and car keys. "I'm going after them!" she told Kristin as she headed for the garage.

"Wait!" Kristin pitched her apple core in the compost bin. "I'm coming with you!"

Phoebe jumped into Chase's yellow electric Venture Automotive SUV, jabbing the button of the garage door opener.

Kristin hopped into the passenger seat and buckled her seat belt. "Let's go!"

"They turned right at the corner." Phoebe screeched out of the garage and into the street. "It's an A-1 cab, I saw that. And the plate begins with H247. Just in case we see more cabs and we lose them."

She peeled down the street and turned the corner, following the cab's route.

"Got it." Kristin scrabbled in her bag for her phone and made a note. "Up there! I see them!"

"Let's hope he doesn't spot us," Phoebe said. "At least he hasn't seen *this* car, because Jamal and Sanjay drove out in Jamal's armored vehicle."

"He's seen *you*, though, Phoebs. If he spots our tail—"

"Yeah, he might recognize me." Phoebe halted at a stop sign. "Well, all we can do is follow him as far as we can and see where he goes."

They drove in silence for a few minutes as the cab turned onto a wider thoroughfare. The taxi seemed oblivious to them—it wasn't driving fast or taking evasive measures. After several minutes, it pulled up to a modest hotel on a commercial street downtown.

Phoebe slowed the car to a crawl. "He's stopping," she said. "There's no place to pull over. And if I pull up behind him, he'll recognize me."

Kristin unbuckled her seat belt. "Go park somewhere," she said. "I'll follow him into the hotel. See if I can learn anything."

"Be careful." Phoebe watched as the shooter exited the cab and entered the hotel. "Don't let him see you. What if—"

"Just *go!*" Kristin hopped out of the car and waited for a break in the traffic. Then she ran across the street and entered the hotel lobby.

Okay. Phoebe took a deep breath and drove around the block. They'd passed a parking lot a few blocks back. If she didn't find a parking space soon, she'd go there.

But she was in luck. Less than a block later, she found a space on the street. *Did James Bond ever plug the parking meter?* she wondered as she fed her card into the slot. Probably not. Probably Q paid all the parking tickets without batting an eyelash. Not that she was comparing herself to James Bond.

The hotel lobby of Phoebe's shooter was surprisingly large, remarkably cool, and comparatively busy. Phoebe glanced around but didn't see any sign of Kristin. Surely she wouldn't go anywhere without her? Or without leaving a message? Phoebe approached the check-in desk.

"Hi." She beamed at the clerk when her turn came, trying to radiate honesty and trustworthiness. "I'm supposed to meet someone. She's visiting a friend who's staying here in the hotel. But I don't see her and I'm afraid I missed her. Has

141

anyone left a message for me?"

"No messages for anyone since I started my shift an hour ago." The clerk's eyeglasses had heavy black frames, giving him something of a Clark Kent vibe. "Who's the guest your friend is visiting? I could ring the room."

"I don't know his name," Phoebe said. "He's Russian, that's all I know."

"Oh, the *Russian*." The clerk grinned. "We've got one of those, all right, a regular. Comes every year around this time. Great guy."

Phoebe blinked. The shooter came *every year*? He killed somebody *every year*? Or maybe he just came on vacation like normal people did, to tour the museums or see the cherry blossoms?

But how could it be best practices for an international assassin to stay in the same hotel every time he came to town? Weren't they supposed to remain invisible?

Clearly there was a lot she didn't understand about international assassination. Maybe she could ask Amos. He'd know.

"That's got to be the guy," she said, refocusing. "Kristin said he'd gotten a bunch of mosquito bites or something on his face, right? He wasn't prepared for the insect life in the park."

"That's right!" the clerk said. "Should I ring his room for you? See if your friend is there?"

"Well—" Phoebe said, stalling for time, just as the elevator dinged and Kristin stepped out. "There she is now!"

Kristin joined Phoebe standing at the clerk's desk.

"How's your Russian friend?" Phoebe asked. "I was afraid I'd missed you."

"*Russians*." Kristin rolled her eyes and grinned at the clerk. "You can't tell them anything. They always know what's best. Am I right?"

"They've got their quirks," the clerk said, smiling back.

Kristin leaned over the desk and lowered her voice. "You tell them and tell them, but do they *listen*? No. They do *not*. Those bites will get infected if you keep scratching them,

I said. Does he *mind* me? I don't have to tell you."

"Those bites do look serious," the clerk said. "I agree with you there."

"Well, you're *different*." Kristin leaned closer and dropped her voice another notch. "If he weren't a friend of my mother, well—" She shrugged.

"Your mother's Russian?" The clerk leaned forward a little bit, too, seemingly mesmerized by Kristin's confidences.

"Bless her soul," Kristin said, blinking rapidly. "Gone now for a year."

"I'm so sorry." The clerk put a box of tissues in front of her. "I'm sure Vlad appreciates your friendship."

"Thank you." Kristin took a tissue and wiped her eyes. "I mustn't keep you from your work. I'm sure I'll see you again. I have to check on Vlad's injuries before he leaves."

"I'll be here!" the clerk said.

Phoebe was amazed at her friend's talent for uncovering information. Kristin was a Mata Hari in Birkenstocks.

"We should leave, Kristin," she said. "We'll be late."

Once out on the street, Kristin shoved the dry tissue into her pocket. "So our guy's name is Vlad, and he's staying in room 604. Where did you park?"

"That was *incredible* work," Phoebe said as they crossed the street. "Plus now the clerk wants to go out with you. I didn't realize you were such a femme fatale."

"My *femme* has been feeling a lot more *fatale* since the whole Nick thing. And I noticed you dropped my name. Not very subtle."

"Subtlety is not always called for. Isn't your mother alive and well and of German extraction?"

"Probably grilling a bratwurst as we speak," Kristin said. "I'll have to call her soon."

"Before you came down, the clerk told me that Vlad comes every year," Phoebe said. "The hotel people like him. Can you believe that? They think he's a nice guy."

"Then it'll be hard to convince them that he's an assassin. If it comes to that."

Phoebe dug out her phone when they got to the bright

yellow SUV. "You drive. I'll call the cops. Let's see if they do something *now*."

But they didn't. Phoebe didn't have the name of the officer who'd interviewed her in the hospital, and without that, she didn't have much, as far as the guy on the phone was concerned.

"Do you have your report number, ma'am?" he asked.

"No," Phoebe said. "He didn't write a report. He said it was a case for the feds. But I was assaulted. Hit by a Taser. Taken to the hospital. And now I have the guy's first name— Vlad—and his hotel and even his room number. I thought the local cops would want to arrest a criminal like that."

"Just now?" the guy asked. "You were assaulted just *now*?"

"No," Phoebe said. "That was *before*. *Now* I followed him to his hotel, so I know where he is. Isn't one assault enough? I still have the holes in my chest from where the Taser barbs went in."

The cop's voice sharpened. "You *followed* him?"

"I *drove*," Phoebe said, still proud of her new license. It felt like a year since she'd passed her test, even though it had been only a few days.

"Okay," the cop said. "Anyway. Listen, without a report, we can't—"

"But I have a witness!" Phoebe said. "My fiancé is a witness to the assault. Well, sort of. Chase Bonaventure. Maybe you've heard of him."

"Fiancé." Evidently the cop wasn't a football fan, or even a follower of the alternative-fuel automotive industry. "What did you say about the feds?"

After a few more minutes of uncooperative sidestepping by the cop on the phone, Phoebe hung up in frustration.

"I'm not getting anywhere with these guys, but the FBI will want to know where Vlad's staying, I'm sure. Or the NSA. Or Homeland. Or even the CIA. *Somebody* will make an arrest. I mean, he's a Russian *assassin*, for Pete's sake! Doesn't anybody *care*?"

"What do the cops do with their time?" Kristin said.

"Although I'm sure they stay busy with thefts and murders and whatever."

Phoebe nodded, peering out the window at the passing scenery. "You know what? We're almost home. That didn't take long. Traffic's light today."

Kristin nodded, glancing at the clock on the dash. "I bet nobody back at the house even noticed we were gone."

But they learned otherwise minutes later when they entered the kitchen.

"Where have you guys been?" Jamal stood at the stove, an apron tied around his waist, stirring something in a big pot. "You abandoned your soup. We were about ready to call the cops."

"Yeah, good luck with *that*." Kristin rolled her eyes.

"Indeed, we have all been most anxious about your safety." Sanjay poured water into the coffee maker and turned it on. "Yuri tried to tell us something, but of course, we didn't understand a word he said. However, he didn't seem unusually agitated, so we were in a bit of a wait-and-see mode."

"Kristin and I had an adventure." Phoebe hung up her messenger bag and keys by the garage door. "We'll tell you over lunch. Is Amos here?"

"Not yet," Jamal said. He banged the edge of the spoon against the side of the pot and lifted it off the burner. "Chase said—"

"Oh, good, you're back." Chase walked into the kitchen. "We were wondering."

"I'm sorry," Phoebe said. "Sanjay said you were worried."

Chase nodded. "I was, but I'd have worried more if just you or Kristin were missing. Both of you gone? I worried about the assassin. Who knows what you two could have done to him."

"Is that a compliment?" Kristin asked.

"I'm not sure," Phoebe said. "I *think* so. So, you want to know what we found out?"

"Please," Chase said. "Tell us while we set the table."

He got soup bowls from a cupboard and piled them on a tray.

She told them about following the Russian assassin. *Vlad*. So good to have a name to go with the face.

"Kristin was brilliant, getting his name and room number," she concluded, pouring herself a cup of coffee. "And I drove!"

"We were careful," Kristin hastened to add. "Phoebe didn't follow too close. He didn't see her, we're both pretty sure of that."

"He saw Kristin, though," Phoebe said.

Kristin nodded. "Unfortunately, yes. I went up in the elevator with him. It was the only way I could find out what room he was in. So now my cover is blown if we have to follow him again."

"*Nobody's following him again*," Chase said, spinning around from taking glasses down. "I can't believe you followed him the *first* time. Did you forget about the tasing already? Here's our plan: we take Yuri to the FBI after lunch, we tell the feds where the shooter is staying, and then *that's it*. We're finished with this business."

Phoebe nodded. She'd be happy when this was over, too, and they could all get back to their regular jobs and home improvements.

And fending off their mothers' wedding plans.

Sanjay took cutlery from a drawer and added it to the tray. "I feel that I must urge a cautionary note," he said. "I believe that we are engaging in a prematurely congratulatory frame of mind. Here is my concern: Phoebe and Kristin followed Vlad the Assassin because they saw him come out of the park, which he must have entered solely for the purpose of locating and retrieving his weaponry. And this he was unable to do, because we had already found and retrieved it."

"Yes, right," Phoebe said. She added some cloth napkins to the pile on the tray.

"And now he probably doesn't have any guns at all, because if he had other guns someplace else, why would he come back for these?" Chase said.

"Precisely." Sanjay frowned at the tray. "With all the

accoutrements that we carry into the dining room, we should consider acquiring some bigger trays."

Chase nodded. "Or a kitchen table. No carrying required."

Phoebe rolled her eyes. "In the meantime, we're safe from whatever Vlad might do, because he doesn't have any guns."

"I believe not," Sanjay said. "Because the assassin's goal of eliminating Yuri remains unchanged as far as we know. Will he give up the goal merely because he lacks the weapons he started out with? I suspect not. That being the case, what means will he use to achieve his ends? What tools will he employ? Because he almost certainly will keep trying to achieve his goal, at least until he is certain that Yuri is beyond his reach. And perhaps not even then."

No one said anything as they all regarded each other.

"*Crap*," Phoebe said.

"He'll get more guns from someplace else," Kristin said.

Phoebe nodded. "That, or he'll use something else. Remember Alexander Litvinenko."

"Poison," Jamal said.

"*Damn*," Chase said, just as another voice said, "Good analysis!" from the doorway.

Everyone whipped around to see Amos smiling benignly at them.

"No one answered the bell, and I know the door code," he said. "Sorry to startle you."

"The doorbell needs repair," Chase said. "We're switching to one of those video doorbells as soon as the alarm company can get out here, which is not until Wednesday. Thanks for getting that literature for us, Amos."

"You're just in time," Phoebe said. "Lunch is ready, and we're hoping to get your expertise on some guns that we found."

Amos raised his eyebrows. "Guns that you *found*."

Phoebe nodded. "Well, really Sanjay found them. In the park."

147

"It is truly a pity that you are unlikely to become a field officer."

"Well, a Russian assassin tased me yesterday, so I'm not as disappointed about that prospect as I might have been at one time."

"I'm sorry to hear that," Amos said. "However, it is mystifying why this Russian assassin went after you. You're not his target. Why put himself at extra risk?"

"We've given up on explanations," Phoebe said. "The FBI can figure it out. That's their wheelhouse, anyway. So, these guns."

"Yes, I'm happy to look at your guns. Where are they?"

"In here." Everyone trooped out of the kitchen and into the blue parlor, where the nylon duffel bag squatted like a fat, black troll on the floor next to a yellow-and-blue chintz sofa.

"We're pretty sure these are the shooter's weapons," Phoebe said. "They're Russian, right?"

Amos bent down and used the flat of his hand to lift the edge of the duffel. "No, not at all," he said, straightening. "These weapons are all of American manufacture."

"*Not* Russian guns?" Phoebe did a double take.

"*American* guns?" Kristin said.

"Oh yes," Amos said. "Although that doesn't mean that they don't belong to your Russian assassin. Almost all the weaponry used throughout the world in wars and clandestine or illegal operations is American in manufacture. Sell to one and all, friend and foe alike, that's the American way."

"But how do American guns get into the hands of a Russian assassin who's here only for a few days?" Jamal asked. "I mean—this quantity, you probably can't carry them on the plane with you, even in checked baggage. And it's not like you can go to the corner and buy night vision goggles and submachine guns. Or can you?"

Amos shrugged, smiling briefly. "Probably not at the corner. But generally speaking, anything you want can be bought on the black market. I suspect that there's a sleeper agent in this operation somehow. Someone in this country who makes the gun buy and leaves the weapons in a locker somewhere. No one meets face-to-face."

"Okay," Jamal said. "But we think that these used to be Vlad's guns, and now they're our guns. So that's still a win for our team."

Amos nodded. "Absolutely. And now all you have to do is keep everybody healthy until you take Yuri to the FBI in"—he checked his watch—"approximately three hours. You say the shooter's name is Vlad?"

Phoebe nodded. "Kristin weaseled that out of the hotel clerk. She was freaking brilliant."

"I wonder if that could be Vladimir Golubkin," Amos said. "One of Russia's premier assassins. He's got to be nearing retirement age by now."

"*What?*" Phoebe said.

Amos shrugged apologetically. "I know him."

Chapter 11

"You know Vlad the Assassin," Phoebe said, trying to as-similate that news as they sat down to lunch. She felt staggered by the knowledge, although why it surprised her, she didn't know. Nothing about Amos should surprise her anymore.

Amos helped himself to bread and passed it Kristin. "We don't exchange Christmas cards, if that's what you mean. We're not *friends*. He was a young shooter just start-ing out when I was approaching retirement. But he came to my attention."

"Is there anything you could tell us about him that would help us—I don't know—catch him? Isolate him? Pro-tect Yuri from him?" She dished out some of the thick lentil soup that Jamal and Sanjay had finished cooking while she and Kristin trailed Vlad to his hotel. It smelled delicious.

"Voice of reason here," Chase said. "We're not *catch-ing* him. The FBI can catch him. Or the cops. Or the CIA. Somebody who is *not us*."

Amos nodded, reaching for the butter. "I don't know a great deal about your guy, if he is Vladimir Golubkin," he said. "You'd do better to contact your colleagues at the CIA who handle Russia."

"Yeah, I'm not besties with anybody in the Russia group." Phoebe handed the soup bowl to Chase. "I could ask

Nattie—she'd help me if she could, although she's not Russia, either. I'm going back to work in a couple of weeks, but I'll be shifting to a new unit, so I doubt anyone would be vested in helping me with this."

Amos nodded. "You must be joining that new outlier group. You're a good fit for it. You and your friend Natasha Wilkinson both. Well, all I can tell you is that as a young man, Vladimir Golubkin was a bright star. He was ruthless, fearless, clever, and deadly accurate."

Phoebe was amazed again that Amos seemed to know all about her new job assignment to a group in the CIA that was so new it wasn't even operational yet. But what he had to say about Vlad the Assassin alarmed her. "That's bad news. From our point of view, I mean."

"Yes. Although he had weaknesses."

"Such as?" Jamal passed the salad to Amos.

"At the time of our evaluation, he didn't handle failure, criticism, or rejection well. Setbacks increased his tolerance for risk, and those risks often involved more injury and bloodshed because it was those times when he made mistakes. Of course, our assessment came when he was in his twenties, just out of his army training. He might have settled down as he matured."

Increased his tolerance for risk. That would explain why she'd gotten tased in broad daylight in front of her house.

"But I'm just speculating." Amos helped himself to soup. "It might not even be the same Vlad."

"Although you think it probably is," Chase said.

Amos shrugged. "Nobody trains *that* many snipers for international assassinations."

"You guys carry on while I update Yuri," Phoebe said. "Maybe he's even heard of this Vlad guy." She leaned forward and started speaking quickly and softly so the others could discuss around them.

"Litvinenko," Yuri said, making a leap in her explanation. The specter of Alexander Litvinenko, murdered by Russian agents with polonium-210—a potent, colorless, tasteless, and odorless radioactive poison—was not something she wanted to think about. What if Vlad had a supply of that? What if he'd brought it to their house? *What if they were eating it right now?*

"What about Litvinenko?" Jamal asked sharply.

"Yuri is suggesting that an assassin who's lost his weapons and is coming unglued and thus taking riskier options might try poisoning us," Phoebe said.

"*What?*" Kristin said, her soup spoon halfway to her mouth.

"You have no need to worry." Sanjay tasted his soup. "The supplies we purchased are as safe as they can be."

Kristin put her spoon back into her bowl. "How can you be sure?"

"How could our Russian assassin, even if he wanted to poison our food, know that we planned to shop today?" Sanjay asked. "We decided only minutes before. And even if he knew that, could he reasonably ascertain at which grocery we would shop? And even if he knew *that*, how could he poison all the food? Because he could not possibly be knowing which apples we would be selecting from the bin. Or even if we would select apples. He would have to be poisoning everything in the store and killing all the customers. That is a task too enormous to be undertaken by a single individual, and a plan too uncertain to attempt, even if he had the knowledge of what store we would patronize, which he did not."

"Argh." Kristin gazed into her soup. "I ate an apple."

"The apples are safe," Sanjay said. "All the food is safe. That is what I'm saying."

Amos tried the thick lentil concoction. "The soup is very tasty. Idli sambar, am I correct?"

"A favorite recipe of my family," Sanjay said. "My mother owns a restaurant, and she taught us all how to cook."

"Sanjay gave me the recipe," Phoebe said.

"My mother would kill me if she knew I was sharing it," Sanjay said. "No one here must ever tell her."

"Danger threatens on all sides." Chase didn't really look

153

like he was kidding.

And why would he be? Phoebe thought. Danger really did threaten on all sides, although probably not from San-jay's mother. Although Sanjay's mother was a force to be reckoned with.

After lunch, they still had a couple of hours before the appointment with the FBI. Yuri went down to the basement to shove his new clothes and toiletries into the shopping bag that Phoebe gave him, Sanjay and Jamal departed to gas up the armored vehicle, and Amos and Chase disappeared to test the doorbell wiring.

"I'm going to call Nick," Kristin told Phoebe as they finished washing the dishes. "See if there's any change in our relationship or employment status. Coach wants to know if I'm accepting my promotion, and I don't blame him. I think this is decision time."

"If you want to talk after, come find me," Phoebe said, folding the dish towel and hanging it neatly on the rack.

Then, with nothing to do until it was time to go, she fol-lowed up on Amos's suggestion to call Nattie about Vlad. But Nattie Wilkinson, her friend since her first day at the agency, didn't pick up. While she was at it, Phoebe deleted a voice mail from her mother, reporting that she'd found a wonderful wedding venue in New Orleans, just perfect for a spring wedding.

As if.

Shortly after that, somebody pounded on the door, which alarmed her, but it turned out to be a delivery guy—a real delivery guy this time—who left a huge box on their porch.

"Should we call the bomb squad?" She peered through the window at the carton outside, which appeared big enough to garage a small car. "Guys delivering boxes have me spooked."

"Nah," Chase said, opening the door. "It's the towels. I got overnight service at no extra charge for a local delivery."

He dragged in the box and tore it open. Phoebe was staggered by the number of towels they'd bought and the array of colors. Well, five bathrooms, lots of houseguests. They needed a lot of towels.

"We could open a store," she said, taking out a blue set. "Look at this beautiful color. So much nicer than it showed on the screen."

"We'll have to tell Mateo to match the paint in the bathrooms to them."

"I should launder them before we use them, right? I'll put a load in the washer right now."

Chase dragged the box upstairs for her and Phoebe happily cut the tags off the towels, started a load of laundry, and recycled all the packaging until *finally* it was time to go to the FBI.

She found Yuri watching a soccer game on the big plasma TV downstairs. "Time to go, Yuri."

He'd been a looming, uncomfortable houseguest who'd endangered everyone, and she'd be glad to see the last of him. Still, she felt a little nostalgic about it, too. They'd had so many adventures since he'd shown up.

"You got everything?"

Yuri touched a button on the remote to turn off the television. "Надеюсь, на новом месте есть такой телевизор."

"You can ask the FBI for a TV like this," Phoebe replied. "It's their job to make you happy."

Yuri nodded and, picking up his bag of belongings with his good arm, followed her upstairs. Maybe he was feeling a little nostalgic, too.

At the door to the garage, Chase enveloped Phoebe in a hug. "I should go in your place. You were just tased yesterday. I don't want Vlad to have another crack at you."

"I'm fine," Phoebe said. "The FBI—Kevin Toth—is expecting me. The Feebs might think something is off if you go instead of me."

"Everything about this venture is off. All right then, how about if we *both* go? There's room in the car."

Phoebe gave him a ferocious hug. "We *talked* about this. You have to stay here. I can't leave Kristin and Amos alone in the house. What if Vlad doesn't realize that Yuri's gone and comes back to do something worse than he's already done? I'd never forgive myself. You're the last line of defense here."

Chase sighed and let her go. "I hate this."

She reached up to kiss him. "I'll be fine. We'll be fine. We'll drop Yuri, and that will be the end of it. We'll be home before you know it."

"I sure hope so."

Phoebe opened the SUV's back door for Yuri, and Jamal hoisted the heavy bag of weapons into the armored vehicle's cargo area. She turned to Kristin.

"You guys be careful here," she said.

"Nothing will happen," Kristin said. "At the very least, the construction crew is a deterrent to assassination. I think it's you guys who are vulnerable."

"There's three of us in the house," Amos said. "If anything should happen, I'm not the fastest runner in the crowd, but I still have a few tricks up my sleeve."

Phoebe grinned. "Probably more than a few. We won't be long."

"Promise me—don't take any risks," Chase said. "Don't put yourself in danger. If it feels wrong, just come back. This Kevin Toth can come over here and pick Yuri up. Jamal, Sanjay—you got that? No risks."

"Got it," Jamal said.

"We will be extremely careful," Sanjay said.

Phoebe helped Yuri with his seat belt, and then they headed out. Traffic was still light, so they made good time to the FBI building, and Jamal was able to park as close as legally permitted, only a block away. After he turned off the engine, they all stared at each other for a second.

Now was the moment of truth. Was Vlad the Assassin out there, waiting to pick off Yuri? Or did he plan to kill all of them? Phoebe didn't like knowing that Vlad might be unraveling. *Deadly accurate*, that's what Amos had said.

She didn't want to die. She hadn't even really started her life with Chase. They'd just bought the house! The new towels were still in the dryer! But she didn't want to live with

Yuri one second longer than she had to, and he had much to offer the FBI. Once they delivered him, the danger would be over.

They unbuckled their seat belts and peered out the windows. Phoebe scanned the area, searching for the guy who'd tased her. She didn't see him, although that would be too simple. Surely he'd be on a roof somewhere. Snipers could fire from great distances—Vlad might be accurate up to a mile away. But they couldn't stall any longer. They had to get Yuri into the building.

"Showtime," Jamal said.

"This could be the most dangerous moment of the entire weekend, the attack on Phoebe notwithstanding," Sanjay said. "This is the last opportunity the Russian assassin has to eliminate Yuri. We must be vigilant."

"Everybody run," Jamal said. "Go as fast as you can in a zigzag pattern. Keep it hard for the shooter."

Phoebe tapped Yuri on the arm, pointed to the door of the FBI building, and told him the plan. He looked pale. Well, probably they all did.

They eased out of the vehicle, pausing for a second behind the open car doors that gave them some cover, waiting for gunfire to erupt. Nothing happened. *Waiting to get us in the open*, Phoebe thought.

Sanjay slung the duffel bag of guns over his shoulder, and they dashed for the entrance, scattering the occasional tourist as they ran. Phoebe's heart pounded, and her mouth was dry with fear. She heard nothing—not traffic or tourists or gunshots. She focused solely on the entrance and how far she had to run. Through tunnel vision, she saw Jamal ahead of her and Yuri beside her, his bright pink cast like a target on their collective backs. Sanjay, carrying the duffel, must be behind her. *Please let him be all right.* She'd never forgive herself if anything happened to him. To any of them.

Every stride that took her closer to the building increased both her fear and her hope. Could she make it? Would everyone get inside safely?

They rushed the door. Jamal yanked it open, using it to

shield himself, and held it while everyone else leaped inside.

They'd made it. Everyone was safe. Phoebe bent over, panting in relief. Sanjay dropped the duffel, which clattered when it hit the hard floor. The men, breathing heavily, grinned and slapped each other on the back. Talk about cheating death! She was as proud of them as if they'd gone hand-to-hand with Vlad and emerged triumphant.

"Duffel bags that size are not allowed on the premises," the security guard said.

"We have an appointment with Kevin Toth at three," Phoebe said, catching her breath. "We have Yuri Severov with us. He's defecting. Kevin Toth is doing the debrief."

"Gonna have to leave the bag outside."

"We have to give it to Kevin Toth," Phoebe said. "Or somebody."

The security guard gave them the once-over. His eyebrows knit over his eyes. Then he seemed to make a decision. He tapped on his computer. Peered at the screen. "You folks aware we're in a government shutdown?"

"*What?*" Phoebe said. A *shutdown*?

The guard nodded, still focused on his screen. "Yup. Budget hullabaloo. Most offices are closed. Or on reduced staffing."

Phoebe stared at the guy, incredulous. Not today! Not the day they were supposed to bring Yuri in. Kevin Toth—that rat bastard! She'd talked to him *two days ago*. He'd *known*. Had to have.

"Was that a sudden action?" Phoebe said. "I just made the appointment with him on Saturday."

The guard shrugged, peering at the keyboard and typing a few more strokes. "What can I tell you? Everything closed as of midnight last night."

No wonder traffic had been light. No wonder Nattie hadn't picked up her phone. No wonder they'd found nearby parking.

The guard squinted back at the screen. "FBI's essential personnel, though," he said. "Law enforcement. National security and all that. So most everybody's in, same as usual.

Even me." He smiled briefly at them.

Thank heaven. Phoebe felt herself relax and realized everyone else had let out a breath, too.

"Except Kevin Toth," the guard said. "He's out for a week for sure. Maybe longer. Measles."

"*Measles?*" Phoebe said, flabbergasted. "That can't be right. They've got vaccinations for that! And he was fine a couple of days ago." The guard shrugged again.

"Sorry, ma'am. Call back in a week or so to reschedule. Anything else I can help you with?"

She closed her eyes, stymied. She wanted to hand off Yuri to someone who could take care of him, keep him safe, and receive the information he was trying his best to give them. And if she brought him back to the house, they'd all still be in danger. Chase wouldn't much like it. Well, she didn't, either. And Sanjay and Jamal had to get back to their security instruction program. They couldn't hang at the house forever.

They were supposed to hand Yuri off today. She really didn't see why they couldn't. Did *all* the Russian defectors have to kill time, couch surfing for days or even *weeks* until the FB-freaking-I decided they were ready to take someone in? Who *were* those people?

Sanjay cleared his throat. "Phoebe. What do you suggest is our next best course of action?"

"Maybe somebody else here at the FBI could take Yuri," she said. "It doesn't have to be Kevin Toth who does the debrief. Maybe they transferred his caseload while he's out. Maybe we can reach somebody—the supervisor!—and find out. And about the duffel bag." Phoebe nudged it with her toe. "We'd really like to get rid of it."

"Good thing I didn't have anything else to do today," the guard said, but he didn't sound mad about it.

"It's full of guns," Phoebe said.

The guard leaped to his feet, grabbed his weapon, and pointed it at them.

Jamal threw up his hands. "Whoa!"

"Don't shoot!" Sanjay said, his hands up. "We are

trying to assist law enforcement personnel by turning in the many weapons of a Russian assassin!"

"That's why we brought them!" Phoebe said, wishing that she'd thought of a better way to tell the guard about the guns.

Yuri stuck his hands in the air, dropping his shopping bag of belongings. "Не стреляйте!"

The guard relaxed marginally, but he didn't put down his weapon. "Russian assassin. Maybe you should explain."

"I'm in the CIA," Phoebe said. "Federal employee. Can you check me out? Verify that somehow?"

But the guard shattered her hopes.

"Above my pay grade," he said. "If our database could handle it, which I doubt."

"Okay," Phoebe said. "Well, we took the guns from the Russian assassin who's after Yuri here. We don't want the guns in our house. Well, we don't want Yuri in our house, either, if we're honest about it, because he's attracting the Russian assassin to us like a killer magnet. I got tased yesterday, and I didn't like it *at all*. And we're worried about what's next with this guy. So we want to leave the guns here. They're just one more thing that could go sideways. Can you take care of that for us? Get rid of them, I mean? Or do whatever?"

"Like a coat check, you mean?" The guard seemed skeptical.

"Well, yes, I guess so," Phoebe said. "But we won't come back to pick them up. We don't want them. Think of them more like a birthday gift. If Kevin Toth is out for a while, can we give everything—Yuri and the guns—to somebody else? The case manager, maybe?"

The guard hesitated, but then he holstered his weapon and sat down at his desk again.

"Guy's out," he said after a minute of tapping on his keyboard again.

The case manager—a civilian, not law enforcement—was furloughed for the shutdown. Toth's supervisor told them to persuade a coworker to take Yuri on. His coworkers—

the ones who answered their phones—told them to call the supervisor. After forty minutes of running in circles, they'd gotten nowhere. Everyone looked discouraged, and Yuri, who had picked up his shopping bag of meager possessions again and held it under his arm, looked a little pathetic, too. Like a refugee. Which he sort of was.

"It seems that we have exhausted our remedies here with the FBI," Sanjay said finally.

Sanjay was probably right.

"He'd be better off in an FBI safe house," Phoebe said. "And we'd be safer, too."

"Should we take him to a hotel?" Jamal asked. "Do you think that's safe enough?"

"No, not really," she said. "Not for a week. Our place is probably still safer than a hotel. Let's go home. I'll call Chase and tell him to expect us."

"An excellent idea," Sanjay said. "Since he is not expecting to have Yuri returning as a houseguest for an indefinite period."

"Rub it in." Phoebe punched in the number.

"Something went wrong," Chase said when he picked up, taking the words out of her mouth. "Don't tell me. Yuri's coming back with you."

"I don't see what else we can do." She filled him in. "I'm sorry, though. It's not really what you expected when we moved in together."

"I suppose Yuri would be killed if we cut him loose," Chase said, "and I'm sorry to say that I'm not as upset about that as I ought to be. Promise me that you'll get on the phone when you get home and try to find someone else we can hand him off to. Who knows when this Kevin Toth guy will recover from the measles? What if he dies of complications and we *never* get rid of Yuri?"

"Don't even *think* it." She disconnected and turned to Sanjay and Jamal. "All good. Now, about the guns."

"You can leave the guns," the guard said. "There's a protocol for that."

"Make sure Kevin Toth or whoever knows these are

connected to Yuri's case," Phoebe said. "It might be important later, when we catch the assassin."

"I thought we weren't catching him," Jamal said.

"Did I say 'catching'?" Phoebe said. "We're not catching."

"Do you want a receipt for the guns?" the guard asked.

"Do I need one?" Phoebe said. "I don't want them back. I just want Kevin Toth to know that we think they belong to our guy. The Russian assassin."

"I'll tag 'em," the guard said.

"Okay," Jamal said. "Now we just have to get back to the car safely."

"I have been thinking," Sanjay said. "I am wondering that perhaps the reason we were not targeted on our dash to the door is that our Vlad the Assassin was not able to reassemble his firepower in time to pursue us to this appointment today. Especially if his weaponry is supplied by a local third party."

"Good point." Phoebe thought for a minute. "If he was waiting for us, why didn't he shoot us when we got here? That doesn't mean we shouldn't run back to the car, though."

"No, indeed. I am not advising we should let down our guard."

Phoebe peered out the glass door, across the plaza, and down the street. She didn't see anyone that could be a shooter, not that she expected to. Was he out there?

"I'll go first and unlock the car," Jamal said. He dashed out the door, beeping open the car as he ran, and then pulled up directly in front, double-parking in the street to get as close as possible to the glass door.

Then Yuri, Sanjay, and Phoebe ran out, zigging across the plaza to the vehicle. Nothing happened, to her immense relief. No shots rang out. No bullets ricocheted. Big thumbs-up there.

For now, they were safe.

"I know you guys thought today would be the end of everything," she said when they were on the road again. She felt guilty, wanting them to stay at her place until Yuri was safely in the hands of the FBI. "You've missed classes and training, and you've already done so much for us. You could just drop Yuri and me and go back to normal life."

Sanjay turned around from his front seat and beamed at Phoebe. "Indeed, no, such a proposition is not part of our plan at all. Jamal and I have become rock stars in the classroom! The envy of all the other students. We have spoken to our instructors, and it is confirmed: we will prepare a class presentation about the steps we have taken to improve your personal protection as well as the protection of the house. This effort will earn us significant extra credit."

"Yuri is extra credit?" Phoebe blinked.

"Ain't that a kick?" Jamal said.

"We feel most fortunate that we are having this unexpected hands-on training, which our classmates might never have," Sanjay said. "We must ask you to sign off on it when the task is completed. Our instructors want to make sure we are not fabricating the whole scenario. Especially the Chase Bonaventure connection. Plus I think there is the autograph factor."

"The company that owns the car and hires me does want the rental fee to be paid for the car," Jamal said. "I checked on that."

"No problem," Phoebe said. "Tell them to send us an invoice. And you guys? Thanks."

By the time they got home, reality had sunk in. Another week—at least—of Yuri in the house while Kevin Toth got over the measles. She didn't want Yuri killed, of course, but her hospitable instincts had limits.

She followed the guys into the kitchen, where Chase waited for her.

"Surprise," she said.

He grinned ruefully at her. "I have a surprise for you, too."

"Oh?" Her spirits perked up a little. "What's that?"

"Phoebe! *Sweetie!*"

Phoebe listened in shock to the enthusiastic exclamation from the next room.

"Sorry," Chase mouthed silently at her.

"Where's my baby?" Footsteps tapped across the entryway. "Where's my little bride-to-be?"

Brenda Renfrew burst into the kitchen, arms outstretched, and beamed at her daughter. "*There* she is!"

Phoebe plastered a smile on her face. "Hi, Mom."

Chapter 12

C hase left the unexpected and unwelcome family reun-
ion in the kitchen and retired to their bedroom. Phoebe
wouldn't appreciate her mom's unexpected arrival for a visit
of undetermined length. If there was going to be a bloodbath
down there, he wanted no part of it.

Phoebe might not forgive him for abandoning her with
Brenda and her overeager wedding plans, but she'd brought
Yuri back, so as far as he was concerned, they were even in
the unwelcome guest department. And given Brenda's history, she'd take up with Yuri, and then they'd *both* be living
in the basement. And wouldn't that be a like a scene straight
out of a movie?

A Stephen King movie.

In the meantime, he still had a company to run, so although he'd taken two weeks off to get settled in DC, he
opened his laptop and got to work.

He wasn't sure how long he'd been at it when he became aware that something was happening. He heard voices.
Loud voices. Phoebe and Kristin were more than capable of
quelling loud voices, but there was a remote possibility that
Russian thugs had gained entrance. More likely, there was
trouble with the construction crew. And in that case, he
wanted to smooth it over, or throw money at it, or do whatever it took to keep repairs on track. So he closed his laptop

to check it out.

Out on the landing, Sanjay and Jamal were standing in front of Yuri, barring him from entering the small purple bathroom. Phoebe was hanging on to Yuri's good arm. Yuri was trying to brandish the baseball bat. Everyone was yelling. He didn't see Kristin, but she was in the melee somewhere because he heard her.

"This man is not the assassin!" Sanjay yelled.

"Not your guy!" Jamal shouted. "Nyet! Nyet!"

"Dude!" the voice of an unknown male bellowed. "What're ya doin', man? You could hurt a person swingin' that bat around!"

"Are you all right?" Kristin called from inside the bathroom. "Be careful!"

Phoebe and Yuri shouted incomprehensible things in Russian.

"What's going on out here?" Chase asked.

Phoebe turned, holding on to Yuri's arm, and rolled her eyes. "Doolie was cutting the hole in the ceiling for the bathroom skylight, and Yuri saw him and decided he was the assassin chopping through the roof so he could drop in and kill him. He took a couple of swings at him with the baseball bat."

"Hey," the unknown male voice said from somewhere in the bathroom. "Doolie here. I'm not the assassin. Maybe somebody could tell that dude."

"Спускаться! Я убью тебя!" Yuri snarled.

"Вы никого не убиваете!" Phoebe said.

"What was that?" Chase asked.

Phoebe sighed. "Yuri said, 'Get down—I'm going to kill you.' You see the failure of logic there. Why would Doolie come down just so that Yuri could kill him? He wouldn't. So I told Yuri that he, meaning Yuri, wasn't going to kill anybody. Well, Doolie, either, for that matter. Nobody's killing anybody, that's my point."

"Certainly not with a baseball bat," Chase said.

"Not with my saw, either." Doolie wisely stayed where he was.

Chase shook his head at Phoebe. "I'm happier than ever that you gave the guns to the FBI."

He eased around the crowd and stepped into the bathroom. A wary young man was just visible through the opening in the ceiling, peering down at them.

"You must be Doolie," Chase said, looking up. "Mateo probably told you that this nutjob in here is our Russian defector. He thinks every stranger is an assassin out to kill him."

"Yeah, we heard about that," Doolie said. "Who knows? Somebody might really be after him. I just didn't think he'd be swinging at me through the ceiling with a bat. I mean, man, I'm on a *roof*. That's *dangerous*."

"Sorry about that," Chase said. "We'll get him out of your hair now."

"That'd be good. We want to get the skylight installed tonight. Rain's in the forecast, and if the roof's wet tomorrow morning, we don't go up. Plus, you know, rain and holes in the roof are not the best combination."

"Understood. Consider it done."

Doolie grinned, sticking his hand through the hole in the ceiling. "Hey, I'm a longtime fan. Sorry about your knee. That hadda suck."

Chase grinned back, shaking hands. "It did, but in the end, it all turned out for the best."

Doolie shook his head. "Team's gonna miss you."

"Coaches and players are working hard. And Washington looks good this year. It'll be a fun season." Chase turned back to the crowd on the landing. "Now we will all go downstairs for dinner, which smells great. *Cher*, please tell Yuri that if he doesn't leave Doolie alone, we will put him out on the curb for the trash collectors."

Phoebe grinned and started chatting to the Russian.

Not that he was so anxious for all of them to sit down together. Yuri would probably complain about something, and Brenda would suggest endless wedding plans, which would annoy Phoebe, not that he could blame her for that.

Not exactly a party mood. And he had at least another

week of this to look forward to—a week of Yuri being annoying and attracting assassins to the house before they could unload him on the FBI.

After that, they'd have only Brenda to contend with. Brenda and her wedding ideas.

But at least Brenda spoke English. And English he understood. Although wedding talk, not so much.

He didn't think there was any kind of translation for that.

After dinner, Phoebe followed him back upstairs, which probably meant she wanted to talk to him privately. These days, if they wanted to have a private conversation in their five-thousand-square-foot, six-bedroom, five-bath, four-parlor house, they had to go to their bedroom to have it. They had a nice sitting area in this room, but he thought cuddling a little would be more enjoyable.

"*Cher*," he said. "Let's get cozy. It seems like I haven't talked to you for months. Hospitals don't count." He sat on the bed and leaned against the headboard, stretching his legs out and rearranging the pillows behind his back.

"Why did Mom have to come?" Phoebe plopped down on the edge of the mattress. "I certainly didn't *invite* her. The magazines with the sticky notes are bad enough. Not that I don't want to *see* her, exactly. I *like* her okay. It's just—"

"You don't want her shoving a wedding down your throat. And the timing with Yuri isn't optimal."

"*Exactly*."

"I get it. But you're her only child. And even though her parenting skills aren't great, she means well and wants the best for you. She wants you to have the things she didn't have." He patted the bedspread. "Scoot up here."

She sighed. "All the things she didn't have, like a wedding."

"I was thinking, a handsome devil like me for a husband."

She laughed, as he'd hoped she would, and crawled up to sit next to him. "Since she's here now, it's a good thing those new towels came today."

He put his arm around her, and she snuggled in against him. That felt better. She gave a little sigh, and he stroked her hair, feeling its silky softness stream through his fingers.

"This is nice," she said.

"It is." He hesitated, not wanting to break the mood. "So, now that Brenda's here."

Brenda's presence would accelerate and magnify what he'd come to think of as the Bridal Magazine Effect—the grumpiness and resistance that Phoebe always displayed after a magazine arrived in the mail. A magazine about marriage. Which Phoebe wasn't ready for.

"What about her?" Phoebe twisted in his arms to look into his face. Already on the alert.

He chose his words carefully. "I gotta agree with you, your mom is pretty relentless. So when she asks me why we're not setting a date, which you know she will do, I want to be able to tell her more than that I'm letting you make that decision. That puts an unfair burden on you, *cher*, being the sole reason for disappointing your mother."

"I'll just tell her you've already got six wives hidden away in Montana. No problem."

He grinned. "I doubt even that would put her off. So I was just thinkin', if we set a date, a *fake* date, a date we don't mean to keep, a date that's five years from now, or even ten, it would shut up *both* our mothers."

In one smooth motion, Phoebe pulled away and got off the bed. Rigid with tension, she stalked to the window and gazed out.

"Setting a date, even a fake one, puts the wheels in motion. And I don't want motion. I want *brakes*."

"I know, and I'm a little worried here about how this tension our moms are creatin' might play out between us," he said. "Your mom was always interested in weddings, ours specifically, but nothing like until we moved in together."

"That's the truth."

"And back when we were in Vegas and lookin' for a way to avoid a long-distance romance when you had to come back to DC to work, I said I'd move here with you on the condition that you agreed to an engagement and living with me. But I didn't realize that agreement would give our moms free rein to hassle you. I'm in hog heaven here, but this arrangement has had some unintended consequences for you. Do you have any regrets about anything?"

She whirled around. "Never! *Never*." She sounded ferocious. Maybe that was good. "You think I felt coerced into living with you? Never! We *agreed*. You moved across the country for me. I moved into your house for you. It was a compromise. And it's worked out great for me. I'm happy to be back in DC and starting work soon. I'm happy with you, I'm happy in this house. What I'm *not* happy about is my mother constantly pushing me. Why should she care when I get married?"

"No reason, *cher*. But your mom wants a weddin', and she can hang tighter than a hungry tick on an overfed hound dog. And I don't want her buggin' you to death. Me either, for that matter."

Her eyes sparkled in anger, her breathing too fast, her voice sharp. "I don't care what my mother wants," she said. "I won't let her dictate my life. She didn't have that much to do with it when I was a kid, and now that I'm grown up, I sure won't let her tell me when or how to get married. If I *ever* decide I want that."

Whoa. If she *ever* wanted to get married? She might not *want* to get married?

"Sweetheart, hey, it's just you an' me here." How to backpedal? Just a second ago they'd been cuddling. Now she didn't want to get married at all? "I'm just tryin' to find a way for you to get the time you want while easin' your mom's overactive matrimonial drives."

"I don't need a *way* to get more time. I just tell Mom to get over it. Period. And if she can't, she can take a hike. She sure knows how to do that."

"Okay." He didn't know what to say to that. This discussion was as old as their relationship. Sometimes Phoebe could take Brenda's interference with amusement, but evidently not when Brenda was in the same house. It seemed like Phoebe's overeager mother had inadvertently set back their marriage plans further than she'd realized.

Phoebe had turned back to the window. To tell the truth, the struggle over the wedding date did seem kind of dumb to him. He suppressed a sigh.

"I heard that," she said. "So you *do* think waiting is pointless."

"Not for you."

"You got married after you knew Tracy for two months," she said. "About the same amount of time as you've known me. And you and Tracy were divorced in about six months, right? And Mom— Well, you know her. She's gone off with a million guys, and each time she thinks he's The One. And it never works out."

"Tracy and I are not the same as you and me. And you and I are not the same as your mother and her guy du jour."

"Of course not. I'm saying that the, the *electricity* that everybody feels at the beginning—it makes everybody feel sure about the relationship until the electricity goes away and everything falls apart. And what *I* want to be sure about is that our relationship won't fall apart."

"It won't fall apart."

She seemed not to have heard him. "Marriage is opening a door to the complete unknown. Beyond it, maybe everything is good. You know, rainbows and unicorns, all that. But half the time—*half!*—it isn't. Maybe what lies behind that door is loneliness, misery, pain, despair—"

"I *get* it," Chase said, wanting the litany to stop. This is what Phoebe thought marriage would be like? Marriage to *him*?

"It's a crapshoot," Phoebe said. "That's what I'm saying."

"No, it's not," Chase said. "Not our marriage. For you and me, when we marry, when we open that door, we will not find misery. Hell, even Tracy wouldn't say that, and she and I were suited for only about fifteen minutes. *Our* future, yours and mine—our *marriage*—is not a fifty-fifty proposition. That is *not us*."

She turned to face him again, her gaze stony, her breathing still too fast. But at least she wasn't looking out the window anymore. She was listening to him.

"I already know you in ways I never knew Tracy," he said. "I know what you want and how much you want it. I know how committed and loyal you are to the things you believe in. I know how smart and hardworking you are. And I think you know as much about me. And that's because we talk to each other. We communicate. We're already a team."

She sniffed, but her face had softened. She didn't look so stormy anymore, he was relieved to see.

"I understand that you feel confident about our future," she said. "But I don't understand why."

"*Cher*, we're exactly alike, you have to see that."

She blinked. "We're exactly alike? You've got to be kidding. You're rich and famous. Raised by nice parents. I'm so not any of that."

"That's just superficialities. Look at the basics. We approach challenges the same way. It seems like we make snap judgments, but the risks we take are based on preparation. We are *ready* when a crisis comes. Take your Empire State Building nightmare. You had to make a snap decision, and at first it looked like the wrong one."

"It sure did."

"But you'd studied for years. And then the CIA trained you. You knew the actors, the situation, the language, the likelihood of a given scenario. You made a decision based on a deep understanding from longtime preparation. And in the end, your decision was the correct one."

"Well, okay, but—"

"Same with me," he said. "That pass to Dan Freer that everybody talks about? It looked like a once-in-a-lifetime execution. But it wasn't as much of a miracle as everyone thinks. Dan and I had practiced that play a thousand times. I knew exactly how high—to the *inch*—he could jump to catch a pass. I knew how high his defenders could jump, too, and I knew that he could beat that. We had luck on our side, sure. Something can always go wrong. But that play worked in a tough situation because we'd prepared for that moment."

"I haven't really thought about us like that," Phoebe said, leaving the window to sit on the edge of the bed again. "I think I'm focused on the likelihood of relationship failure because that's what I know. I mean, my mom, obviously. One hundred percent relationship failure there. For decades."

"You are nothing like your mom. One reason I fell for you was that you'll fight to the last inch before you let a relationship fail."

"*Really?* Why do you think that?"

"Way back, when you found Trouble on the side of the road. When I said that you couldn't take him to the plant, you quit your job working' for me. Remember?"

"How could I forget?" She grinned at the memory.

"Yeah, and you really needed the money, too, but you chose to hang on to that mangy dog rather than the nice, cushy job at the extortionate salary I was paying you. And I knew right then that if you'd go to the mat like that for a dog you'd just met, think how you'd stick by a guy you cared for. Through thick and thin, that's how."

"Oh." She looked thoughtful.

"And deep down, whether you've thought about us in those same terms, I think you feel that certainty, too. You *know* that we're right together."

"You're right that I haven't thought about things that way."

"Tell me something." He reached out to play with her fingers. "What's the worst that could happen? And how would that make you feel?"

"The absolute worst would be if we got married and divorced. I'd be crushed. I don't think I'd ever get over it."

"Well, of course I would be unforgettable." He grinned at her. "That part's easy to understand."

Phoebe laughed, but her laughter died quickly. "Part of it would be about the loss of you," she said. "But there'd also be the realization that I failed. That I failed as a human being. As a person who could—who has the capacity to—"

"Love somebody? Love someone deeply?"

She nodded, her eyes filling with tears. He reached for her hand.

"Like your mother failed," he said. "Failed in her relationships with men and her relationship with you."

She sniffed, grabbing a tissue and wiping her nose.

"*Cher*. Sweetheart. It'll never happen. That dumb dog proves it. All your friends. Kristin, Sanjay, Nattie. For Pete's sake—they stick to you like glue because you are loyal and true and a wonderful friend and you are a wonderful fiancée and you will be a wonderful wife whenever you decide you want to add that to your résumé. Hell, you got me to accept Yuri living in the basement, and if that's not a triumph, I don't know what is."

She smiled, but it was a little shaky at the edges. "You know what? I feel better."

"I believe in us. Our success. Our forever. We won't always see things the same way on every decision. Marriages have bad patches. I've seen it with my own folks. But if you talk and care about the other person and are kind, you come out stronger. My folks are solid. My brothers, too. They're happy. And so are we. We're good now, and we'll be good later, too. In fact, I think we'll get better as we age. Like fine wine."

Phoebe grinned. "Wine, huh? Well, maybe. I hope so. I feel sure of this moment. I'm just not quite sure about the forever part. And that's what I want with you. Forever. And until I *am* sure, I don't want to rock the boat."

"I know. But I believe. And in time, I think you'll see that we'll be even more successful in marriage than we are right now."

"Well, that's what I'm talking about," she said. "More time."

"We're on the same page, then." But in truth, he wasn't sure that they were. And if Brenda persisted in pushing Phoebe to the altar, he was afraid that she'd back off altogether.

Not getting married soon—or even at all—was one

thing. He could live with that, if they were all in on the commitment side of things. He knew plenty of committed couples who lived together without the benefit of marriage. He himself would prefer to get married, but if Phoebe didn't want the legalities, he could go along.

But if she didn't believe in him—if she couldn't find a way to "forever" and decided to leave him altogether—that would be different. Devastating.

He hadn't known Phoebe for long, but he loved her totally and absolutely, for her heart and courage and brain, for everything she was. He couldn't imagine not living with her for the next half dozen decades, figuring out everything he didn't know about her so far and finding out what their life would be like down the road. He loved her with his whole being, for the long haul.

He didn't want to think that she might not love him back the same way.

Chapter 13

Phoebe woke to find the other side of the bed empty. Chase must have gone out already for a run, which he tried to do most days. She hoped he had taken Trouble. You couldn't be too careful with Russian assassins out there tasing everybody.

She took off the little Band-Aids that covered her Taser wounds and inspected the area. No redness, so all good there. The back of her legs where they had abraded on the pavement had started to itch, so that was probably a good sign, too.

Progress.

She stepped under the shower and let the water pour over her for longer than was strictly necessary to get clean, and when she stepped out, she toweled off with one of the new towels, a big white one, fluffy and soft, with a pretty, deep cobalt-blue trim, color-matched to the bathroom. *Nice.* They'd made some good choices. And the towels had been on sale, too.

Kristin was already in the kitchen, pouring water into the coffeepot when she got there.

"Hey." Phoebe got a mug from the cupboard.

"Morning."

They stood together in companionable silence until the coffee finished dripping, and Kristin poured some first into

Phoebe's mug and then her own.

"The sunroom's nice this time of day," Phoebe said. "Let's sit in there."

Kristin grinned. "Yeah, the sunroom's a lot less formal than the dining room."

They carried their mugs across the entryway to the sunroom at the back of the house and settled into the overlarge chintz furniture. Phoebe sipped her coffee. Very strong, just how she liked it.

They sat in silence for a minute, savoring the moment before Chase came back and everyone gathered for breakfast. Phoebe thought about the problem that was Yuri.

"I'm worried about what the FBI will say when they find out that Yuri doesn't have as much intel as we'd originally led them to believe," she said finally.

"The FBI will still take him, though, won't they?"

"I certainly hope so," Phoebe said. "The data is valuable even if there's not as much of it. But he can't be worth as much to the FBI. What if they don't take him? Or they take the intel but don't offer him asylum or witness protection? All that."

"You're afraid that he won't ever leave your basement."

"In a nutshell. I mean, they'll do *something* with him, but—"

Kristin shook her head. "I don't see what we can do about it except be as persuasive as possible with the FBI."

Phoebe nodded. Sipped her coffee. Thought about it some more. Then she settled her cup on the end table.

"Okay, here's something. I have an idea."

"What kind of idea?"

Phoebe flashed a grin. "Probably a bad one. The whole plan depends on you. So, no pressure if you don't want to do it."

Kristin perked up. "Really? Me? Of course, I want to do it. Tell."

"Well, Vlad broke into Yuri's room and stole all his stuff and the data with it. We know where Vlad's staying. How about we steal the data back?"

Kristin choked on her coffee. "You want to steal data from an armed Russian assassin? How do you propose that we'll do that? And live to tell about it?"

"The data has to be in Vlad's hotel room, right?" Phoebe said. "Would he risk shipping Yuri's suitcase back to Moscow? Like with FedEx or something? Maybe leave it in a locker someplace? He might, but I think he'd keep it with him. He'd want to keep an eye on it, wouldn't he? I don't know. Maybe I'm wrong. But I think we should make the effort. See if we can find it."

"Again," Kristin said. "How will we do that? And I'm doing this by myself?"

"I'll be with you, but you have to do the heavy lifting. Vlad has to leave his room sometimes, right? For meals and whatever. To go out and tase me. Whatever errands a Russian assassin has to do."

"Riiiiight," Kristin said slowly.

"So we break into his room when he's gone. I'll ask Yuri for descriptions of his stuff, but it's probably all in his suitcase. Vlad would just have thrown everything together when he stripped Yuri's room. I mean, Vlad's an *assassin*. He doesn't have to be neat about a theft."

"I'm not necessarily *against* the idea," Kristin said, frowning. "But don't you think that Vlad will be even madder at us and desperate to find Yuri if we steal that data? The retribution could be fierce."

Phoebe nodded. "It could be. It's a risk, for sure. I think it'd be worth it if we could get the data back, and not just because it would get Yuri out of the basement. The analysts could really use the information he's got."

"So how can we break into Vlad's room? And how will we know when he goes out?"

"That's where you come in," Phoebe said. "The hotel clerk likes you. He's our way in."

"I don't know if he likes me enough to give me the key to a guest room."

"We'll have to play that part by ear," Phoebe said. "But my idea is to say we want to surprise him."

Kristin raised her eyebrows. "Oh, I think we'll surprise him, all right."

They concocted a story about working with Vlad, and Kristin called the hotel and talked to Gordon, the hotel clerk, who was very happy to hear from her. He reported that, in fact, Vlad had left the hotel, probably to eat breakfast, which he preferred to take at the local diner rather than their own dining room. With that news, Phoebe ran downstairs to consult with Yuri, and five minutes later they were on their way. They had to move quickly, because Gordon had told Kristin that Vlad didn't usually stay out for meals much longer than an hour or so.

If they were going to get that data, now was the time.

Vlad sat on a red vinyl stool in the diner he'd come to think of as "his" and dawdled over breakfast, pondering how to save his mission. So far it had been a colossal failure. First he'd missed killing Severov at the State Department when his shot had gone wide. And then he'd lost all his weapons. Because of that, he hadn't returned to the State Department yesterday to eliminate his target, as he and the Boss had agreed over the weekend that he would. What was the point? How could he shoot Yuri Severov if he didn't have a gun?

He'd tried to contact his American weapons supplier to get more weaponry. He'd prefer the long-range sniper rifle that he usually used for work, but even a simple handgun would be fine. At this point, anything that could shoot straight would do. But either the contact did not respond to messages that didn't come from Moscow, or they were trying, and perhaps failing, to find him some new artillery. Maybe locating replacement long-range sniper rifles for a Russian assassin was not as easy as it appeared, even in America.

One thing that was both good and bad was that he'd confirmed that Severov was staying in the Agarwal-Renfrew safe house. When he'd emerged from the park after failing to recover his weapons, he'd clearly seen the Russian defector standing there in the open doorway. And Cher had run out of the house, too, and watched him as he made his getaway in the cab. So at least he'd *found* Severov. Now he just had to figure out a way to get to him.

Because now he also knew that Severov had top-notch, round-the-clock security, and a lot of it. What had been added to the mix just since yesterday was a group of marksmen who moved constantly around the property, monitoring foot and vehicular traffic and staking out weapons caches. Those snipers might look like they were construction workers putting on a new roof, but he knew subterfuge when he saw it. In reality, they were setting up their shooting positions. That was an unexpected setback.

Vlad had not called the Boss yesterday to report success, as he surely would have been expected to do, because he'd had no success to report. The absence of a call would concern the Boss. If he didn't figure out this situation soon and get matters taken care of, he could not expect a hero's welcome when he got back to Moscow.

Vlad sighed. Nothing about this job augured well for his future.

"Everything okay here, hon? You don't seem that hungry today." His usual waitress in the frilly turquoise-checked apron glanced at Vlad's plate as she poured a coffee refill, splashing a little in the saucer. The fact that she recognized him was a bad sign for his mission and a bad sign for her, too. First rule of professional assassins: go unnoticed. If she was overly observant, he'd have to kill her. Not that he thought the waitress was engaged in counterintelligence. Ha! Counter intelligence. That was a good one.

"Iz good," Vlad said, smiling at his own joke. The food was as delicious as always, but of course, everything was not "okay." Not that he could tell her about the missing guns and his unsuccessful effort to kill Yuri Severov. As sympathetic as the waitress seemed to be, she might not be all that understanding about the complex issues of international assassination.

She tilted her head, considering him. "You know, you're not lookin' so good. Did you walk into something hinky?

Because whatever it was, I think it got infected. Maybe you need to see a doctor."

Vlad didn't know what "hinky" meant. "Iz good."

"Okay." The waitress moved away. "Just sayin'. The emergency room will take you even if you can't afford to pay."

Well, that was good to know. The bug bites did make his face feel like it was on fire, not that he had time to consult a physician. He had work to do.

As he finished his meal, he thought about his options and the time he'd need to accomplish his goals.

And how he was going to kill Yuri Severov.

"Where's the closest place to get some Mylar balloons and a cake?" Phoebe asked when she stopped at a red light. If their plan was to pretend to be Vlad's work colleagues, she wanted to make it look good. Kristin thumbed open her phone and searched for possibilities.

"There's a big supermarket up here, three blocks to the left," she said. "They claim to have a bakery, anyway."

"It doesn't have to be fancy," Phoebe said, turning left with the arrow. "Anything in a pink box will do."

Fifteen minutes later they were on their way again, a large pink box on the back seat, a bunch of Mylar balloons floating against the roof and blocking Phoebe's view out the rear window.

"Are you ready to practice your feminine wiles?" Phoebe asked as they approached the hotel. Traffic had been light coming in, and she found a parking space on the street not far away. *Thank you, government shutdown.* In case Vlad might see her and recognize her, she'd tucked her hair under a wide-brimmed sun hat and put on a pair of heart-shaped sunglasses. That was the best disguise she'd been able to muster on short notice.

Kristin applied some lipstick in the rearview mirror. "I'm not sure I have any feminine wiles. What if Gordon doesn't let us into the room?"

"He'll let us in," Phoebe said. "He's got it bad for you.

We just have to be quick. Vlad could come back any minute, and we're already thirty minutes into our hour window."

She grabbed the balloons and Kristin took the cake. Then they crossed the street and entered the hotel.

"Hi, Gordon," Kristin said, smiling at the clerk. "It's great to see you! I'm so glad you're working today!"

Gordon looked like he'd won the lottery. "Good to see you. Are those for me?" He grinned, pointing at the balloons and cake.

"You're so *funny*." Kristin reached out and tapped Gordon's hand, laughing as she did so. "No."

Gordon flushed, gazing at her, a silly smile on his face.

Holy crap, Kristin was good at this. Forget Yuri. *Kristin* could be a spy.

"We brought these for Vlad," Kristin said. "It's his last day at work, and he's been such a treasure! But he slipped out before we could have his party. He's always so modest! So I thought I'd deliver the cake and balloons. As a surprise!"

Gordon glanced at the balloons Phoebe was holding. "Why do the balloons all say happy birthday?"

"The party was a last-minute idea," Kristin said, which was no more than the truth. "These balloons were all the store had on short notice."

Phoebe tried not to fidget. They needed Vlad's room key, and the sooner the better, before he came back and caught them in the lobby or—even worse—his room. That would be a surprise party that none of them would want to celebrate. Phoebe kicked Kristin's ankle, hoping she got the message.

"So—*uh*—" Kristin sucked in her breath when Phoebe's running shoe made contact. "What do you think, Gordon? Can we put this stuff in Vlad's room to surprise him?"

"Sure," Gordon said. "Let me see the cake so I know you're not taking a bomb up there. Ha! Not that you would. But I have to check. Security, you know."

Kristin put the cake on the countertop, and Gordon carefully slit the tape that held the box lid closed. The cake, iced in a garish blue frosting, had a screaming red CONGRATULATIONS!

written in a wavering script across the top. Miniature flowers and flags in neon colors packed the top and sides. It was unbelievably hideous.

"Looks, ah, good," Gordon said, closing the lid and retaping the box. "I'm sure Vlad will appreciate the sentiment."

"We hope so," Kristin said.

"I'll call housekeeping to let you in." Gordon reached for the phone. "I can't actually give you a key."

Phoebe's heart sank. Now they'd have to outmaneuver a maid somehow, too. At least maybe they could do that outside of Gordon's immediate range of vision.

"Should we meet her up there?" she asked.

"Yeah, that works." Gordon nodded, the phone tucked under his chin. He pointed to the elevator bank down the hall. "Head on up."

Kristin reached out and patted his hand.

"*Thank you*," she said. "We certainly appreciate it, and I know Vlad will, too."

"You know, maybe we could—"

"Let's *go*, Kristin," Phoebe said. "We have to get a move on. For the surprise, you know."

"Here's my number," Gordon said, scribbling something on a card and shoving it at her. "Just in case."

"Why, thank you!" Kristin said. "I'll be in touch!"

"*You'll be in touch?*" Phoebe whispered as they waited for the elevator.

Kristin shrugged. "Or not." The elevator arrived, and she punched the button for the sixth floor. "He is sort of cute, though, isn't he? Not that I'm looking."

"He is," Phoebe said. "He reminds me of a golden Labrador. Friendly. Eager."

Kristin shook her head. "Never. Those glasses! Clark Kent. Nerdy superhero."

Phoebe rolled her eyes. "If you say so."

The doors closed and the elevator started up.

They got out on the sixth floor and headed down the hall. Room 604 must be where the maid now stood, watching them as they approached.

"The maid isn't that big," Phoebe said, keeping her voice very soft. "If we have to, we can take her down. Or I'll steal Yuri's bag and run. It's not like Vlad will call the police to report a robbery."

"*We're not tackling the maid*," Kristin hissed.

That was all the time they had before they reached the door to room 604.

"For the party," Phoebe said to the maid, pointing to the cake.

"*Si*," she replied, unlocking the door and entering the room with them.

Rats, Phoebe thought. The maid wasn't going to leave them alone in the room. Of course not. Professional to the core.

She glanced around. The room had not yet been cleaned. The bed was unmade, and towels, presumably wet ones, lay across the wrinkled sheets. An opened suitcase sat on the luggage rack, clothes spilling out onto the floor. In the closet alcove, Phoebe saw a green roller bag—a closed one—that answered to the description Yuri had given her of his suitcase. *Bingo*. Now she had to figure out a way to roll it out of here.

She tied the Mylar balloons to the arm of the desk chair, and Kristin cleared a space on the surface to put the cake. The maid stood stoically near the doorway. Phoebe wanted to break the ice with the maid, get her on their side.

"*¿Conoce a Vlad?*" she asked the maid.

The maid shrugged. Continue in Spanish or switch to English?

"He won the prize," Phoebe said in Spanish. "He gets the balloons and the cake, and one request. Guess what he asked for? Clean clothes! He wants us to take his clothes to the laundry. I guess he didn't plan well for his trip. He said it's all in his suitcase. Don't worry. I'll return it!"

Would the maid buy that whopper of a fib? It was totally lame, but it was the best she could do on short notice.

Phoebe grabbed the handle of the roller bag, holding her breath. The maid shook her head and put out her hand.

185

"*No lo tome*," she said.

Well, too bad. She was taking the bag whether the maid liked it or not.

"*Phoebe*," Kristin said, urgency in her voice. She'd been standing by the window. "We have to go *now*."

"Don't worry." Phoebe smiled at the maid and started toward the door with the roller bag. She truly didn't want the maid to worry. She was worried enough for the both of them.

"*No lo tome*," the maid repeated more forcefully.

"I *must*."

"*Muchas gracias*." Kristin strode to the door and opened it for Phoebe, who pushed the roller bag over the threshold, holding her breath. Would the maid yell or call Gordon? As she passed the housekeeper, Kristin handed her a bill, Phoebe didn't see how much, because she was already heading down the hallway.

Controlling the urge to run, Phoebe strode to the elevator, Kristin right behind her. She'd bet anything that Yuri's toothpaste tube full of microdots would be in there. If not, well, at least Yuri would have his clothes back.

The elevator came, and they rode down to the first floor. Now all they had to do was get past Gordon, not to mention Vlad, who must be inside the hotel by now. But they'd never make it back to the car, just over a block away. Vlad could outrun them, especially since they had to drag or carry the roller bag.

"We have to hope there's a taxi," she told Kristin. "We won't get away otherwise."

Kristin nodded. "I saw a cabstand at the side entrance. It's our best shot."

It wasn't just their *best* shot. It was their *only* shot.

Vlad returned to his hotel, content with his breakfast but deep in thought. As he crossed the lobby to the elevator, the desk clerk gave him a big smile. Those Americans! Always so damn friendly. It was *exhausting*.

"Hi, Vlad," the desk clerk said, winking at him. What was that about? What was the matter with him?

"What?"

The desk clerk smiled more broadly than ever. "I understand you've done an outstanding job at work."

What? Now he must endure the insults of this, this nogoodnik? When Vlad had just been worrying about the complexities of completing the mission? Which so far had been unsuccessful? What could this person possibly know? And how could he know it? No one knew! At least, no one *should* know. Had the boss sent someone to punish him? Worse, eliminate him?

"Don't worry," the clerk said as the elevator dinged. "I don't know anything. Oh, look! Here's a friend of yours now! Kristin! Someone's here to see you! *Hey!* What do you have there?"

What was this fool talking about? And who was this Kristin?

Vlad whirled around, confused but expecting the worst, and saw two women—really only their legs—disappear around a corner, dragging Yuri Severov's roller bag behind them. One of them stuck her hand in the air, waving at them, *mocking him.*

They had stolen the traitor's roller bag. With all its data. The data that he, Vlad, had retrieved so efficiently.

With a roar, he tore across the lobby after them, ran down the hall to the side exit, and slammed out the glass doors to the street.

Without looking back, Kristin waved at Gordon as they ran out through the side entrance. Outside at the cabstand, Phoebe flung open the back door of the only taxi and hurled the suitcase inside.

"Let's go!" she said, jumping in behind it as Kristin leaped into the front seat.

"Go, go, *go!*" she said.

"Where to?" the cab driver asked as he screeched away from the curb.

Phoebe peered out the rear window to see Vlad rush out onto the sidewalk. She heaved a sigh of relief as she turned back around. They were already through the green light. He'd never catch them now.

She told the cabbie the intersection near where they'd parked, and he stared at her through the rearview mirror in disbelief.

"Lady, that's not even two blocks from here," he said.

"Just go, okay? If you promise not to go back to that cabstand for another hour, we'll make it worth your while."

"You got it."

Once at their car, she hoisted Yuri's roller bag into the cargo area. Kristin hopped into the passenger seat, and Phoebe pulled away from the curb.

Mission accomplished. They'd recovered all the data, and Vlad hadn't caught them at it and wasn't following them now. At least she didn't think so.

She checked in the rearview mirror. No sign of Vlad behind them in a car or anywhere else.

"I think we're safe," Kristin said, turning around to look, too. "I think we got clean away. Also, you owe me a hundred."

"That's what you gave the maid?" Phoebe laughed in relief. "Worth every penny." She checked the rearview mirror again. "You know, I think we *are* home free. And you were *great*!"

"You, too," Kristin said, turning back to face forward. "Watch out, Russian assassins! Phoebe and Kristin are on the job."

Chapter 14

Vlad watched the taxi screech away, barely making it through the yellow light at the intersection, and disappear into the flow of traffic.

They were gone. And with them, Severov's data.

His mouth went dry as a film of sweat broke out on his forehead. What could he do now that the suitcase was gone? What could he do now that the Americans had the data?

Blind with fear and rage, faint, his heart pounding, his hands trembling, Vlad inhaled deeply, trying to control his breathing as his instructors had taught him so many years ago. What could he do? *What could he do?* With the loss of the suitcase, he had *nothing*. No dead traitor. No guns. And now, no data. Nothing to protect him from the wrath of the Kremlin, secure his mission, or enable him to achieve his goals.

The shock of it riveted him to the spot until a car horn alerted him that he was standing in the street. As he entered the hotel, the full impact of his failure weighed on him like chains in the gulag. Three days after he'd taken his best shot at Severov, the traitor was still alive and at large, having taken refuge in a safe house protected by America's finest security detail. And now they had the data, too.

And he was without a plan of action. Without weaponry. Without contacts.

Numb with disbelief and despair, he took the elevator up to his room, where he was so startled to find a bunch of Mylar balloons hugging the ceiling that he almost overlooked the pink bakery box sitting on the desk. *What was this?*

Terror gripped him. As surely as he knew his own name, he knew that if he opened that pink box, it would explode. And those balloons were stuffed with anthrax or sarin or even the radioactive polonium that had killed Litvinenko. Had Agarwal and Renfrew decided to dispatch him on their own? Or were they working with his enemies back in Russia? Had some other Russian assassin come to eliminate him for not yet killing Yuri Severov?

Fury ripped through him. Who did the Kremlin bosses think they were? He had never once missed a target! Never once failed to perform as ordered! And now, only three days overdue, his bosses were ready to kill him! Him, Vladimir Golubkin, the most accurate and deadly of all the Russian assassins!

It wasn't as though the failure was even his fault. He'd had bad intel! Had they told him that Severov was protected by Sanjay Agarwal and Phoebe Renfrew? No, they had not. Had they advised him that Severov had an armored car at his disposal and a group of bodyguards so fierce that they put the Cossacks to shame? No, they had not! Had they thought to mention the relentless attack dogs that guarded the compound? *No, they had not.*

Had he known these things, he would have proceeded differently.

But now somebody in Russia wanted him dead. He had to get out of here fast, before the bomb went off, and then find a place where he could hide until he killed Severov, even if that entailed tearing off the traitor's limbs one by one with his bare hands. And then maybe the Russian higher-ups would let him live.

Perhaps ten seconds had elapsed since he'd stepped into the room. He could hear the clock ticking in his head. *Get out now.* Before that pink box could do its worst.

He grabbed his suitcase and held it closed under his

arm, not pausing to zip it, articles of clothing trailing out of the opening. He had to go. He could do nothing about Severov's stolen suitcase now, and the first rule of international assassination was, survive the operation. He thought the bomb would not go off until he opened the pink box—the better to ensure that it killed him—but you never knew what Russian assassins might do. It might be on a timer. And if it was, he had to act quickly.

He left the room and jogged to the stairwell. The stairs would be quicker than the elevator and safer, too, if the bomb exploded. His mind churned as he ran, jumping the last three steps of every flight, taking the landings hard, losing a sock or two with every jarring thump.

The exercise cleared his brain, so by the time Vlad got to the ground floor, he had questions for the desk clerk. Even with the bomb set to explode, he needed answers.

He'd had only the briefest glance at the backs of the pair who'd stolen Severov's roller bag. The question was, who were they? Who would have had the nerve to enter his hotel room, leave a bomb in a box and poison in the balloons, and steal the traitor's suitcase?

The obvious answer was that it was Severov's protection detail—Agarwal and Renfrew or their minions.

But could they be in the employ of the Russian bosses? How otherwise would Agarwal and Renfrew know where he was staying? Perhaps they were working in concert with another Russian shooter who'd been kept informed of his movements.

But why would the Boss take this step? Vlad hadn't spoken to him in the past twenty-four hours, so he couldn't know that Severov was still alive. Vlad might be running three days late on his assignment, but he was still the best assassin in Russia. After twenty-five years of faithful, discreet, and trouble-free service, even the Boss wouldn't dispatch him without proof of failure.

Severov's protection must be working on its own. Russia could not be involved. In some way, this was a relief. Moscow was not trying to kill him. His pension, so far, was secure.

The bad news, however, was that Severov's American security team had thwarted Vlad at every step. And now, somehow, they'd figured out where he stayed, and then they'd gotten into his room. Tried to kill *him*.

A fresh surge of rage exploded in his gut and flooded his brain. Those interfering Americans! One step ahead *again*! How *dare* they interfere? How *dare* they challenge his actions! *Russia* decreed the fate of traitors! Not Agarwal and Renfrew! They would find out what it was to challenge him, Vladimir Golubkin! For this effrontery, they would pay. For this insult, they would *die*!

Vlad's skin itched with a scorching heat, and he clawed at his face as he stormed into the lobby. He saw with grim satisfaction that the perpetual smile of the lobby clerk faltered.

"Mr. Golubkin," the clerk said. "Vlad."

He hated how the clerk glanced from his face, which—Vlad examined his fingers after he'd scratched it—was bleeding, to the unzipped suitcase from which, he realized, his Hello Kitty pajama bottoms trailed.

The clerk nodded to his suitcase. "Checking out?"

"Iz time laundry," Vlad snarled, not that it was any of the fool's business. "Who you allow in room? Waz Phoebe Renfrew, yes? Sanjay Agarwal?"

"Uh," the clerk said. "We let your coworkers in with the cake? To celebrate your work victory?"

"Waz Phoebe Renfrew," Vlad said. "Sanjay Agarwal. Yes?"

"I didn't learn the other woman's name," the clerk said. "Kristin is the person I talked to."

Vlad didn't know any Kristin, but Renfrew might have given a false name. Or been the other, unknown woman. But that it was Renfrew, he was certain.

"Is everything all right?" the clerk asked, looking upset now. "I apologize if I did the wrong thing. They seemed so pleased and happy with your work."

Vlad struggled to control his temper. He didn't want to

give anything away now. But when the hotel blew up, Vlad hoped the bomb would shred this idiot clerk.

"Iz good," Vlad said, gritting his teeth. "Surprised only."

"Oh, excellent news," the clerk said, visibly relieved. "I'm so glad. They wanted to thank you for a job well done."

Vlad felt his rage build at the insult. A job well done! Renfrew and Agarwal *knew* that the job *wasn't* done, well or otherwise. They were *mocking* him. *Jeering* at him.

"They zed that?"

"Oh yes!" the clerk said. "They were so excited to surprise you. You know, I'm worried about your face. It might be infected. Maybe you should see someone."

He was going to see someone, all right. He was going to see Renfrew and Agarwal! He was going to put an end to this—this arrogance! Right now! They dared to ridicule *him*? To the *hotel clerk*? He would show them and the hotel clerk, too! When the bomb went off, they would know who was the winner and who was the loser!

"I will." A red mist surrounded his vision as he stormed out to the side street where a cab had parked at the curb, the driver standing outside his vehicle, unwrapping a sandwich.

He straightened when he saw Vlad. "Taxi?"

Vlad hefted his suitcase and, using it like a battering ram, bashed the taxi driver in the chest, shoving him backward into the street and knocking him down. Then he tossed the suitcase into the passenger seat, jumped into the cab, and roared away.

Chase stood at the window, looking out, trying not to worry. He wished Phoebe and Kristin wouldn't go out without telling anyone where they were headed. They were both smart and resourceful, and they were probably fine. But this was the second morning in a row they'd taken off without explanation. That gave the assassin another chance to find them. And the bottom line was that an assassin with a gun could take down two women without any trouble, no matter how smart and resourceful they were.

Minutes later, he saw the yellow SUV come down the

street and pull into the garage. And then Phoebe and Kristin entered the kitchen, laughing and exuberant.

"We've had an incredible morning," Phoebe said as she hung her messenger bag on the hook. "Wait till you hear! Were you waiting for us? I didn't think we were gone that long."

He put his coffee cup in the sink and took a deep breath, nodding at the green roller bag. "I gotta say, if you've been out shopping, I think you could have done better."

Phoebe laughed. "That's Yuri's suitcase. We got his data back! At least I think we did. We haven't taken the time to check for sure. But we got all his stuff, so at least he has his own clothes and toiletries now, if nothing else."

"You did *what*?"

Phoebe nodded. "Yeah. Kristin was great. We called the hotel to find out when Vlad was out. They said he'd be gone about an hour for breakfast, so we had to fly. And then Kristin's friend at the front desk told us we could go in, so we did."

"He's not my friend," Kristin said.

"The ruse worked pretty well, all things considered," Phoebe said.

"But then just as we were coming out, Vlad came back," Kristin said. "We had to run for it then, but we got away clean in a cab."

Chase took a deep breath. "I'd been wondering if I'd be scraping dead bodies off a sidewalk somewhere. Sounds like I had reason to worry."

Phoebe looked stricken. "I'm sorry! I didn't realize—"

"The man's an *assassin*, Phoebe. The Taser wasn't enough for you? You could have been killed! Both of you! Have we not decided that we will not be taking unnecessary risks?"

She didn't look stricken anymore. Her chin had come up and her shoulders had rotated back. She stood as straight as an arrow.

Her voice was cool. "When exactly did we decide that?"

"You know we did!"

Kristin edged toward the door. "Um, I'll just—" she said, disappearing faster than a Russian assassin at a law enforcement convention.

"I'm sorry that I scared you," Phoebe said, not sounding at all sorry. "When you didn't leave a note for me this morning, I decided you'd gone out for a run."

"Don't make this about me!"

"I'm merely drawing a comparison."

He felt his anger subside. Of course, he'd gone for a run without leaving a note. And of course, she was going to take advantage of a situation if she could, even if it was dangerous. He knew that about her. It was just who she was.

He realized that he'd been holding the tension in his shoulders, and he rolled them back to release some of it. He realized, too, that his anger was gone, replaced by relief and regret that he'd been so sharp.

"I'm sorry I yelled, *cher.* I guess I was more worried than I realized."

She was instantly contrite. Her chin came down. "I see that. I'm sorry, too." And then she crossed the room and put her arms around him. So that was good. And she wasn't going to hold his anger against him. Also good.

He held her close. Breathed her in.

"You know, it's kind of a novel experience for someone to worry about where I am," she said, sounding surprised. "I've never had to think about that before. Nobody's ever paid any attention to my whereabouts."

Sometimes he could throttle Brenda. "Putting you on notice," he said. "I'll worry. Your friends, too."

She leaned up to kiss him. "It would have been great if you'd been there. Kristin wanted us to tackle the maid, but I was against it."

"I did not want to do that!" Kristin yelled from the other side of the door. So she hadn't gone upstairs after all. "That was your idea!"

"I knew that," Chase said. "Kristin, you can come back in now, if you want. I'm done yelling."

"Sorry to upset you, Coach," she said, coming back into

the kitchen. "Going to Vlad's hotel seemed safe enough because he was out. But it was a close shave at the end, so you aren't wrong about the danger. However, the upside is that we're pretty sure we've got the data."

Chase nodded. "Which, despite my concerns for your personal safety, is great, because we sure as hell are not keeping Yuri in our basement forever."

"Well, that's what I think, too," Phoebe said. "I've been worried that he might not be a good enough prospect for the FBI. What if they don't let him defect? Which is why we ripped off the suitcase, even though it *was* risky and it'll probably make Vlad furious, too. Let's get Yuri up here to see if everything's there."

Chase dragged the roller bag into the blue parlor and hoisted it onto the coffee table, and Phoebe went to the basement steps.

"Yuri!" she yelled. "Я получил твой чемодан! Поищем данные!"

"Я иду!"

"He's coming," she said when she got back to the blue parlor.

In a few seconds, Yuri came charging up the stairs.

"Наконец!" He unzipped the bag, which revealed the shaving kit sitting right on top. He opened it and saw the toothpaste, shampoo, and shaving cream. He visibly sagged in relief, but he unscrewed all the tops to make sure.

"Микроточки безопасны," he said.

"The microdots are safe," Phoebe translated.

"I'm happy to hear that, because I would strongly prefer it if you didn't try a stunt like that again," Chase said.

"No, and I don't think we could pull it off again, either," Kristin said. "It was a pretty shaky plan to begin with."

"But it's done, and it worked." Phoebe beamed at him, and he couldn't resist that sunny smile. His heart softened looking at her, her cheerful warmth erasing the dread he'd felt when he realized she was gone. "And now all this spy business has made me hungry. What do you say about pancakes for breakfast? I feel like celebrating."

Chapter 15

Breakfast was nearly ready when the doorbell rang. Chase checked his watch midflip of a pancake. Only nine thirty. Too early for morning callers unless it was Amos for some reason. Everyone looked at each other in surprise and, in some cases, alarm.

And no wonder, given events of the past couple of days.

Kristin paused from counting out silverware. "Who could that be?" she asked, giving voice to what they all thought.

Phoebe poured the rest of the water into the coffeepot. "Vlad's Tasering Service," she said, sounding grim.

"I'll get it!" Brenda called from the dining room. Too late, Chase realized he'd heard her little clicking heels on the hardwood floors of the foyer.

"No!" he roared, as Phoebe shouted, "Mom! *No!*"

"Don't answer the door!" he yelled as he bolted out of the kitchen, Phoebe right behind him.

Brenda could be killed out there. Vlad knew where they lived now, and if he had a gun—

Chase charged into the foyer to see Brenda standing at the wide-open front door, the covering sheet crumpled on the floor. A flushed and angry Nick Balasco faced her from the porch.

"Who are you?" each asked the other simultaneously.

Just what they needed. Another houseguest. This time,

a pissed-off houseguest.

"I'm Nick Balasco," Nick told Brenda. "I'm looking for Kristin Seiler. Is she here? She's supposed to be here."

"She's here," Phoebe said. "I'll get— Oh, here she is now. Kristin. Nick's here."

Not that she needed to tell Kristin that. There he was, suitcase in hand, on their front porch. And there was Kristin, as pale as a ghost, staring at him.

"Better come in," Phoebe said to Nick. "Vlad the Assassin likes to shoot first and ask questions later. Although he might be gunless right now. We're not sure about that."

"What?" Nick said sharply, whipping around. "Shooting? Vlad the *who*?"

"*Get in here.*" Phoebe took his arm and pulled him into the foyer, and Brenda slammed the door behind him. Nick dropped his suitcase and glared at them all.

"We need to get a few things straight," he said, jabbing a finger at Kristin. "When were you planning to come back? Or *weren't* you? And besides that—what the hell is happening here? Vlad the *who*? What are you *talking* about? And what are those construction workers doing, trying to stop me when I got here?"

"Hey, Nick, relax," Phoebe said. "Kristin's fine, we're all fine, but it's a long story. You must be tired after the red-eye. We're in the middle of making breakfast if you're hungry, unless you'd rather get some sleep first? Then you guys can talk."

"Why do you have a suitcase?" Kristin asked.

"I came straight from the airport," Nick said, sounding calmer now. "I want you to come back to the hotel with me so we can talk. You know, clear the air."

Chase didn't want to be inhospitable—that's why he'd insisted on six bedrooms, after all—but he was glad Nick had gotten a hotel. They had enough drama, not to mention danger, without Nick contributing his two cents.

"So, Nick," he said. "Everything okay back at the office? What's going on?"

"What's going *on*?" Nick said. "I came to talk to Kristin.

We weren't getting anywhere on the phone. What's going on *here*?"

"You told me before I left that you'd said everything you had to say," Kristin said. "That's why I decided to come out here for a while. To help Coach and think things through. You said you'd leave the decision up to me."

"And have you decided?"

"Can we not discuss this in the entryway in front of everybody?" Kristin said, sounding harassed. "Nobody else cares about our problems."

"Nick, why don't you have breakfast with us?" Phoebe said. "The pancakes are almost done. And you guys can talk after."

"I'm not here for breakfast or to sleep," Nick said. "I'm here to take Kristin home with me. This afternoon, I hope."

That was news to Chase, and judging from the expression on Kristin's face, news to her, too—and not necessarily welcome news.

"Okay, well, you guys figure it out," Phoebe said, clearly taken aback. "Breakfast is almost ready if you want it."

Kristin nodded and led Nick upstairs without looking back.

"Еда остывает. Давайте есть."

Phoebe nodded. "Yuri's right—the food *is* getting cold."

"And all this excitement has made me hungry," Brenda said, heading into the kitchen. "Or hungrier, I should say."

"Pancakes coming up," Chase said, following her in.

Hearing Yuri complain about the cold breakfast reminded Phoebe that she'd promised Chase to call the FBI to see if someone other than Kevin Toth could debrief the Russian man. Now seemed like a perfect time, especially if their re-theft of Yuri's data infuriated Vlad so much that he'd attack them with any weapon he could find. Best to get Yuri out of the house before Vlad developed any ideas.

"The coffee should be almost finished dripping," she told Chase. "I meant to call the FBI, too. I'll do it now, before the day gets away from me again."

"Good idea," Chase said. "The rest of us can get

breakfast on the table."

"I met Nick and Kristin on the stairs," Sanjay said, coming into the kitchen. "We will have many hands to thwart Vlad as well as make breakfast."

They crowded into the kitchen, and Phoebe headed into the blue parlor, where she made herself comfortable on the blue-and-yellow-chintz sofa. Ten unprofitable minutes later, she'd been bounced from one FBI phone tree to another—the government shutdown at work again—without making any headway. She wanted answers. How could she get them?

She could call Aaron Picone in Vegas again. He'd given her Kevin Toth's name in the first place. Picone might not like her, but he was an FBI agent, sworn to protect and serve and all that. He'd help her, even if begrudgingly.

"Renfrew," he said when he picked up. "Don't you have any other agents on speed dial?"

"Aaron, so nice to hear your voice."

"Yeah, yeah," Picone said. "What is it this time?"

"I have a problem," Phoebe said. "Kevin Toth has the measles."

Picone snorted. "No shit? That's funny. I'll have to call and give him a hard time."

"You do that. In the meantime, the Russian defector is still in my basement, and nobody else out here will take him—FBI agents, I mean—because of the government shutdown. And now I have a Russian assassin on my butt and a house full of people, and I'm worried that something will happen. Something not good."

"Russian assassin?"

"Yeah, it's a lot to process. Name of Vlad Golubkin, sent here to kill Yuri. He—Vlad, I mean—has been surveilling our house. And he tased me. I had to go to the hospital."

"You *have* been busy." He tapped on his keyboard, and Phoebe knew he was checking the database for Vlad.

"Yes. So—can you direct me to someone other than Kevin Toth? When I was at headquarters, everybody passed the buck, and now I can't get past the phone tree."

The tapping on the other end stopped. "How do you

know the assassin is Vlad Golubkin?"

"Amos Glenwethering told me," Phoebe said. "He's a neighbor. Retired CIA. Russia expert."

The tapping resumed.

"How do you spell it?" Picone asked. "Glenwethering, I mean. Golubkin, I got."

Phoebe spelled *Glenwethering*. The tapping picked up and stopped again.

"Ah," Picone said.

"So can you help?" Phoebe asked.

"I'll make some calls," Picone said. "Toth is my only personal contact in the DC office. No promises."

"Whatever you can do," Phoebe said, curtailing her disappointment. As long as they had Yuri in the house, they'd all be a target for whatever Vlad had in store for them.

Picone tapped a bit more. "Are you back at work now?"

"A couple more weeks," Phoebe said. "I think if I were back officially, this would be easier. I tried handing Yuri over to the CIA, but they're busy with the Chinese climate change dissidents."

"Yeah, I heard about that," Picone said. "Well, good luck. I'll be in touch."

She disconnected the call on a sigh. Maybe something would materialize, maybe not. She headed into the kitchen, passing Yuri, who was carrying syrup and butter into the dining room.

"Smells good," she said as she joined the controlled chaos of the kitchen.

"Breakfast is ready," Chase said. "What's up?"

"Calling the FBI in DC got me nothing but endless phone trees. Maybe Picone in Vegas can help—he said he'd try, but he doesn't know any agents personally except Toth."

"That is most unfortunate," Sanjay said, putting the big platter of pancakes on a tray.

"It all sounds very exciting, sweetie," Brenda said, forking bacon from the stove. "Although I don't think I understand all the details of what you're up to."

"Seriously, Mom?" Phoebe felt like they'd been living

with Yuri for months, if not years. She'd all but forgotten that Brenda had arrived only yesterday afternoon, and while they'd certainly discussed their situation over dinner, evidently Brenda had missed a few points.

"I don't know what's going on, either," Nick said. "Just what you said in the hallway."

Phoebe was happy to see that Kristin's face was unmarked by tears.

"The story in its essentials is relatively straightforward," Sanjay said. "Yuri Severov is a Russian defector with whom Phoebe and I became acquainted when he jumped in my cab and Vlad the Assassin shot out the windows. For lack of better options, Yuri is now living here in the basement. Vlad has found out where Phoebe lives and has been inching closer to us—hence all the precautions we're taking—and in one kidnapping attempt, tased Phoebe. We have tried to deliver Yuri to the FBI to debrief, a plan that has experienced multiple unavoidable delays. We were able to steal a cache of his weapons, but we are uncertain of what else he might have acquired, so we are unlikely to take unnecessary risks in the expectation that he might have been able to replace much of his firepower. Does anyone want to add anything?"

"Not me," Phoebe said. "You got that dead on, so to speak."

"What's the worst that can happen?" Brenda asked, taking napkins out of the drawer. "Yuri stays with us for another week or so, right? That's it?"

Us, Phoebe heard with dread. Brenda was saying *us* in reference to their house. No, no, *no*. Wrong. So, so *wrong*.

"Right," Chase said, turning off the stove. "Yuri stays here and we try to keep him safe until we can deliver him to the federal government, while Vlad figures out a new way to eliminate him and finds the weapons to do it."

"Which puts us all in danger." Phoebe snagged a piece of bacon from the platter.

"Vlad's persistent, you have to give him that," Kristin said, taking a big container of yogurt from the refrigerator. "And devious. Willing to take chances, right? *Clever* is how

Amos described him to us."

Sanjay grabbed the teapot. "That is correct."

"I have the orange juice," Jamal said, taking it out of the refrigerator.

Brenda picked up the coffeepot, beaming at everyone in the kitchen. "Time to eat. We have to keep up our strength if we're going to fight off Russian assassins."

Everyone laughed, but Phoebe didn't find anything funny as she led the way into the dining room. Chase had been right to be upset earlier. The house was too full of people she didn't want to see hurt, and no one really knew where the next attack would come from.

Because one thing seemed certain: Vlad would be only too happy to injure them all if it meant he could kill Yuri, too.

After everyone ate breakfast and cleared away the dishes, Kristin and Nick went back to the TV room to talk—*argue*, Chase was willing to bet. Brenda went upstairs to make bridal plans and then drive Phoebe crazy with them, and Sanjay and Jamal joined Yuri in the basement to practice martial arts maneuvers. Everyone in the house was accounted for, matched up, paired off, and otherwise occupied, leaving him alone with Phoebe in the yellow parlor. The novelty of it struck him with some force.

"At last, we're alone, with nothing on our to-do lists and no assassins at the door," he said, settling down on one end of the chintz sofa.

Phoebe turned back from the window where she'd been standing. "I know," she said. "What should we do today? I feel sort of at a loose end."

Smiling, he quirked his eyebrows at her. "I know something we could do."

Phoebe grinned back, that mischievous, I-know-what-you're-thinking grin that made him want to follow her anywhere.

"We did that already this morning," she said. "Twice."

He laughed outright. "And how fantastic it was, too."

"Phoebe?" came a bright voice. "Are you down here, sweetie?"

"Where can I hide?" Phoebe whispered.

"Too late now," Chase said. "Buck up and take your hits like a woman."

"*There* you are!" Brenda frisked into the room, her kitten heels clicking on the polished floorboards, her arms full of a tall stack of magazines. "I swear, this place is so big, a person could get lost in it! Although your house is totally beautiful, *of course*. Just so *big*."

She plunked down on the sofa between them and piled the magazines next to her on the cushion. "Don't let me interrupt," she said. "I know you're making plans. That's what I'm doing, too! I called Claire—she is a *sweetheart*, Chase! I simply *love* your mom!—and we're thinking—"

Time to go. If Phoebe needed him to rescue her, she'd have to holler, because full-body Velcro and Gorilla Glue could not make him stick around for an in-depth discussion of bows or whatever it was that wedding planners talked about.

"That's my cue," he said, standing. "I'll let you ladies get on with your huddle while I make some calls."

His smart, hardworking, budget-bashing Phoebe glared at him with burning reproach. He could read the accusation in her eyes: *Coward.* That's what she was thinking. Good thing he didn't care, or all that animosity might bother him some.

And then she smiled, an evil smile, which was scarier than a swarm of fire ants goin' up your pant legs after your jewels.

"Sure, you take off," she said. "I know you're busy. You know, Mom has a real knack for decorating. I bet she'd be willing to help you figure out your office space. She could help you scope out what's available and choose carpeting and paint. And furniture. And office supplies. Whatever you need."

"Oh, I *would!*" Brenda said. "Name your time. Maybe later today? Or tomorrow morning? Around the wedding plans."

"Uh, sure," Chase said, as he headed toward the door. *In her dreams*.

He escaped the parlor with barely a second to spare.

Phoebe and Brenda both watched him go, and then they looked at each other.

"*Men*," they said at the same time and then laughed.

"I sure scared him out of here," Brenda said.

"You sure did, Mom. That said, you know we're not planning my wedding, right? Chase and I aren't ready to get married."

"Not this *minute*. But *planning* it takes a long time— even a year or two, to do it right," Brenda said. "And by that time, you *will* be ready."

"Yeah—no," Phoebe said. "Here's the thing—"

She paused as Kristin, followed by Nick dragging his suitcase, walked through the foyer, past the yellow parlor where they sat, toward the front door. *Was Nick leaving*? So soon? He'd only just arrived.

"Excuse me for a sec, Mom. I have to go see—" She jumped up and dashed into the foyer. Kristin had opened the front door, and Nick was stepping over the threshold.

"Goodbye, Nick," Kristin said. "I'm sorry I can't do what you want, be what you want."

"I'm sorry, too," Nick said. "I—"

"Kristin?" Phoebe said.

"Phoebe," Nick said. "Sorry to have barged in on you like this. I'm leaving. Kristin and I have decided that—"

"Here's your cab coming now," Kristin said, peering down the street.

Nick turned to spot the cab. "That was fast."

Phoebe stepped off the portico and stood out on the lawn, waiting for the cab to pull up. It was coming up fast, all right.

Way too fast.

Chapter 16

Phoebe watched Nick's cab barrel up the street, traveling way over the speed limit and much too fast and erratically for a residential neighborhood. Nick shouldn't take that taxi no matter how quickly he wanted to get away. The cabbie was driving like a maniac.

Within seconds the cab accelerated and—to Phoebe's shock—jumped the curb, plowing up the incline of their yard.

"Watch out!" she shrieked, leaping back. Two men in Mateo's crew dropped the cases of slate roofing tiles they were carrying and jumped out of the way.

The cab's front wheels lurched over the shallow terracing, struggling to make the ascent, but the chassis caught on the stonework and the cab got stuck. The driver spun the wheels, digging up the patchy lawn.

What on earth was going on?

"Hey!" Phoebe yelled, taking a few steps down the terracing. "Stop it! Get off our lawn, you bozo!"

Chase appeared at the front door, holding the bat. "What's happening out here? Nick said he called a cab, and—"

"The cab went over the curb and now it's in the yard," Kristin said. "Maybe the steering's busted."

"Or the driver's nuts," Phoebe said.

"Or drunk," Nick said. "Or high."

"Or a murderous idiot," Kristin said.

"And he's wrecking the lawn," Brenda said behind them.

"What there is of it," Chase agreed. "What the hell is he doing? Phoebe, back up, will you? Stay clear of it."

"Should I call the cops?" Mateo yelled from the cab of his pickup.

"Might as well try," Phoebe called back. "Maybe they'll come. There's always a first time."

Trouble wriggled his way out to the porch, barking his head off, and Kristin grabbed his collar.

Nick started down the sidewalk toward the cab, dragging his roller bag. "I'll ask him—"

"Nick!" Kristin said. "Be careful!"

Jamal and Sanjay came out to stand on the lawn. "What's happening?" Jamal asked.

"Nick's cab driver left the road," Brenda said. "In more ways than one. Jerk."

"This taxi operator has lost all sense of direction, not to mention decorum," Sanjay said with disapproval, gazing at the cab still stuck on the terracing. "One could expect that remaining on the roadway would be a reasonably simple test of one's navigational skill."

"You'd think," Phoebe said, standing hands on hips, glaring at the driver. Her mother was right, for once. The cabbie *had* wrecked the lawn. She squinted at the cab, but the glare on the windshield prevented her from seeing the driver, or if only one person occupied the taxi.

Mateo got out of his pickup, his phone still stuck to his ear, and approached the porch. "Cops aren't picking up. Should I give him a push? To get him off that terracing?"

Phoebe glared at the stuck taxi. "I don't trust him not to run you over."

"The driver's main intention seems to be to destroy your landscaping in its totality." Sanjay frowned at the cab. "That is astonishing and incomprehensible."

Yuri edged out onto the portico, staying behind the

small crowd that had gathered there. "Что происходит?"

And wasn't that the sixty-four-thousand-dollar question? They'd all like to know what was happening.

"Таксист сошел с ума," Phoebe said. *The taxi driver is crazy*, which seemed true enough.

Yuri had made a makeshift sling from one of their new towels, a pretty, soft yellow floral, to support his pink cast, and now he looked a bit like a giant Easter egg. She supposed that the sling was more comfortable for him, but she hoped that he didn't ruin the new towel. That set worked perfectly in Sanjay's yellow bathroom.

Nick ducked down by the taxi's passenger-side window to gaze inside and knocked on the glass. The cab's engine had been emitting a high-pitched whine as the driver spun the wheels in the dirt, but with Nick's approach, both sound and action ceased for perhaps five seconds. And then the driver revved the motor. The engine roared and the taxi surged forward, jumping over the terraced weed patch, shoving Nick back.

"Nick!" Kristin shouted as Nick stumbled and dropped his suitcase and then tripped over it. His arms windmilled furiously as he tilted on the edge of one of the terraces, but he couldn't regain his balance and fell hard to the terrace below, landing awkwardly on his shoulder and hitting his head against the decorative stonework. He lay stunned among the weeds as the taxi headed full throttle right at Yuri on the porch.

Brenda screamed.

"Nick!" Kristin ran to where he lay.

"Run!" Chase shouted, but Yuri remained rooted to the spot. Chase jumped in front of the Russian. Holding the bat like a major league outfielder, he stepped into his swing and smashed the bat into the windshield. Tiny cracks frosted the glass in every direction, creating a network of fissures that obliterated visibility but didn't break the glass.

Should have shot it out, Phoebe thought. *That works*.

With all the cracks, the driver couldn't see through the windshield. That would surely slow him down. Maybe he'd come to his senses.

The cab backed down the yard, bounced over over the curb, and shot out into the street, coming to a rest, its engine idling, when it hit the curb on the far side. It sat there like an evil creature waiting to spring on its next unwary victim.

Yuri needs to get back in the house.

"Скрывать! Возвращайся в дом!" she yelled, but for some inexplicable reason, Yuri did not run inside to hide. Instead, he ducked sideways and stood in front of the house.

Not in front of the window! If the cab went after Yuri again and hit the building and broke the mullioned window, it would cost a fortune to repair. If it could even be repaired to look as good as it did now.

"Everybody get in the house!" Chase yelled.

"I'm still on hold with the cops," Mateo said. "What's going on with *them?*"

"I'll try, too," Brenda said, disappearing inside.

Good luck with that, Phoebe thought. *It's federal,* the police would say and then go back to doing whatever they did when they weren't coming to their house.

Sanjay pulled Nick to his feet, staggering under his weight, and Jamal went to help him drag the sluggish and injured Nick up the lawn and into the house. Kristin followed with Nick's suitcase, releasing Trouble. Mateo and the two guys who'd been slinging tiles up the pulley gizmo to Doolie and the three guys on the roof also came to stand on the porch.

"What's this guy's problem?" Mateo said. "It's like he's deranged."

"No kidding," Phoebe said. The idling cab creeped her out. What was that driver trying to prove? Why was he attacking them? Chase hadn't taken his eyes off it, either, and he still held the bat poised at his shoulder, ready to swing again. So he was worried, too.

A weird, muffled pounding came from behind the cab's windshield, growing in intensity. And then, like a creature in a horror movie, a fist shoved through the cracks of the glass. The arm jerked hard from side to side, breaking out the little pieces of safety glass, widening the opening until, with no glass in his way, the driver could see out. And they could see in.

Phoebe squinted at the pocked face, the bleeding and infected pustules. She knew that face. *Of course.*

"It's the shooter!" she said. "It's *Vlad the Assassin!*" And as though Trouble knew what she'd said and didn't like it, he streaked toward the cab, barking like a creature obsessed.

"Trouble! *Come!*" Phoebe called and ran after the dog, but Trouble didn't obey.

"Phoebe!" Chase yelled. "Forget the dog!"

Vlad revved the engine and tore forward, across the street, over the curb, and up their lawn again. Trouble ran right at the vehicle and, at the last minute, dashed sideways. The cab bounced against some broken terracing, which altered its trajectory, and smashed into one of the stone planters that lined the entryway. The planter broke, scattering chunks of rock, dirt, and dead leaves across the sidewalk.

Phoebe ran up the lawn to the portico, hot fury burning behind her eyes. How dared Vlad try to hurt her friends and wreck her house? And he'd almost run over her dog. Ruining the lawn was one thing. But there was a construction crew here. With scaffolding and other expensive equipment and materials. Now the planter. Not to mention the tasing. And the *shooting.* She was *done with it.* She wanted the cab *off her property* and Vlad *arrested.* And if the cops wouldn't arrest him, she was perfectly willing to rip his head off with her teeth and let Chase use it for a football. And if the CIA or the FBI or, for that matter, the freaking *NFL* didn't like it, *tough.*

She grabbed Trouble's collar, pushed the agitated dog into the house, and slammed the door. Then she glanced around, looking for something she could use as a weapon. The construction workers had dropped some boxes of tiles, and some of the slate was broken. She picked up a piece. It had a nice heft to it. It could do some damage—to Vlad or his taxi. At this point, she didn't much care which.

The engine whined as the taxi's front wheels spun, trying to get some traction.

"Get off my lawn!" she yelled, hurling the piece of slate at the cab. It smashed on impact, scattering stone chips and chunks across the yard and even inside the vehicle. "Go! *Get out of here!*"

She heaved another piece of tile at the cab, which didn't go anywhere, but the action made her feel a lot better. When Chase ran up to the driver-side door, holding the bat ready, she desisted. She wouldn't risk hurting him with flying chips of stone, and maybe he could get some results with this guy.

"What the hell are you doing?" he bellowed at Vlad. "Get out of the car! Get out!" He grabbed the handle of the taxi door and tried to wrench it open, but it held fast.

Vlad jammed the taxi in reverse, and the engine screamed as the tires finally found purchase. The car leaped backward off the planter pedestal, yanking Chase's hands off the door handle. He staggered against a bristly hedge but didn't fall.

"Chase!" Phoebe threw a last tile at the retreating cab. The sharp slab bounced off the hood and into the taxi.

That had to hurt, she thought in satisfaction before she dashed over to check on Chase.

"Are you hurt?" she asked him, looking for injuries.

"I'm fine," he said, working free of the entangling shrub. "Just annoyed."

"Ah, sweetie?" Brenda came out of the house and pointed down the street. Phoebe whirled around to see what her mother was looking at. The rogue taxi was across the road again, but some kind of delivery van was pulling up to their front curb. What was that?

The van bore a huge DRESSES TO TRESSES logo on the side panel, which included an enormous picture of a bride with curly blond hair—the kind of hair Phoebe would never have—wearing a poufy white dress—the kind of dress Phoebe would never wear. The van parked in front of her house.

No. *No.* Oh no, no, no, no, *no.*

"You *didn't*, Mom," Phoebe said. "Say you didn't."

"This is what I was trying to tell you," Brenda said. "Before."

Two blond women wearing matching pink polo shirts jumped out of the van, opened the back doors, and pulled out a rolling rack of frothy white wedding dresses. The taxicab, much worse for wear now, idled in its spot across the street, waiting to do whatever evil it was going to do.

"No!" Phoebe yelled, waving her arms at the van. "Don't come any closer!"

The women waved back as they pushed the rack into the street and then slammed the van's doors closed.

"Stop!" Phoebe shouted as she took off across the lawn, or what remained of it, to warn them. "Put those dresses back! Get out of here!"

"Come in!" Brenda shrieked, tottering after Phoebe, her kitten heels sinking into the fresh, torn-up dirt of the front lawn. "We've been waiting for you! Hurry!"

The Weddings from Hell ladies paused for a second, uncertain, as Phoebe and Brenda descended on them, yelling contradictory orders, but then they shrugged, maneuvering the clumsy rack up the driveway. Yuri stepped out from behind the bush he'd staked out and headed down the driveway to help them. Although why he would and what he could do with his arm in a yellow floral towel sling, Phoebe didn't know.

"No! Stay back!" Phoebe yelled at him, forgetting to speak Russian.

The garage door rumbled up, and Kristin, holding a garden rake in front of her like a Girl Scout storm trooper, marched out of the garage, followed by the armored car, Sanjay at the wheel.

What a good idea. Sanjay and Jamal were a lot more protected behind the wheel of the armored car than the rest of them were standing out here in the yard. Although their attack would be a lot like bumper cars. With wedding dresses. And, maybe, a rake.

Kristin eyed the taxi across the street and stomped over

to where Phoebe stood on the driveway with her mother and the wedding planners with their dress rack. They'd been halted in their sweep up the drive when they met Sanjay's armored vehicle emerging from the garage.

Phoebe nodded at the yard implement. "A rake?"

Kristin shrugged. "Coach has the bat. Your place is pretty lame as weapons go."

"Weapons?" one of the wedding planners—Blonde #1—said. "What do you mean, *weapons*?"

"We should go," Blonde #2 said, glancing at Vlad's damaged taxi idling at the curb. "This doesn't seem like a good time."

"It's a perfect time!" Brenda said. "Come in! Hurry!"

Yuri joined them on the driveway. "Блондинка хорошенькая."

He'd come down the driveway, out here in the open, because he thought the blond lady was *pretty?* On the other hand, maybe he was right. Vlad hadn't shot at anyone, so maybe he didn't have a gun and Yuri was in no more danger than the rest of them.

That would be a relief. Still, she didn't want to encourage him.

"Она уходит." If she had anything to say about it, the wedding dress ladies would be leaving immediately. Maybe Sanjay and Jamal could scare them away. She turned to Kristin. "Why aren't you in the armored car with Sanjay and Jamal? Seems a lot safer."

"I didn't want to be a passenger," Kristin said. "What could I do from the car?"

"You could have brought me a garden trowel or something, then," Phoebe said. "I'm defenseless here."

Kristin grinned. "And not only in regard to Vlad the Assassin. You've got wedding planners now, too."

"Assassin?" Blonde #1 shrieked. "There's an *assassin*?"

"No assassin!" Brenda said. "He's—he's a cab driver! And—and *Swedish*!"

"Swedish?" Phoebe said. "I wouldn't say he's Swedish. More like, you know, Russian."

"Let's reschedule," Blonde #2 said firmly. "Make an appointment. Come to our office."

Sanjay beeped the horn. *About time*. Phoebe wanted nothing more than to force Vlad's cab out of the neighborhood and, preferably, out of her life altogether. But first, the wedding planners had to move that dress rack off the driveway so Sanjay could get out.

"I'll call you next week," Phoebe said to Blonde #2. *When hell freezes over*. "We'll set something up."

"Push the dresses around the car and into the garage!" Brenda said to the wedding planners, skittering up the driveway. "Go around!"

"Great!" said Blonde #1, jerking forward on the dress rack, pulling it toward the house.

"Wait!" said Blonde #2, jerking back to return the rack to the van.

Phoebe turned to Kristin. "I hope Sanjay runs over those dresses." She kept her voice down. "Rolls right over the entire rack of those wretched things."

"That would ruin them," Kristin said.

"A girl can dream."

Blonde #1 won the jerking contest, and following Brenda's directions, the wedding planners swerved left to go around the armored car just as Sanjay, inching back, also swung left. The rear fender of the car banged into the clothes rack, catching one of the dresses in the vehicle's bumper. Sanjay idled the armored car in the driveway while the wedding planners tried to free the dress, tugging gently at lace pleats or whatever was stuck.

Well, *crap*. Jamal and Sanjay needed to get out of that mess and go after Vlad, who would not be idling at the curb across the street for much longer. Phoebe glanced at the damaged taxi and saw Chase head down the lawn toward it, bat in hand. If that lunatic Vlad hurt Chase, she would— Well, she didn't know what she'd do. But she'd think of something really bad. She ran after Chase, scooping up a piece of broken slate on the way.

But before either Chase or she could reach the damaged

cab, Vlad stomped on the gas. The taxi whizzed past them, jumped the curb, and accelerated over the lawn, again heading straight for Yuri, who stood in the driveway, holding the dress rack steady in his good hand to prevent the imprisoned dress from tearing.

"Watch out!" Phoebe screamed.

The wedding planners, Brenda, Kristin, and Yuri all jerked their heads up and saw the danger bearing down. The wedding planners fled to their van, Brenda to the garage, Yuri to the shrubbery again.

Not the shrubbery, Phoebe thought in panic. Get away from the *window*. Get in the *garage*.

Kristin didn't move. She stood ready, her face fierce and determined, holding her rake in front of her.

The rack of wedding dresses, abandoned where it stood in the driveway, one gown still enmeshed in the fender of Jamal's armored car, rolled gently downhill as far as the entangled dress would let it go. But Sanjay charged straight for the charging taxi, dragging the rack of dresses behind him.

Fear tied Phoebe's stomach in knots as she watched the two vehicles speed toward each other like medieval jousters. She didn't want anything to happen to Sanjay or Jamal, and their armored car should have the advantage in a collision. But anything could happen.

At the last second, when the two cars were so close that Sanjay and Jamal must be able to see each infected mosquito bite on Vlad's face through the taxi's broken windshield, Sanjay hauled the steering wheel hard to the left, sending the armored car into a controlled spin. Its back end came around and smacked the taxi's driver-side fender. The rack of wedding dresses, still attached to Sanjay's bumper, swept around the armored car in a full and surprisingly graceful arc and hit Vlad's taxi on the driver side before falling over sideways onto the torn-up lawn.

The dresses separated from their hangers and fluttered softly in the dirt and weeds. Some of the gowns broke free altogether and billowed toward the street like foamy tumbleweeds. The wedding planners shrieked and ran after them.

Phoebe hoped the Weddings from Hell ladies had good insurance. Those dresses would never be the same again.

Kristin stepped up and thrust her rake through the windshield of the cab, now halted by the armored car, and jabbed Vlad with it. Chase joined her with his bat, which was shorter but more powerful than the rake. Phoebe pounded her piece of slate on Vlad's trunk—not that she thought it would do much to stop the assassin. But it was crowded up around the windshield with both Kristin and Chase taking a whack at it, and the hammering sure felt good.

The cab spurted back, and Phoebe jumped aside just in time to avoid being hit squarely in the chest.

"*Cher!*" Chase said. "Are you hurt?"

"I'm fine, but he's making me really mad. What does he think he's doing? He won't get Yuri this way. Not unless Yuri jumps in front of the cab and waits to be run over."

"Vlad's lost control. That's clear."

Vlad had driven over some of the frothy wedding dresses to get away from them. Now he accelerated forward, driving over the dresses again and banging into Sanjay's rear bumper. The armored vehicle scarcely rocked from the impact. Kristin hadn't budged from her spot, and now she swung the rake in a wide arc against the taxi's passenger-side window. Chase hefted the bat and slugged the window on the other side.

"Good going, guys!" Phoebe said. Her slate tile had been broken in her last attack, and now she looked around for something she could use as a weapon.

Kristin smashed the rake against the cab with a very satisfying thunk, but the return force was equally strong. She couldn't hang on to it, and it flew out of her hands, falling to the ground several feet away, directly behind the taxi.

"Stay back, Kristin!" Chase shouted.

Vlad backed up several feet, evidently planning to smash into Sanjay's armored car all afternoon, and drove over the rake. He hit the edge of the prongs, which dug into the threadbare tire. The taxi lurched forward again, heading straight for Yuri, who still stood behind the shrub in front of the window. The rake handle shot up and bounced against the fender and then broke out of the tire, leaving a savage tear in the rubber.

That cab was toast.

But what was Yuri doing still standing there in front of the window? Couldn't he have moved away? Anywhere at all? Anywhere that wasn't in front of her window? Phoebe's heart sank as she said goodbye to the mullioned panes.

Engine whining, the taxi lurched forward. But in a leap that a gazelle would have envied, Yuri jumped out of the shrubbery. With two long running steps to gain momentum, he stretched out and dove for the covered portico. He made it to shelter but didn't stick the landing, falling with a smack on the concrete and sliding a foot or more, his arms out-stretched. He shrieked in pain.

That had to have hurt his broken arm, but he'd shown remarkable survival skills, and at least he was alive. Thumbs-up there.

Vlad backed up out of the shrubbery with a crunch of broken branches and the ear-tingling screech of something scratching metal. The cab listed to one side where the rake had damaged the tire, but the engine roared as Vlad retreated, driving over the wedding dresses again. One of the gowns floated up and caught on the windshield wiper, billowing out over the taxi's roof and obliterating his view through the hole where the windshield used to be. Vlad stopped.

"Now we've got him!" Chase said, running toward the taxi. "He can't see!"

But they'd underestimated the assassin. An arm reached up through the broken windshield and grabbed a handful of frothy tulle. Vlad yanked hard, trying to dislodge the acres of fabric by pulling the gown into the cab. To no avail. The dress, with its multiple layers of filmy white stuff, shifted around, but there was too much of it. It didn't unstick from the windshield wiper blade, and even with most of it inside the cab, it obliterated visibility.

They had him.

But then Vlad stuck his head out the driver-side window

218

and drove away. The dress flapped out the broken windshield while the dress's train shot over the roof like Supergirl's cape in midflight. Sparks flew as the Russian steered the cab down the street, one tire ruined, the wheel on its rim.

"That'll stop him!" Kristin said.

Sanjay sped after Vlad, trying but failing to avoid the few remaining wedding dresses that still littered their yard. He bounced the armored SUV over the curb and into the street after the escaping assassin.

Finally this attack would end. Sanjay and Jamal would catch Vlad, and they would turn him over to the police. All of them would be safe. And in a few days, when Kevin Toth was over the measles, Yuri could get full-time protection from the FBI.

Even better, the wedding dresses were ruined. The wedding planners would never come back.

Happy endings all around.

And then the unbelievable happened.

Vlad tore the wedding dress and the wiper blade off the taxi and tossed them away, but the gown's full skirts and train caught the breeze. The dress soared into the air and streamed out like the sails of a clipper ship in a strong wind before landing squarely on the windshield of Sanjay's armored car and clinging there.

Sanjay hauled hard right to avoid the thing, but, blinded by fabric, he drove straight into the Dresses to Tresses delivery van. The force of the collision caved in the door of the van, and Sanjay used precious seconds to get out of the car and rip the dress away.

By then, Vlad had screeched down the street, tires shooting sparks and the radiator spouting steam, turned a corner, and disappeared. Sanjay jumped back in the car, stomped on the gas, and turned the corner after him.

Phoebe watched them speed away. If anybody could catch the assassin, Sanjay and Jamal could. They'd trained for it. And on the upside, Vlad couldn't go far. His taxi was too damaged.

So even if they hadn't actually caught Vlad, they'd

prevented him from killing anyone. They'd deflected him from damaging their house. The lawn was wrecked, but her mullioned windows were still intact.

She'd call that a win.

A car door slammed, and she turned to see a different cab at the curb and a shaky Nick emerge from the front of the house. This must be the cab he'd called, the one he'd been expecting when Vlad drove up. Then she became aware of the wail of an approaching siren, which must mean that the cops Brenda had called had decided to come. Too late, of course, but still. Arriving had to count for *something*.

The squad car pulled up, and the two cops flung open their doors, leaped out, and drew their weapons on the cab driver.

"Hands up!" they yelled. "Get on the ground!"

The cab driver looked around in confusion. "Me? Why? What did I do?"

"*Get on the ground!*"

The cab driver knelt, hands on his head. Well, this was simply *all wrong*. Phoebe trotted over, staying away from the cops' line of fire.

"Officers!" she said. "You've got the wrong cab! The right cab is getting away!"

"You! Get on the ground!" The cops shifted, pointing their guns at her. Couldn't they tell a bad guy from a good guy? You'd *think*.

"Hey," Phoebe said, putting out her hands. "The cab that attacked us drove off a second ago. You can probably still catch him. Nobody here is a bad guy. We're the people who called you."

"Officers, I'm Chase Bonaventure, and you've got the wrong cab," Chase said, jogging up. "The cab you want got away."

"We got a rogue cab at this address!" the lanky cop said. "You're *who*?"

"*Chase Bonaventure*," the cab driver breathed, still kneeling on the ground. "Oh, my God. It's Chase Bonaventure."

"Who's Chase Bonaventure?" the shorter cop said to

the cab driver. "*You're* Chase Bonaventure?"

"Of course, *that* guy isn't Chase Bonaventure!" Kristin walked toward the curb, holding the broken rake. "*That* guy's the cab driver! *This* guy's Chase Bonaventure!" She nodded her head to Chase, who shook his head. "The quarterback? Las Vegas Rattlesnakes?"

"Put down the weapon!" the lanky cop yelled.

Kristin dropped the rake.

"It's a *rake*," Phoebe said, drawing the cops' guns to her again. "Not a weapon. Well, it *could* be a weapon, but it's broken. So, not a weapon. Anymore."

"*Chase Bonaventure!*" the cab driver said. "It's an honor! Could I have an autograph for my, ah, son?"

The cops frowned at each other.

"Don't tell me you're baseball fans," Phoebe said. "Who'd have believed it?"

"Basketball," the lanky cop said. "What are you talking about?"

"Football," Phoebe said.

"DC's not much of a football town," the cab driver told her.

"So I've been led to understand," Phoebe said. "Especially in the postseason."

"No lie," the cab driver said.

"The squad's expecting good things this year," Chase said. "I know a few of the guys."

"Chase Bonaventure," the shorter cop said. "*Hold* on. The Rattlesnakes quarterback? The *Las Vegas* Rattlesnakes? What are you doing out here?"

"I live here now," Chase said. "This is my house. And—"

"Phoebe, honey?" Brenda had abandoned an urgent talk with the wedding planners and trotted over. "What's going on here?"

"The cops got the wrong cab," Phoebe said.

"Well, for Pete's sake," Brenda said. "That's just silly. Are you *sure* you want to live here, sweetie? This kind of thing would never happen in Vegas."

That was probably true. The cops there would certainly

know who Chase was, anyway. And would take his word for it when he told them they were detaining the wrong cab driver.

"Officers," Chase said. "There's been a misunderstanding. You want a damaged taxi driven by a Russian assassin with injuries to his face. Not this driver in this cab. Which, as you can see, is in perfect condition."

"Thank you," said the cab driver.

"Russian assassin?" The lanky cop raised his eyebrows. "You got a Russian assassin running loose around here in a taxicab?"

"*Yes*," Phoebe said. "I'm with the CIA, and—"

"Oh, so it's *federal*," the short cop said. Both officers holstered their weapons. "No wonder it sounds cuckoo. We don't do federal, lady, and—"

"The part where the nutso tried to kill us and tore up the lawn isn't federal," Brenda said. "We need protection!"

The cab driver took a risk and stood up, brushing himself off.

"Cab's gone, you said." The short cop sighed.

"Yes. My daughter and Chase, her fiancé, and their friends forced it off their property."

"With a rake?" The lanky copy grinned.

"Yes." Kristin glared at the cop. "With a *rake*."

"And a bat," Chase said. "Don't forget the bat."

"Okay," the lanky cop said.

"I want to file a report," Phoebe said.

"Yeah, no." The short cop got back into the squad car. "What you got here, whatever it is, is federal."

"The assassin's coming back," Phoebe said, following him to the vehicle. "He didn't get what he wants. How are we supposed to stop him? We got lucky this time."

"You're cops, right?" Kristin said, stepping up to the window. "You drive around. Can't you drive around and look for a bashed-up taxi driven by a maniac? He wouldn't be hard to spot."

The short guy nodded. "We can do that."

"*Thank* you," Brenda said.

He fired up the engine. "But we're not your target law enforcement. You're CIA? Call those guys. Or the FBI, or Homeland, or whoever. This stuff's beyond our pay grade."

"Or you could get a new rake. That seemed to work." The lanky cop chuckled and got in on the passenger side. He leaned out the window as the short cop shifted gears.

"Seriously, folks. Call the feds." He squinted at the trashed lawn. "Also maybe a landscaper."

He rolled up the window and the squad car drove away.

Phoebe glared at the retreating vehicle. The cops wouldn't help.

They'd have to figure out a way to get the job done themselves.

Chapter 17

Vlad tore around the corner, pressing the accelerator to the floor without getting any more speed out of the taxi. Of course, the tire was shot, the wheel was riding on its rim, and clouds of white vapor poured out the front. Those problems took a toll on performance. The taxi's mechanical failings, combined with its physical condition—windshield gone, hood smashed, trunk dented, not to mention its bright yellow paint job and bold lettering—made it easy to spot.

That was not good.

He had maybe ten seconds' lead on his pursuers. When he saw an alley up ahead, he swung into it, hoping the men in the SUV behind him wouldn't see him make the turn. And then, halfway down the alley, he got the break he needed. Someone had left a garage door open, and the garage was empty. He pulled into it, jumped out of the vehicle, and yanked down the garage door.

Trembling from the adrenaline rush, he leaned against the door and peeked out the window, waiting to see if the security team passed. Thirty seconds went by. Then a minute. Then two.

Then he saw them. Driving slowly, the guy behind the wheel of the black SUV peered into yards and driveways.

They kept moving.

He waited again, another five minutes.

Nothing.

He'd lost them.

He was safe. For now, anyway.

And then his phone trilled. *Unbelievable.*

He yanked the device out of his pocket and stared at the encrypted display, although of course, a message on this phone could come from only one person. The Boss.

He glared at the phone. If he'd had something to report, *he'd have reported it*. When the job was done, *then* he'd report it. In the meantime, that idiot jerk sitting in his comfortable heated chair back in Moscow wanted results? He could just *get in line!* And *wait his damn turn*!

With a savage stab, he sent the call to voice mail. *There.*

Now that the immediate danger had receded and his heart rate slowed, he started to think. He had no gun, and he was going up against a crack security team of at least seven trained professionals, plus the five-man sniper team on the roof, all of whom knew what he looked like and what he was driving. The taxi was damaged. And the next time, they'd be waiting for him.

He couldn't do anything about the damage to the taxi's radiator, but at least he could change the tire. As he worked, he formulated a plan. He still had cards to play. He didn't have to *overpower* Severov's security team; he had merely to *outwit* them. His intelligence, insight, and perseverance had led to decades of flawlessly precise assassinations. He could get the job done here, too, despite all odds, and demonstrate to the Boss what he was capable of.

Twenty minutes later the tire was changed. However, the cab, like the traitor Severov, didn't have long to live. He needed to allocate its last minutes carefully if he wanted to maximize its value, which meant that he couldn't drive it to accomplish everything he needed to do before nightfall. However, all the time he'd spent riding around on the city's busses had not been wasted. He knew exactly where he needed to go and how to get there.

Vlad let himself out of the garage's side door and glanced up and down the narrow alley. Nothing. No black

SUVs. No cops. Nobody.

He walked through the yard and to the front of the house, where he spotted two newspapers lying on the porch. His first stroke of luck. The homeowners were out of town. The garage would stay empty until tomorrow. Long enough.

He turned left and reached the thoroughfare. His new plan would be his last shot. His last opportunity to kill Yuri Severov.

He wouldn't waste it.

Chase gazed at his battered band of warriors, now slumped in chairs scattered around the blue parlor. Nick had taken off for the airport in the cab with the football-worshipping taxi driver, upset that his plans for Kristin had gone awry and annoyed that he'd flown across the country for nothing. Chase didn't blame him. He had a lot of sympathy for a guy who'd been blindsided in love, because, hell, the same thing had happened to him.

However, Chase was relieved for a couple of reasons that Nick had left. Kristin would be happier, for sure. And everyone at the house was in danger, and having one less person to worry about was an improvement in their situation.

Everyone else was accounted for, including the construction crew, who were already back on the roof, hard at work, and Sanjay and Jamal, who had returned, embarrassed that they hadn't found Vlad after he'd driven away.

"How could we have missed him?" Jamal asked. "He simply vanished."

"His disappearance is inexplicable," Sanjay said. "He had the narrowest of leads, and the condition of his vehicle must have impaired his ability to gain ground on us—quite the reverse, in fact. And beyond his inability to increase speed, his vehicle emitted unmistakable sounds. One minute, the rasp of his tire rim striking the pavement was impossible to miss, and the next minute, we heard nothing."

"Don't worry about it," Chase said. "You forced him off the property, that's the main thing. He'll be back. We'll get another crack at him. So how is everybody? Who's hurt?"

They passed the first aid kit around and helped each other with disinfectant and Band-Aids. No one was seriously injured—but luck had had a lot to do with that. What about tomorrow? How could they get the cops either to go after Vlad or provide some security?

"We should take it easy while we can." Chase closed up the first aid kit after everyone was patched up.

"I'm all for that," Kristin said, standing up. "I think I'll lie down for a while. Read, maybe. Or nap."

"I have some calls to make," Brenda said, her voice too bright. That didn't sound good. She was hatching something.

"*No wedding plans*, Mom," Phoebe said, confirming his fears. "Do *not* call wedding planners of any kind. No one who sells or rents dresses or venues or anything. Call *no one*. Do *nothing*."

"Well, sweetie," Brenda said. "You know I—"

"*No wedding plans*," Phoebe said again, her voice steely. "Do not make reservations or down payments or promises. Do not speak for me. Do *nothing*. Am I clear?"

"But Phoebe, honey," Brenda said. "I was talking to Claire, and she said Chase will want a big wedding because he has a large family and a lot of friends. All those football players! And business associates! He'll want everyone there, and big weddings are not simple matters to arrange. Unless, of course, you're British royals. I'm not sure what they do."

Dammit. Now Brenda—and by extension, his own mother—was trying to lay this wedding crap on *his* doorstep. And that was going one step too far.

"Wait a second, Brenda," Chase said. "Phoebe's right. Until we know exactly what we want, until we're *ready* to make plans, we're not moving forward with anything. Our wedding, when it happens, will be what *Phoebe* wants. *And* what I want."

But really, he wanted whatever Phoebe wanted. He just wished she wanted to get married a little quicker. Then all this hassle would be over.

"In any event, we have to smooth things over with Dresses to Tresses," Brenda said. "They have a lot of ruined merchandise on their hands."

"Write a check if you have to," Chase said. "I'll cover it."

"Oh! Thank—" Brenda started.

"*No, you won't,*" Phoebe said fiercely, turning on him with a sudden fury. "You and I had *nothing* to do with that, and you are *not* paying for it. That was Mom's doing, and if that company doesn't have insurance to cover work-related damages and they go after her, then Mom can figure out how to pay for it. It's on *her*. *Not* on you."

Okay. Nothing like having all the women in the house mad at him, especially his own fiancée. How could he get out of here? He was sick to death of discussing the wedding, arguing about the wedding, and worst of all, not having a wedding.

"Я хочу сон," Yuri said, standing up.

Even Yuri had picked up on the vibe. That lucky rat bastard could go down and hide in the basement, away from everybody. He wished he could do the same.

Sanjay stood up, evidently more than ready to join Yuri in abandoning him to the rage of the womenfolk. Not that he blamed either of them.

"Chase's suggestion that we all rest for a while is a most judicious one," Sanjay said. "My belief is that the best use of my time would be to prepare something sustaining for dinner. I'll be in the kitchen."

Jamal jumped up. "I'll help."

Sanjay nodded and turned to Chase. "Call us if you need anything."

"I will," Chase said. "And thanks for everything—going after Vlad and cooking, too."

"Do not mention it," Sanjay said. "I am happy to help in whatever capacity is most needed, either the culinary arts or protective services." He followed Jamal across the entryway and into the kitchen.

"I'll be off, too," Brenda said, bustling out of the room.

"I don't like the looks of that," Phoebe said, glaring after her.

"She's probably going to—" But then, for the life of him, he couldn't think of one thing Brenda could be doing that wasn't about his and Phoebe's nonplanned, nonscheduled wedding.

"Yeah." Phoebe smiled wanly. "She's figuring out how to ensnare us in a big wedding by next week. I'm not having it."

"I know." He got up and went to sit next to her on the sofa.

She leaned away from him and poked her finger in his arm. That wasn't good. And she had a strong finger.

"I *mean* it," she said, warning in her voice. "You are *not* paying for that fiasco with the wedding dresses or anything else she comes up with. I will *not* support her tricks."

"I get it."

"I hope so," she said. "Her maneuvering really pisses me off."

"I see that."

"*Okay*." She leaned back against the arm of the sofa and glared at him.

"I just—"

"No," Phoebe said.

"Even if it—"

"*No*."

"Okay," he said. "I promise."

She gazed at him with that unwavering CIA stare that had brought international kidnappers, data thieves, and the Secret Service to their knees. He tried to look resolved and stalwart. Whatever she saw seemed to reassure her, if marginally.

"Okay," she said, more calmly this time, rearranging herself to lean against him, so that was an improvement. "I'm sorry I yelled, but you are *not* paying for Weddings from Hell. I'm drawing a line."

"Yeah, I figured that out."

"You're smart. I like that in a fiancé." She smiled, turning up her face to kiss him. She was still riled up, so the kiss had a lot of energy.

He might as well take advantage of it, so he closed his eyes and deepened the kiss. He enjoyed the—surge, somehow, of her lips and savored the softness of her mouth, feeling a deep connection in his center, a humming in his blood. He cradled her head, her bright hair sifting over his hands, finding a response that felt both exciting and calming—thrilling but centered. He couldn't describe it, except that it was somehow *right*. Like the focused adrenaline he'd felt before a game, or now when he negotiated with his international business partners. He didn't know everything about this woman yet—he might need decades to discover everything about her—but he knew without a doubt that she was the right one for him, for now and always.

She broke off the kiss, sitting up a little straighter, bouncing a bit in her seat. So, still riled up.

"You know what I think?" she asked, not waiting for an answer. "I think there's something up with this house. Like magic. It draws people in. And then they stay."

Jesus, he hoped not. Although the way things were looking, she might be right.

"I don't think it's the house," he said. "I think it's you."

"*Me!*" She jerked upright faster than a bottle rocket.

Chase grinned, enjoying her shocked incredulity. "Sure. People gravitate to you because you fix trouble. And while you're doing that, many of those people stay at your house. I suspect that if they didn't stay at your house before, it was because you've never had a house. So that's why this whole thing comes as a surprise to you."

Their dog Trouble, hearing his name even in his sleep, raised his head to see if a walk was imminent. Seeing no leash, he decided it wasn't and put his head down again.

She flopped back against the sofa cushions. "That's the weirdest thing I ever heard."

"It's no weirder than house magic. This is your life, Phoebe Renfrew. This is your *story*. We'll keep a diary, and in ten years, we'll see if I'm right."

She clunked her head on his shoulder. "You better not be."

"Why not? We're a team, we've got some chops, and our house is strong. Amos and Sophie lived here, remember? The house can take anything you throw at it."

Phoebe nodded, her brow furrowed. "I think so, too. So, okay. While we're thinking about strong houses, what can we do about Vlad?"

Chase exhaled. "There's no telling what he'll do next, but some things are a given." He picked up her hand. "For starters, he doesn't have a gun, because if he did, he'd have shot us today. In fact, I doubt that he has any weapons at all, so what his strategy will be for killing Yuri, I have no idea. Unless he thinks he can get up close and personal and strangle him. And since he's losing it and making bad decisions, I wouldn't put that past him."

"What if he gets a gun?"

"I don't think he'll get a gun by tomorrow."

"Doesn't have to be tomorrow, does it? Could be next week. Or he could come back in that taxi and drive right through one of our windows."

"He could. Although then he'd be trapped in the house and significantly outnumbered. Besides, he's accelerating his attacks. He must be getting anxious to get back to Russia."

"He could release some kind of poison."

"I'm not sure what kind of poison he could get at, say, Walmart. What kind of poison can a person get on the open market?"

"This conversation is depressing me," Phoebe said, sounding gloomy. "We have to think of a way to protect ourselves. Maybe we could weaponize the front yard."

He saw a lifetime of weird weekend activities opening up before him. "Tire spike strips. Those'll work. If he decides to drive over the yard again, I mean."

"Good idea!" Phoebe dug out her phone and did a quick search. "Shoot. You can't get tire spike strips at Walmart. Or anywhere brick-and-mortar as far as I can tell. It looks like you have to order them. Maybe so they can investigate you. That would be fun. *Not.*"

"And ordering would take too much time," Chase said.

"Want to go buy a bunch of rakes? Kristin was remarkably effective with hers. We could plant them around the yard. We just have to tell Sanjay and Jamal where they are so they don't drive over them if they get in a smash-the-invader game with Vlad again."

"Let's do it. They'd be better than nothing. I was thinking of giant boulders along the perimeter, but rakes would be a lot easier. And we could get more bats. Kristin said we didn't have enough weapons."

"If we're going to buy more bats, let's get enough to field a team."

They let Sanjay and Jamal know where they were headed, then drove to Walmart and bought a bunch of rakes and bats and some other things they needed. When they got home, they laid the rakes prongs-up in the patchy lawn and scattered loose dirt and leaves over them to conceal them as best they could.

"I feel like a regular homeowner," Phoebe said with satisfaction when they were done. The underground irrigation system had come on while they worked, soaking the ground, and she pulled off her muddy gloves and surveyed the area with pride. "Taking care of my place. My yard."

Chase straightened up from laying the last rake. "Planting rakes in the yard to repel Russian assassins is not what regular homeowners do. Trust me on this. Normal homeowners mow the lawn or trim the shrubs."

"Well, special circumstances." Phoebe shrugged. "Let's go in and see what Sanjay and Jamal made for dinner. I'm starving."

"I'm putting this in the ten-year diary," Chase said, heading into the house. "*Weaponize front lawn with rakes*. First entry."

"Next week we'll trim the shrubs, I promise." Phoebe grinned, running to catch up with him, and took his hand as they went indoors.

Vlad took the bus, making several trips to various big box stores to buy a couple of cans of black spray paint and all the parts he needed to make a bomb. He was not an explosives expert, but he knew enough to get by. He could make a bomb big enough to kill and small enough to conceal, which was the important thing. He'd blow up the safe house and everyone in it during the night. Yuri Severov, *done*. Renfrew and Agarwal, *done*. Cher, Running Man, Rake Woman, Driving Men Crushing His Taxi, Suitcase Man Who Fell Down, Vicious Attack Dog, Sniper Team on the Roof, *done*. Everybody done.

As a solution, he didn't much like it. Bombs, especially homemade ones, were inexact. They could go off too soon, too late, or not at all. They could take out too much or not enough. Even with the best information in the world—which he didn't have—and the time for planning—which he also didn't have—he still might not eliminate his target.

And bombs were noisy and messy. They drew cops, which he didn't want.

But he had no other alternative. No store would sell him a gun, not without residency. Poisons were too hard to get, at least for the best ones. He'd be happy to knife that traitor Severov—and with the big pink cast he was wearing on his arm, he'd be slow and easy to kill. But how could he get into the house? It was too well-protected with all the security personnel, as well as the attack dog and alarm system.

No. A bomb was not his first choice of weapon, but it would get the job done. He would make sure of that.

He needed most of the afternoon to get all his purchases safely back in the garage. Only then could he start work. First, the taxi. To move under the cover of darkness, he needed an inconspicuous vehicle. Not a damaged, bright yellow taxi.

He opened the garage's side door to get some ventilation in the cramped space, uncapped the black spray paint, and set to work, covering the taxi's logos and as much of its bright yellow finish as he could. The spray paint spritzed everywhere in the small garage, choking him despite the paper face mask he'd bought, but in the end, the taxi was unrecognizable. It sat there like a splotchy storm cloud, paint dripping off fenders, doors and hubcaps. He didn't care. The cab didn't have to be beautiful. It simply had to be dark.

When the taxi was painted, he unwrapped his bomb-making materials and spread everything out on the garage floor. He had batteries, detonators, and fuses. He had burner phones. He had the ingredients for gunpowder. He was good to go.

As he worked, he plotted. He'd rest for a couple of hours. And then at three or four in the morning—when every-one in the house was asleep—he'd blow the place up. Every-one would die. And he'd be out of there and back on a plane to Moscow.

That reminded him that he had to call the airline and change his ticket for first thing in the morning.

An hour later, the mission was accomplished. He was set.

Let the fun begin.

Chapter 18

We should set a watch tonight," Chase said. "At least through the night. And every night until Vlad is caught or the FBI takes Yuri off our hands."

Phoebe watched him pace in front of the fireplace in the yellow parlor. Sanjay and Jamal had made one of Sanjay's mother's favorites, a vegetable and chickpea soup, and a Lebanese chicken-and-rice casserole flavored with cinnamon that was a signature dish of Jamal's mother. Having such a nice meal at the end of a trying day had perked them all up.

So at least *somebody*'s mothers were helping out, although in absentia.

The night was still young, but Brenda was already in bed—or at least that's where she'd said she was going when she went upstairs. For all Phoebe knew, she was lining up caterers for their nonexistent wedding. However, everyone else, including Amos, was seated around the room. He'd dropped by after he heard about Vlad's attack and the destruction to their lawn—how he'd found out about that, Phoebe didn't want to know—and now he was the only one who seemed relaxed and bemused. Well, this kind of siege was probably old hat to him.

She was keyed up, like she thought the rest of them were, expecting that Vlad would make his next attempt on

Yuri's life sooner rather than later.

"Зачем устанавливать охранника?" Yuri asked. "Bang, bang."

"What's he saying?" Chase frowned in Yuri's direction. "Although I have a pretty good idea. Bang, bang—I get that."

Phoebe nodded. "He wants to know why we don't have guns. He thinks if we shot Vlad, it would solve all our difficulties."

"But create new ones," Kristin said.

"Too bad we gave all those guns back to the FBI," Jamal said. "We could use them now."

"If we shot him, we'd have to prove self-defense, though," Phoebe said. "And if Vlad doesn't have a gun, that's a problem."

"Besides, it doesn't seem very sporting," Kristin said.

"And on a practical note, does anyone in this room even *own* a gun?" Phoebe asked.

They all looked at each other.

"I do," Amos said.

Phoebe's heart sank. Vlad could hurt them, probably in ways they hadn't even thought of yet, and despite Chase's assurances that the Russian assassin would not have been able to obtain a firearm, Phoebe wasn't so sure. But the thought of shooting him down made her feel slightly sick. Then they'd be no better than the man they were trying to stop. Although how they would stop him was still a big question.

"But I'd rather you didn't borrow it," Amos said.

Sanjay cleared his throat. "To further the discussion about conducting a watch, as Chase has suggested, I concur. A watch is most advisable at night when the assassin's target could be sleeping and at its most vulnerable."

Jamal nodded in agreement. "What Sanjay said."

"I think Vlad'll probably attack tonight," Phoebe said, turning to Amos. "Don't you?"

"You think *tonight*?" Kristin took a deep breath. "It's almost dark *now*."

"His Russian handlers must be pressuring him for

results," Amos agreed.

"I'd say so." Phoebe remembered only too clearly how her own bosses at the CIA had once pressured her. "I bet he was supposed to be here only for a day or so, and now he's been here for, what? Four or five days. Because he shot out Sanjay's cab on Saturday at noon and now it's Tuesday night."

"Our training informs us that our most expeditious security precautions should incorporate walking a perimeter around the yard, perhaps also with the occasional foray out into the street," Sanjay said. "The goal is to keep Vlad as far away from ourselves as possible."

"You guys are the experts," Chase said. "We'll need to be careful. Stick with a buddy at all times for extra safety. And let's take Trouble when we go out. He's too friendly to be much protection, but he'll bark at strangers if you show anger or fear. And he knows Vlad and doesn't like him."

"Plus, we got more baseball bats, so we have weapons," Phoebe said. "We should each take one of those. And don't forget about the rakes we planted in the yard. Don't trip on them. They're supposed to stop Vlad, not us."

"For how long tonight should we keep watch?" Kristin asked.

"Until light," Chase said, calculating. "Ten hours. We've got five people, two people per two-hour shift. Everybody gets four hours altogether. Amos, I appreciate your expertise in the spy game, but I'm leaving you out of this. It's our fight."

"A kind way of letting an old man off the hook," Amos said. "But I agree with you. I don't want to leave my Sophie all night with only the nurse. I'll call or drop by in the morning on my constitutional and see how you made out."

"We'll have the coffee on," Chase said.

"I want the first watch with somebody," Phoebe said. "I'm too wired to sleep."

"How are we going to split up?" Kristin asked. "I'm used to seeing Sanjay and Jamal work together, but they have security training, and the rest of us don't. Although, of course, as a former star athlete, Coach, you have superior strength and conditioning."

Chase grinned. "Nice save, Kristin."

Kristin grinned back. "Thank you. And for myself, despite a lack of training and superior physical skills, I wield a mean rake."

"You do," Jamal said. "Very mean. And Phoebe hurls a mean piece of slate."

"Well, I was riled up." Phoebe watched Chase fill out a chart.

"Here's how we'll do it," he said, handing it to Phoebe to pass around. "See what you think."

Phoebe had drawn the first watch with Sanjay.

"Okay," she said, taking a deep breath. "Sanjay, we're on."

"Stay alert, and *stay safe*," Chase cautioned again. "That's our first priority."

Phoebe glanced at him and saw the warning in his eyes. He thought she might do something risky.

He was worried about her. The thought gave her a warm feeling.

Well, she planned to be careful. She didn't want to get hurt, but she wouldn't let Vlad kill Yuri if she could do anything to stop it. Killing people for a *living*, for *money*, was indefensible. And Yuri could give the FBI a lot of useful information about Russian hacking into American organizations. And if by protecting Yuri they could also turn Vlad over to the police, so much the better. The world would be a safer place as a result.

"Vlad is tougher than he might seem at this moment," Amos warned. "Don't forget—he took a big hit this afternoon, but somehow he got away from you. He's out there somewhere, regrouping. Don't sell him short. His back is against the wall. He could still do serious damage to you all, even without a gun."

Phoebe nodded. Her throat was tight from the tension in her back and neck. What Amos said was true—and they were underprepared and undertrained compared to the Russian.

But what choice did they have? None. Vlad was coming after them. And no one in law enforcement was coming to help.

Vlad had the advantage of skills and training and experience.

They had the advantage of numbers.

The battle was on.

Chase handed Phoebe one of the bats they'd bought that afternoon, stifling a prickle of anxiety. She was a language analyst for the CIA, not a field officer, so she didn't have any training in defensive or offensive maneuvers or anything else that could help her in this situation. Tonight she'd be on foot, armed only with a baseball bat and a flashlight, searching for a trained assassin who'd probably be driving a beat-up taxi—unless he'd stolen another car—and might even have a gun. The potential outcomes of that uneven matchup chilled him to the core.

But Sanjay would have her back, and this was a part of the job she wanted to do. He just had to hope that nothing went wrong.

Chase had decided to take the watch patrols when he thought Vlad would be most likely to attack—the later three-to-five and five-to-seven shifts. Those early-morning hours would be the time when everyone would be most tired or most likely to be asleep. Vlad would know that and try to take advantage of it.

He thought. *Hoped.* He wanted to be there when Vlad made his move.

"A dog is a most useful ally in terms of improving one's security profile," Sanjay said as he clipped Trouble's leash to his collar. "However, I'm afraid our most faithful and energetic watchdog here will get extremely tired as well as bored if we walk him continuously around the perimeter for ten hours."

Chase handed him a flashlight. "You might be surprised. That mutt never seems to tire."

Phoebe hefted her bat across her shoulder. "Ready?" she asked Sanjay. "Let's hit the road."

"Be careful," Chase said again, kissing Phoebe hard. "Sanjay, good luck."

"We will remain alert and vigilant, and we have our phones," Sanjay said. "At the first sign of any efforts by Vlad the Assassin to do us or your property any harm, we shall do what we can to neutralize such actions, as well as alert the police, the FBI, and you."

"Good man. Jamal and Kristin will relieve you in two hours."

Phoebe wiggled her bat. "But if Vlad comes at us, I'm going to beat the stuffing out of him. I'm tired of his crap. Just so you know."

He could only hope that the evening would be that simple. But he was pretty sure it wouldn't be.

Phoebe and Sanjay walked with Amos to the end of their block, checking all the parked vehicles to make sure that none was a damaged taxi with a Russian assassin sitting inside, watching them. None was.

She worried when Amos took off for home, wondering if he'd be safe and if they should walk him all the way. But he assured them that he'd be fine and promised he'd call when he arrived, so they turned around. Fifteen minutes later, he did call, and that was the last excitement they had on their first watch.

For two hours they led Trouble around the house without spotting anything unusual. Patrolling the deep backyard was difficult, because the back of the house—like all the houses on the street—was perched at the edge of a steep slope. The incline was heavily wooded and dotted with rock outcroppings, and in the dark, even with flashlights, they couldn't see to the alley below. Navigating down to it was difficult, made more so by the darkness, and getting back up again was exhausting. Trouble loved it, however, and saw it as a wonderful game they could all play. He raced up and down the embankment twice while she and Sanjay struggled to the top for what must have been the tenth time.

Phoebe stopped to catch her breath. "Maybe we should

let Trouble run around on his own and we could go to bed. He'd bark if he saw Vlad."

"That would be an excellent solution if only he didn't also bark at unknown nighttime wildlife," Sanjay said. "And sometimes the breeze."

Phoebe laughed. "And to think he used to be such a quiet dog."

Sanjay smiled. "He was probably more insecure when you first found him abandoned and wandering out on the road in Vegas. Now he's more confident of his future and acts more naturally."

"That'll be helpful if he spots Vlad."

They took a couple of short forays down the block, looking for anything suspicious, but no damaged taxis showed up. Vlad did not appear in any other car or on foot. Trouble sniffed at interesting but nonthreatening smells.

"Nothing," Phoebe reported when they got back at eleven. "Quiet as a mouse, except that the next-door neighbors seem to be binge-watching old horror movies."

"They want horror, they could help us." Kristin took Phoebe's bat from her. She was on the second watch with Jamal. "Although I guess as movie themes go, we're more action-adventure."

"Sort of like *Home Alone*," Jamal said. "Rather than, say, *The Terminator*."

"I wouldn't know," Chase said. "I'm more of a rom-com man myself. You guys ready? Be careful out there."

"Always." Jamal picked up a bat and Trouble's leash and followed Kristin out the door.

As they walked to the back edge of the property and headed down the steep grade, Trouble trotting alongside, the others watched from the kitchen window.

"Did you get any rest?" Phoebe asked, her eyes glued to the dark yard, trying to follow Kristin and Jamal's progress. The night would be even more dangerous if they weren't physically ready for it—if they were too tired to respond efficiently.

"Too wired," Chase said. "But Sanjay and I take the

next watch. I'll lie down until then."

"And now I'm off to try for a few z's myself," Sanjay said. "I'll set my alarm in the event I manage to sleep." He left them in the kitchen and headed to his room.

"I hope that when Vlad makes his move, he makes it when I'm on watch," Chase said. "It's one thing for him to go after me, but I don't want anyone else to get hurt out there. Vlad and Yuri are our problem, not Kristin and Jamal and Sanjay's problem."

Our problem. She felt warm hearing that, because really, Vlad and Yuri were *her* problem. Chase, much less her friends, hadn't asked for this grief. But Chase had made *her* problems *their* problems. She slipped her hand into his and squeezed it.

"I'm feeling guilty about sending everybody out there to protect us," she said. "Maybe we should have called a private security company instead."

"I thought of that. But then Sanjay and Jamal might think that we didn't respect their training."

"I have every confidence in Sanjay. Jamal, too."

"I do, too. And I doubt private security would send out more than two guys anyway. As it is, we've got two trained—or mostly trained—guys on our side, plus you, a terror on wheels, plus Kristin the bulldog. And Yuri's not much good with his broken arm, but he can still do some things. Hell, even your *mother* can do some things."

"You think I'm a terror on wheels?" She loved that idea.

"Absolutely. *Especially* on wheels. You terrify me all the time."

"Oh, good. That's the effect I was going for."

Chase laughed and leaned down to kiss her.

"I wish we knew what Vlad was up to," he said when he let her go. "But I guess we'll find out soon enough." He turned away from the window. "Until then, let's see if we can get some sleep."

Contemplating his improvised workshop, Vlad was irritated that the garage failed to yield a suitable container for the bomb that he wanted to build. In a perfect world, he'd have access to better supplies—C-4, at least—and he wouldn't need a large volume of explosive material.

But he couldn't buy C-4 or anything close without raising dozens of red flags, so he'd had to settle for the less-effective materials he *could* get. He needed more of those for the same bang, so now the bomb, instead of being small and compact, would have to be large and bulky. But it could still get the job done just fine.

In the revised large-and-bulky-bomb scenario, he'd prefer to stuff the taxi with his bomb materials, park the taxi next to the front door of the safe house, and watch the whole building go sky-high when he pushed the button. But he couldn't risk driving the car up to the front door and leaving it there. Renfrew and Agarwal and the rest of Severov's security team were undoubtedly keeping a watch on the place, and someone would notice a taxi at the front porch, even at three in the morning.

Since he couldn't use the damaged taxi as a bomb container, he needed something else that was large but easy to transport. Preferably something—perhaps several somethings—that he could hide behind the shrubs or leave around the corner of the building, something that would look like it belonged there. Something like oil drums. Oil drums would be perfect.

The garage did not have any oil drums, but it did have trash and recycling bins. These containers were more than big enough to do the job—and they had wheels—but they also had hinged lids. Therefore, some of the bomb's force would be expended upward through the lid, rather than outward. However, now was not the time to be choosy. The bins would work.

Both receptacles were full of trash, but it was fully dark, lights visible in some of the houses that lined the alley, although no one was outdoors or in their yards. He dragged the bins out the side door of the garage and tipped them over in the alley, leaving a pile of soggy, stinking refuse in the roadway. Leaving the mess wasn't a problem. He'd be long gone before anyone complained. If anyone did.

He brought the bins back inside and put enough combustible materials inside to make a nice explosion. Then he rigged the burner phones he'd bought to detonators and attached them to the bins, taped the lids closed, and loaded them into the trunk of the damaged taxi.

He'd set aside enough material to build a couple of baby bombs, because even a small blast could cause some damage and increase fear and confusion in its targets. What to put the material in? He poked around the garage for a suitable container and saw some cardboard boxes on a shelf. Perfect.

Dumping out the contents onto the floor, he filled the boxes with the last of the bomb material. To each, he added a simple spring-loaded pressure release switch that he built from a mousetrap he found on a shelf. The simple IED would have a hair trigger, but it wouldn't need another phone to detonate. A good bump would do it. Always an upside. Then he taped the boxes closed.

There. Finished. When he called those phones attached to the detonators on the bin bombs, *boom*. When the box bombs got nudged, boom again.

He checked his watch. Only ten o'clock. Still plenty of time. He'd stretch out in the taxi and get some sleep, safe and secure that his plan was foolproof.

Dawn—and victory—would come soon enough.

Chase was on the three-to-five-o'clock morning watch with Kristin, Phoebe safe at home in bed—he hoped—after her second shift with Jamal. Everything was still quiet in the neighborhood. Kristin was visibly flagging, perhaps still affected by the jet lag of her trip from Vegas only a few days ago. So much had happened in the last past seventy-two hours, it seemed like she'd been in DC longer than that.

For himself, the edges of exhaustion nibbled around his eyes, but he was too edgy to feel tired. He didn't see how he could have been mistaken about Vlad attacking tonight. But here it was—four o'clock in the morning, and no sign of the assassin yet. Could they have been wrong?

They struggled up the last few yards of the slope that was their backyard and walked through the side yard to the front of the house. Kristin stumbled on a clod of dirt that had been churned up when Vlad destroyed their yard that morning. Chase took her arm to steady her.

"I'm not much good out here right now, I'm afraid." She couldn't conceal a huge yawn. "Way too tired. Sorry about that."

"I'm sorry to keep you up," Chase said. "This isn't even your fight."

"The *hell* it's not." Suddenly energized, she stopped dead in her tracks. "Phoebe is my friend, and okay, you're my boss, but I'm sorry, you're my friend, too. Your fight is my fight, Coach. And this is my country as much as it is Phoebe's, and I can worry about it as much as she does. We've got a Russian inside your house trying to defect with information that will show how Moscow is threatening us, and an assassin going around trying to kill him and everybody else in his way, and I'm not letting that stupid jerk get away with that kind of crap. That is *not happening*. And I'm taking the VP job, too. By the way. As if you didn't know."

He was touched by her loyalty and impressed by her convictions, doubly glad she'd decided to take the VP job.

"Sorry, Kristin. I just don't want you—or anyone—to get hurt. But I appreciate your help more than you know. And I'm glad that you're taking the promotion. It'll be good to have you here in DC."

They paused at the front sidewalk. Across from them, the park loomed, dark and forbidding now that they thought Vlad might be hiding there. Cars lined the street on both sides. None of them was a damaged taxi. Should they walk down the block and peek inside all the vehicles? He glanced at Kristin again. She really did look beat. But he could leave her here to sit on the front stoop and keep guard, and he could walk the block by himself. He didn't think Vlad would get the drop on them in the next few minutes. Unless he had a gun, of course.

And then a deep *boom* reverberated off the houses on

their street, and halfway down the next block, a fireball arced into the sky. Trouble barked at the commotion, straining at his leash.

Kristin whipped around and peered down the roadway. *"What was that?"*

"Something exploded. Go in the house and call 911. Wake everybody. Be ready to vacate. Or if Sanjay and Jamal say to get out, then go."

"You think it's Vlad."

"Yeah. But why did he do something down the street? Why isn't he *here*?" He handed her the bat he'd been carrying.

"Wait. Where are you going?"

"I want to check it out. People might need help."

As Kristin headed into the house, phone to her ear, he ran down the block toward the fire with Trouble, who was eager to get to the scene. If that asshole Vlad had hurt innocent people, he'd make sure the Russian assassin never saw daylight again.

Chapter 19

The first cardboard-box bomb was more trouble to set off than he'd initially imagined. Because it was built with a spring-loaded pressure switch—essentially an IED—Vlad had to trigger the switch when he was far enough away not to get hurt himself. He'd placed the bomb on the roof of a car, expecting the device to destroy the vehicle when it went off and, he hoped, cause as much confusion to the neighborhood as possible. But then he spent many fruitless minutes tossing rocks at the box, trying to hit it. He didn't have to strike the box hard, but it did need a push. And it was a lot harder to hit a smallish box from a distance in the dark than he'd expected.

Finally he hit the box with enough force to spring the switch. With deep satisfaction, Vlad watched the first small bomb go off, igniting the fancy car. He anticipated with amusement the anger the car owner would feel when he saw his prized vehicle reduced to a pile of charred, twisted metal and melted upholstery.

As his eyes adjusted to the dark again, he saw Running Man and Vicious Attack Dog charging down the street toward the blast, no doubt to check out his accomplishment. So, as he'd anticipated, the security team at the safe house compound was, in fact, keeping watch. If they had not been, Running Man would not have been able to arrive so quickly, and fully dressed.

He'd hoped the blast would attract more of Severov's protection detail—perhaps Agarwal, too, and some of the sniper team—but even with only Running Man pulled away from the compound, this was the moment when the guard would be reduced in force. The other team members would be sleeping, or in disarray. Now was the time to make his move, while Running Man was away from the unit. The safe house wouldn't be weakened for long.

He left the burning vehicle and plunged down the steep slope to the alley where he'd parked the damaged taxi. He got in and drove into the next block as quickly as he dared—the vehicle's damaged radiator was already spewing steam—and parked behind the dark safe house. As he glanced up, a light blinked on in one room. So they were stirring.

No time to waste now.

He popped the trunk and hauled out both bomb bins and the second cardboard box bomb. Tucking the box under his arm, he hauled the first heavy trash bin up the rocky incline to the side of the house, struggling to keep the bin upright. The effort cost him too many precious minutes and made him sweat so much that droplets poured down his face and dripped into his eyes. The humidity in this cursed city was enough to drown a man. If the mosquitoes didn't kill you first.

He couldn't wait to get back to Moscow and the deep, penetrating cold of a Russian winter.

He peeked around the side of Severov's safe house to the front. No one was out there. No guard and no dog. He positioned the bin at the end of the house by the garage. If he went any closer to the kitchen or front door, he and the bin would be visible through those big fancy windows. He didn't want that. He didn't want them to see anything suspicious at all.

Then, carrying the cardboard box bomb under his arm, he crawled under the windows, trying to get as close to the front door as he could. That turned out to be a time-consuming error of judgment. He'd thought he could push the box bomb along the hard-packed earth of the lawn, but the ground was soggy from what must have been an overactive irrigation system, because no rain had fallen in the past forty-eight hours, and no weather was so humid that the ground turned to mud. In resignation, Vlad held the box off the ground with one arm to keep it dry, leaving him to hurry as best as he could while he crawled on his knees and one hand toward the front door.

And then he put his palm down hard on the tines of an upturned rake, which hurt more than he would've thought possible, and the rake handle flew up and hit him on the shoulder and forehead before it fell against the window. He almost dropped the box, too, which would have set the bomb off and killed him, while not guaranteeing the traitor's death. For several critical seconds, Vlad froze, waiting for someone to challenge him, nursing his injured hand. It was bleeding, and maybe he'd torn a ligament or something, although he couldn't tell in the dark. But his palm was raw and throbbing.

Finally, several precious moments later, when no one stepped out to the porch or opened a window, he placed the box by the bushes near the front door in the driest spot he could find. In the dark, no one would see the box bomb in the shadow of the shrubbery.

So far, so good. He crawled back to the side of the house and stood, taking a second to glance down the street at his handiwork. The car fire a block away was still burning nicely, but he could hear sirens in the far distance. Certainly fire trucks, and probably police, too.

He had to hurry now.

He hustled back down the slope to the alley and dragged the second bin up the backyard and around the other side of the house, a task made more time-consuming and difficult with his injured hand. Conscious that he needed to hurry, he positioned the bomb at the corner, where he hoped it would bring down that end of the compound. With the big bombs on either end of the structure and the small one in the middle, the multiple blasts should take out the entire building, killing everyone inside, including that treacherous traitor, his initial target, Yuri Severov.

If the demolished car down the street was anything to go by, this house and its inhabitants didn't stand a chance.

Phoebe woke from a deep sleep, wondering if she'd heard something outside. Then she thought of Vlad and, suddenly worried, sprang from bed to peer out the window.

Chase, holding Trouble's leash, was sprinting down the street, away from their place. Of Kristin there was no sign. From her angle, though, she couldn't see what Chase was running toward.

What had happened?

She hadn't bothered to undress when she lay down to sleep, so she thrust her feet into her shoes and charged out the door. She met Kristin in the hallway, dashing up the stairs two at a time.

"Explosion down the street!" Kristin said. "Do you have a landline? I can't get through on my cell."

"In the TV room. Vlad's work?"

"Has to be, right?"

"I'll get Yuri," Phoebe said. "Let's meet in there."

She bolted down the hallway, but not before she saw Sanjay, wide awake and also fully dressed, emerge from his room. Maybe they'd all slept fully clothed. Probably by now they were all sensitized to noise and threats.

She barreled down the stairs and into the basement, where Yuri lay sleeping on the foldout sofa, dead to the world. Well, probably it was a lot quieter down here. Or else the Russians were sounder sleepers. Or not as worried about assassins.

"Yuri!" she said, shaking his shoulder. "Yuri! Вставай! Произошел взрыв! Это мог быть Влад!"

Yuri opened his eyes and blinked at her. "Влад? Черт возьми."

He got it in one. *Vlad, dammit* was right.

He swung his legs over the edge of the sofa, rubbing his eyes. He had gone to bed fully dressed, so evidently Russian IT hackers did fear international assassins. Unless, of course,

Yuri always slept fully dressed. Which, the way he looked most of the time, he might.

She pulled him upstairs and into the TV room, where everyone else had already congregated.

"First responders are on the way," Kristin said, hanging up the landline. "The dispatcher knew about the explosion already. I told them that we think it was deliberately set by a guy who's really after us. They're going to come here and check on us when they're done down there."

"I hope they are sufficiently aware that they might be heading into a trap," Sanjay said. "If Vlad set multiple bombs and responders aren't wearing those bombproof suits, they could be seriously injured, if not killed, when Vlad sets the bombs off."

"I'll call them back." Kristin picked up the phone again.

"We should get out of the house," Jamal said. "If a bomb's been planted around here, we're sitting ducks."

"Right," Phoebe said. "As long as we're pretty sure he doesn't have a gun, right? We don't want him shooting us one by one as we go out the door."

"I'll go first," Brenda said, standing up. "He won't consider me a threat, so he might hesitate to kill me. It might gain us a little time."

Amazement, shock, and admiration flooded Phoebe's brain. That was an incredibly brave and selfless thing for her mother to offer. In that second, Phoebe was proud of her.

"Mom—" she said.

"Miz Renfrew," Sanjay said. "Thank you for your extremely generous proposition, but I am sorry. It is unacceptable."

"Nope," Brenda said, marching to the door. "I know I'm right. So I'm doing it. I'll go out the front. If he shoots, you go out the back."

Brenda led the way out of the TV room, down the hallway, and into the entryway, where Phoebe caught up with her.

"Mom, no," she said, talking Brenda's arm. "I'll go first. It's my responsibility. Besides, who's going to pick out my wedding dress if you get hurt?"

Brenda brightened. "You're going to let us plan your wedding after all?" she asked. "Oh, that's fantastic! Kristin, did you hear? You *must* be maid of honor! Because Phoebe said—"

As Brenda turned to talk to Kristin, Phoebe grabbed a bat and flung open the front door, determined to take the first step across the threshold. But she was careful to stand well to the side so she wouldn't be a target for anyone out there. Let Vlad show his position by shooting at the open door.

Not that he had a gun.

Or probably he didn't.

When Chase arrived at the scene of the car bomb down the street, he checked out the small but avid crowd surrounding the burning vehicle, thinking that Vlad might be among them. He'd never seen the Russian assassin, but those infected mosquito bites on his face couldn't have healed yet. He'd be obvious.

But no one standing there looked like they had a bad case of chicken pox. And in the meantime, Trouble was going nuts, whining and barking and pulling at his leash.

Uncharacteristic of him. Usually the mutt was a happy-go-lucky friend magnet. And now the dog wanted to get away—toward the neighbors' house. Chase wondered briefly if that was the house where the horror movie buffs lived. Maybe they had a dog. Maybe that was it.

Or maybe it was the accelerant Vlad had used to get the car to burn like that. The sharp odor of gasoline still lingered in the air.

Or maybe it was Vlad himself.

"Got something, boy?" he asked the dog. "Let's check it out." He unsnapped the leash, and Trouble took off across the street, up the lawn to the neighbor's house, and around the side of the building. Chase ran after him. The dog clearly was on a mission.

Trouble ran down the incline at the back of the property, down to the alley, where he pranced and whined. Chase followed as fast as he could. When he reached the alley, he saw a crapped-out, death-star-black vehicle parked in the next block.

His block.

And maybe that was a taxi light at the top.

Vlad. He'd painted the taxi.

And now he was doing something at their house.

Maybe—probably—leaving a bomb, if the car bomb on this block was anything to go by. And *that* bomb had been set to distract them—him—from Vlad's real goal.

The car bomb had been set to draw him away from his house. Away from Phoebe. So Vlad could inflict the maximum damage on their house and everybody in it.

He had to be stopped.

"That's Vlad!" he told the dog as he took off running. "Let's go!"

They tore down the alley, both running hard but Trouble in the lead. As they approached the parked taxi, Chase saw that its trunk was open and empty. A man—*Vlad*—was running down the slope of their backyard, away from the house to the damaged vehicle. He was empty-handed.

So any bombs he'd built were already in place around his house. They'd already been set.

He had to get to Vlad before the assassin could detonate them. If not—he couldn't think what would happen if he didn't. That just wasn't an option.

He was almost at the taxi—only a few dozen more yards—but Trouble was ahead of him. Even dark as it was, the assassin had to have seen them. Now they'd find out if he had a gun or not.

Vlad got to the taxi and reached into the trunk for something before he slammed it closed. As Trouble leaped for the assassin's leg, growling and barking, Vlad whirled around, raising his arm, a tire iron in his hand. Chase felt sick.

"*Hey!*" he yelled, trying to distract the Russian.

Vlad glanced up, which gave Chase the split second he needed. He launched himself at the assassin, grabbing him around the knees and taking him down to the pavement with a hard thump. Vlad went down but hung on to the tire iron, and with one swift, sure move, swung it across his body, cutting the air like a scythe and catching Chase on the shoulder with unbelievable force.

Intense pain sucked the breath from his body and numbed his entire arm. Trouble leaped in, biting Vlad's arm and hanging on. Vlad struggled to get free, kicking Chase and wrenching his arm away from the dog. Chase tried to hang on and wrestle the tire iron away, but his arm wasn't working right.

Then with a huge lunge and a kick, Vlad broke loose. He surged to his feet, taking Trouble with him, swinging him into the air until the dog let go. Then he staggered into the taxi and revved the engine, sending plumes of white mist spewing from under the hood.

Chase staggered to his feet, but by then Vlad had angled the taxi up the embankment toward the house instead of heading down the alley for a quick getaway. Why would he do that? The steep slope, covered in rocks and trees, was almost unnavigable.

He wanted to see the bombs go off.

There was no other explanation for it. Vlad planned to blow up the place, and he wanted to watch his handiwork.

Trouble took off after the damaged taxi, racing up the backyard slope toward the house. Chase stumbled up the slope after him, trying to shake off the numbness in his arm. Only one light was on in the darkened house, and as far as he could tell, Phoebe—and everyone else—slept on, unsuspecting.

He broke into a run.

When no one shot at her, Phoebe, bat in hand, left the house, stepping off her front porch onto the lawn. She didn't see Vlad. She took a few steps toward the sidewalk and looked down the street in the direction she'd seen Chase running. She didn't see him, either, but she did see the remnants of a fire and heard the crackle of flames. The wail of sirens was audible, too, and behind their house, maybe in the alley below, a car revved its motor.

So that was where Chase had gone—down to a fire. Kristin had said there'd been an explosion. That must have been what had awakened her.

The good news was, Vlad wasn't here. He hadn't shot at her, and she didn't see the taxi anywhere on the street, either.

As she turned to gesture to the others to come out, she saw Chase tear around the corner of the garage, arms pumping, running hard, toward her.

And from the other side of the house, she saw the blackish hulk of a damaged taxi belching white smoke roar up their side yard, turn sharply, bounce over the broken stonework, and head toward the front of the house. The taxi's headlights flashed across her and strafed the bedraggled landscaping of their front lawn.

Trouble stretched out, running hard, barking like mad, followed on its bumper.

"Trouble!" she yelled. "Get over here!"

The dog didn't listen. He jumped at the vehicle, still barking. One bad turn, one flick of the wrist, and Vlad would hit him.

Enough. She was furious at Vlad for trying to hurt them, run them down, and kill them. She was angry at the damage to her property. She was enraged that Russian assassins got to ride roughshod in her city. Where was border control when you needed them? Didn't those people bother to check passports anymore? Was Homeland just too tired and too busy?

Somebody had to stop Vlad.

Evidently she was the one to do it.

She shouldered the bat and took a stance, prepared to blast Vlad and his stupid taxi out of their lives forever. Vlad was not getting away with his stupid crap any longer.

"*No!*" Chase roared. "*Move away!*"

What was he talking about? She wasn't moving. *She was ending this.*

Vlad revved his motor. *Good.* She was ready.

She adjusted her position and waited for Vlad to get closer.

Vlad couldn't believe his eyes. Running Man was charging full-tilt around the side of the garage, hell-bent, it looked to Vlad, on stopping the taxi bare-handed. He thought that blow with the tire iron had put him down, maybe for good. But it hadn't even slowed him down.

However, no unarmed man on foot stood a chance against a trained Russian assassin in a vehicle. Vlad did a sharp turn on the lawn to point the taxi's headlights at the front door of the safe house. Yuri Severov, surrounded and protected by most of the security team, stood under the portico. Alone on the lawn stood one incredibly foolish woman, facing him down with nothing but a baseball bat. That was Cher, the woman he'd tased. He wondered where Agarwal was. Perhaps even now the wily trained agent was aiming a rocket launcher at him from the roof.

He couldn't worry about Agarwal, and Cher was doing him a favor by making herself so obvious. He'd run her down and then blow the place up, taking them all out.

Vlad stamped on the gas pedal and accelerated toward Cher. Instantly he realized he'd driven over something. He felt a bump and a pull on his steering, and then something smacked the underside of his car.

What was that?

But with a sickening feeling, he knew what it was—a rake. A booby trap, planted in the yard. The same kind of booby trap he'd hurt his hand on in the shrubbery only minutes before. The same booby trap that had ruined his tire yesterday.

He'd driven over a damn rake and punctured his tire. Again.

He glared at the woman, who waggled her bat and grinned at him with an evilness that only Rasputin could have matched.

She was mocking him.

White-hot rage flooded his eyes. Determined to kill her, knowing how much he'd enjoy it, he put the accelerator to the floor again. The cab sagged to one side, hampered by the rake caught in the tire. He didn't care. He was killing her now. Once and for all. The Kremlin would thank him for it. The entire Russian *nation* would rejoice.

He kept the pressure on the accelerator, and the engine strained. The cab broke the rake handle and surged forward. And then he ran over a second rake, puncturing the tire on the other side. He felt the tire go, felt the cab dip in the front.

It was time to make the call. Time to set off the bombs. Time to have some fun.

He stamped on the accelerator and punched in the first number.

And despite the damage to his tires, the vehicle responded. Not as fast, of course. But it *went*. His plan was still working.

He was almost upon her.

Now she would die.

Chase tore around the corner of the garage, fear clogging his throat, sidestepping at the last second to avoid a trash can with a taped lid that was sitting out there, blocking his way.

What was that? They never left the trash cans outside, and who would tape down a lid?

A bomb maker.

As the headlights of Vlad's taxi swept over the yard, he saw Phoebe standing alone on the lawn, a bat to her shoulder, her eyes on the taxi. Everyone else was bunched up on the porch. Behind her—out of everyone's line of sight—was a box. Who'd leave a box in the shrubbery, a box that hadn't been there during delivery hours?

A bomb maker.

On the far side of the house, he saw another trash can—another taped lid—nestled against the landscaping.

A third bomb.

In one split second as he reached the front of the house, he saw everything, the moving, flowing scenario, just how he used to see the football field in his playing days. Then he'd scrambled in the pocket, looking for a way to get rid of the ball, while the receivers ran their routes, trying to get open to catch it.

This scenario was the same. He had several play

options, none of them good.

Time slowed to a crawl as he weighed them. Every detail before him was frozen in the hairbreadth of a moment.

He yelled at Phoebe to move away. If they all went out the back door, or out into the street, they wouldn't be as exposed as they were standing right next to a bomb.

Phoebe shifted her stance, but she didn't move. She didn't see that the biggest danger was behind her in the box bomb, not in front of her in Vlad's taxi.

Vlad had turned the car and pointed it at the house. With a final rev of the motor, he drove straight at her. In a few yards, he'd hit her.

Chase had one chance. Once chance to save Phoebe. Once chance to make the play of a lifetime. Phoebe's lifetime. Maybe his, too. One chance.

That was all.

He chose his option.

And put the play in motion.

As he charged past the garage, he leaped, low and fast.

The garage blew up.

The blast from the trash can nearly threw him sideways, and chunks of brick and wood and glass shot up into the air and rained down on him. But he was already airborne, moving away from the center of the blast, stretching out low, his body parallel to the earth, arms extended to their maximum.

As he leaped, straining to reach his goal, he calculated his position in space and to the other objects around him—his relationship to Vlad's taxi, the box, Phoebe, and the porch. In the critical second, he reached out with one hand, scooped up the wet box, and in one continuous, swift motion, tossed it hard in a flat, strong arc toward Vlad's approaching taxi.

His throwing arm ached with the pain of ten thousand tackles, thanks to Vlad's tire iron. But he'd thrown in pain before, and he'd always thrown at moving targets. This target was no different. Events could always go sideways, but he'd had twenty years' practice of throwing footballs to receivers downfield. He could only hope that Vlad would catch the toss.

The leap had taken him this far, but the force of gravity was pulling him down before the play was over. Willing himself to fly just a little farther, Chase grabbed Phoebe to carry her away from the impending explosion. He wrapped his arms around her head and twisted midair to cushion her hips, doing what he could to soften the blow of landing and the upended rakes in the yard. As they headed toward earth and Vlad barreled down on them, he saw the assassin's horrified face through the taxi's broken windshield. A split second later, they hit the wet dirt in a tangled roll, and the bomb sailed through the open windshield of the damaged cab and exploded.

And then Chase felt nothing but pain. Hot, sharp, overwhelming pain. His limbs were immobilized, blinding white light obliterated his vision, and a roaring filled his ears.

And that was all.

Chapter 20

Seconds later, after the noise had dissipated and the smoke had cleared, Phoebe opened her eyes. Chase had wrapped himself around her tighter than a boa constrictor around its lunch and hit the ground first, rolling them away from the blast. Her wrist was throbbing, and she'd probably be pretty bruised in the morning, but she wasn't seriously hurt.

Chase, however, didn't look so good. His eyes were closed. His skin was pale. His breathing, to her inexperienced ears, sounded shallow.

"Chase! Chase, honey!" She worked her hands free from the vise of his arms and stroked his face. He felt cold and clammy. "Talk to me! Are you all right?"

He opened his eyes and blinked a couple of times. He seemed to think for a second.

"Yeah," he said on an exhale. "You?"

"I'm fine. I don't know about anybody else."

"What about Vlad?"

She gazed over at the smoldering taxi, which had come to a halt across the yard. It slumped on one axle, a sludgy, grayish-black, useless pile of metal, dented and windowless, hunched over on their poor lawn like a depressed vulture. The passenger-side door had been blown off. The fender was mangled. The bumper, either from the rakes or the bomb, had ripped away and fallen to the ground. Vlad lay motionless in the damp grass and weeds beside it. She didn't see any blood, but then, it was pretty dark.

"He's not moving. I can't tell if he's breathing."

"You think he's dead?"

"I sure hope not. I want him out of our *lives*, not out of *existence*."

"We should call the cops," he said. "Or an ambulance."

"I don't think we have to call." And in fact, as she watched, she saw the flashing lights of squad cars down the block. "They're almost here already."

"That might be for the car fire down the street," Chase said.

The entire house contingent rushed over to them. Kristin had taken hold of Trouble and had him on a leash. He whined at the restraint.

"Phoebe! Chase!" Sanjay said, bending down. "How badly are you hurt? Do you need an ambulance?"

"Chase does," Phoebe said, worried about Chase's color and temperature.

"I'll make the call," Brenda said and went back into the house.

Sanjay took one of Chase's arms to help him up, and Phoebe flinched when Chase sucked in his breath.

"Other side," he told Sanjay. He sounded tired. "This side got whacked."

"Oh no." Phoebe rolled to all fours but gasped when she put her weight on her left hand.

"Wait a sec," Kristin said. "What's wrong with *you*? Besides all the scrapes and cuts I can see, I mean."

"I did something to my wrist. I don't think it's too bad. Maybe a sprain."

Kristin helped her up, and they joined Chase, who'd walked carefully to the porch with Sanjay and slumped on the bottom step. Sitting down, even on the cement stairs, was a huge relief.

"Is Trouble hurt?" Chase asked. "He took a chunk out of Vlad in the alley. Vlad tried to hit him. I *think* he missed.

Can't be sure."

"He's not acting like it, but I'll check," Kristin said. She started to go through the dog's fur, checking for cuts or possibly broken bones.

Yuri sat down with them, his yellow towel sling still miraculously supporting his pink cast. Phoebe doubted that the bright floral towel would ever recover its fresh newness after he was done with it. They'd have to buy more towels. Because, who knew, she might need a towel sling herself.

"Это конец," he said.

"Теперь вы в безопасности." Phoebe smiled at Chase. "Yuri says it's all over. We're safe now." They *were* safe, too. She was hugely relieved about that.

"Well, there's another bomb over there," Chase said, his voice weary. "So there's that."

"*What?*" Kristin yelped, scaring Trouble.

Phoebe jerked around. "*Another bomb? Where?*"

"At the other end of the house. In the trash can that's taped up."

Phoebe leaned over to look around Chase, and sure enough—there it was.

"We have to do something!" she said. "It'll go off!"

"I don't think so," Chase said. "Not if it hasn't by now. Vlad triggered the first one. And he's out. So I think we're fine."

"I'll go tell Brenda to ask for the bomb squad, too," Kristin said, heading inside.

Phoebe glanced at Chase again. He really did seem exhausted.

"If the ambulance doesn't come exceptionally soon, we'll take you to the hospital," Sanjay said. "Should Jamal's armored car prove to be undrivable because of damage to the garage from the blast—although those vehicles are built and guaranteed to withstand a tremendous force—we'll call Uber. Have no worries."

"What is *keeping* those EMTs?" Brenda said, coming back onto the porch.

"And the bomb squad." Kristin joined her and stared

down the street. "I mean, they're in the *next block*. I could run down there and get them up here."

"I'll call again." Jamal pulled out his phone. "That was some leap you made there, Coach. Dan Freer couldn't have done better."

In one split second, Phoebe had a horrifying thought. With a surge of adrenaline, she lunged up and smacked Jamal's hand as his fingers hovered over the keypad, sending his phone flying.

"Ow, ow, ow!" she yelped, staggering back and holding her wrist. "Ow!" She eased herself back down onto the front step.

"What the *hell?*" Jamal stared at her.

"That bomb by the garage—that was a cell phone detonator, wasn't it?" she asked, bent over her arm. "It wasn't on a timer, because the garage bomb went off just as Chase passed it."

Sanjay went very still, his eyes locked on Phoebe.

"I would think so, yes," Jamal said. "Why?" And then as shock registered on his face, she saw that he understood what she meant.

"*What?*" Brenda demanded. "What are you talking about?"

"The bomb over there in the recycling bin," Phoebe said. "It could be set off by a cell phone call."

Brenda paled. "Good Lord. No one make any calls! No cell phones! Stay away! We have an unexploded bomb out here!"

Kristin tied Trouble's leash to the porch. "You know what? I'm going to move that bin out into the street. That'll be safer for the neighbors, too."

"*No!*" Brenda said. "Leave it there! Don't touch it! And you know what, Chase, honey? You don't look so hot. I'm getting you a blanket." She trotted back into the house.

"I'm going over there to pick up my phone so it doesn't get wet," Jamal said, edging away. "But I will not touch any buttons. I will be very, very careful." He picked up his phone and turned it off before wiping it gently and tucking it into his pocket.

"Well, I'm not positive that any call would set it off," Phoebe said. "But we might as well play it safe. The cops'll tell us. They have to show up here pretty soon."

"I wouldn't count on it," Chase said.

Brenda came out with a blanket, and Phoebe saw Chase wince when she put it around his shoulders. He must have hit the ground harder than she'd thought. And then when he moved, she saw the blood, and her stomach clenched. How was he really? And *where was that ambulance*?

"I'll see if I can start the car," Jamal said.

He and Sanjay stepped off the porch and headed over to what was left of the garage.

Kristin glanced down the street. "Here come the cops. Finally."

"Why would they rush?" Phoebe said. "It's federal."

Two squad cars parked in front of their place, and the two officers they'd met earlier, carrying what appeared to be heavy suitcases, slogged up the messy slope of their front yard, their leather shoes sliding on the wet grass, weeds, and broken rock, and headed over to where Vlad lay motionless on the ground. Two guys in jackets and ties approached the porch.

"I'm Detective Orlando Ramirez of the Metropolitan Police Department," the shorter cop said. "This is my partner, Detective John Silkes. You folks all right?"

"Chase needs an ambulance," Phoebe said. "And we need the bomb squad. We're afraid to use our cell phones because there's an unexploded bomb over there in the recycling bin." She pointed to the other end of the house.

The cops glanced in the direction she pointed but didn't seem surprised.

"You're fine," Ramirez said. "We turn off cell service to an area when there's a bomb threat. You couldn't call in or out on a cell right now if you wanted to."

"Oh," Phoebe said. "Good to know. On the downside though, I think Vlad might be dead."

"Vlad," Ramirez said. "That would be the Russian

267

assassin you told the officers about earlier. He's the guy lying over there on the lawn?"

"Yes. Vlad Golubkin." Phoebe glanced over to where the two uniforms had opened their suitcases. They'd taken things out and attached them to Vlad, and now they seemed to be probing him. That had to be positive, right? Ramirez and Silkes turned to check out the scene, too, and the two uniforms glanced up and gave the thumbs-up.

"He's still cookin'," Ramirez said. "Paramedics are on their way. Bomb squad, too. They'll get rid of that thing for you."

"Thank you." Phoebe leaned back against the porch, suddenly exhausted. The adrenaline rush, plus maybe hunger and the lack of sleep, had done her in. She was just so *tired*.

"*Cher*," Chase said. "Ambulance is here."

Phoebe jerked upright, aware that she'd been leaning against Chase, whose shoulder probably didn't need the aggravation.

"Sorry," she said. "Did I hurt your shoulder? Or anything else?"

"Nah," he said with a smile. "Anyway, you've only been out for a minute or two."

Phoebe grinned, tucking her good hand under his good arm. "I would have hated to miss any of the excitement." She gazed out at the yard, which was now swarming with paramedics and guys in giant white padded suits. One of them lumbered over to the porch.

"Could have been a lot worse," he said cheerfully, shoving back his headgear. "That little baby bomb got wet. Really diminished the effectiveness of the blast. The other two were pretty crude."

"It took out our garage," Phoebe said.

"A little C-4 or Semtex in a bucket that size that sealed better could have taken out your whole house and most of the neighborhood," the guy said. "So what happened? The little one went off before your guy got it placed? Or what?"

"It got placed," Phoebe said. "Chase threw it back into the car before it went off."

"I'll be damned. Never heard of that before."

"Well, he's Chase Bonaventure," Phoebe said. "So, yeah."

"Chase Bonaventure," the guy said. "Do I know you?"

"No," Chase said.

"*Heck*, yeah," Phoebe said. "Star quarterback of the Las Vegas Rattlesnakes for ten years? Three-time Super Bowl champion? *That* Chase Bonaventure?"

"*Cher.*"

"Sorry," the guy said. "I'm more of a hockey fan myself."

"You don't know what you're missing," Phoebe said.

"I guess not, if you can throw a bomb in a box through the window of a moving vehicle," the guy said. "Okay, well, we did a sweep for more bombs and you're clear. So we'll be off. Take care now." He lumbered away to join the rest of his crew, which had loaded the last bomb into a heavy enclosed trailer. He got in, backed over the lawn, and drove away.

Phoebe had been watching the activity in the yard as they talked. Paramedics had arrived in the two ambulances now parked in the driveway, and a couple of the EMTs strapped Vlad onto a gurney. They fiddled with plastic bags full of clear liquid on rolling poles that they attached to him with tubes. So he wasn't dead. That was good news.

More paramedics trundled two gurneys over to the front porch.

"Now it's your turn," one of them said cheerfully. "Who goes first?"

"Chase," Phoebe said. Why were all these first responders so chipper in the face of mayhem?

"*Chase*," the second EMT said, pulling out a tiny light and shining it into his eyes, flicking it from one eye to the other. "Somebody said you were Chase Bonaventure. *The* Chase Bonaventure? Look left. Now right. Good. I *thought* so! Holy cow. Wait till they hear about this back at the station!" He edged back Chase's shirt and checked the wound.

"Yup, you'll need a couple of stitches," he said

269

buoyantly. "Let me stick something on there in the meantime. That game against the Steelers! That was one hell of a throw!"

"Dan Freer makes a quarterback look good." Chase winced when the paramedic finished his exam and moved Chase's shirt back into place.

"How does that shoulder feel?" the guy asked.

"Hurts like hell," Chase said.

"I think you separated it," the guy said. "You'll have mega bruising, too."

"Wouldn't be the first time."

The female EMT rotated Phoebe's bad wrist, and the pain made Phoebe forget about everything else.

"I don't think it's broken, but they'll do an X-ray at the hospital," the EMT said. "I'm going to give you both something for the pain."

"Is this what modern couples do on Saturday nights now?" Phoebe asked Chase. "Matching morphine shots? Couldn't we simply have settled for tattoos?"

"We could, but it's only Tuesday," Chase said, offering up his arm. "Tuesday is morphine night."

The paramedic took a syringe from her bag and administered the painkiller to Chase and did the same for Phoebe. Then she popped a lever and the gurney lowered.

"Let's get you on this thing, and we'll get you to the hospital in a jiffy," she said.

Phoebe was already feeling the effects of the painkiller, so getting on the narrow gurney with her bad wrist was a little trickier than she'd expected. But once she and Chase were settled, the EMTs pushed the gurneys down the sidewalk and over to the driveway where the ambulances waited. The other paramedics had finished working on Vlad and were pushing him toward the driveway, too.

They were about to meet Vlad in the driveway, she realized. One way or the other. A showdown, like cowboys in a Western drama. Only without guns. Just rakes and baseball bats and one broken-down, stolen taxi.

All the EMTs pushing gurneys came to a halt at the

pavement, where they stopped to open the ambulance doors and jockey for position. Trouble had somehow gotten loose from the porch, and now the dog sat next to Vlad's gurney and showed his teeth. At least Trouble would make sure Vlad didn't escape.

Phoebe glanced over at the Russian. Beneath the infected mosquito bites, his skin was pale, but his breathing was obvious now.

"What's wrong with him?" she asked a paramedic.

"Almost everything," he said. "You name it, he broke it. They'll do tests at the hospital."

"He's an international assassin, you know," Phoebe said.

"I do know," the paramedic said. "The cops told us. He won't be doing much assassinating for a while, though."

"I hope not," Phoebe said, feeling mellower by the second. "He wanted to kill Yuri—our friend over there in the pink cast—because Yuri's defecting from Russia. But he couldn't defect this week because of the government shutdown, so he's been staying at our house. I'm with the CIA, so it sort of works out okay."

"Holy crap," the EMT said. "That I *didn't* know. CIA, huh?"

"Yeah," Phoebe said. "It's federal."

She considered the Russian, lying so still on the gurney. What would happen to him? Surely he'd be arrested. Would he stand trial here? Elsewhere? She had no idea. She'd ask Kevin Toth when she and Yuri went to the FBI next week.

As she gazed at Vlad, his eyelids fluttered and then opened. He took a deep breath. Opened his mouth. Turned his head to see her better.

"*Cher*," he said, his voice weak but clear. "*Cher*. Wait."

Vlad was exhausted. He hurt everywhere, but mostly he was exhausted—physically and, worse, mentally. He had lost. He had not killed Yuri Severov, who was standing right over there with his stupid pink cast. And how had the defector gotten that cast in the first place? It was a mystery.

Someone had hurt him, but that someone was not he.

Not only had he not killed Yuri Severov—and now never would—he had not managed to penetrate the safe house in any significant way. He had succeeded in blowing up the garage of the compound, but that was irrelevant for his mission. Cher and the Running Man were, it was true, going to the hospital, but they did not seem seriously hurt. Despite his best efforts.

Why had he failed? What did they have that he did not? Better tools? Training? Brains? Strength? Courage? Cher had stood alone out front in the yard with nothing but a base-ball bat, daring him to run her down. Running Man's throw had put the bomb back in his car. Then there was all the rest of it: the superior driving of Agarwal and the other guy. The combined battle skills of these other agents standing around now, including an attractive, middle-aged woman in—unbe-lievable—fur slippers. The concealed rooftop sniper team, giving nothing away.

That had to be it. Somehow, in this country, these peo-ple had cultivated extraordinary powers that made them bet-ter agents. Better protectors. And probably, if they put their minds in the other direction, better assassins.

How could this be?

He flashed on the diner where he'd eaten all his meals, remembering the pancakes with real maple syrup; the rich, apple-smoked bacon; the fried eggs with their creamy, runny yolks; the crispy breakfast potatoes. The hamburgers and french fries, the meatloaf and mashed potatoes, the fresh sal-ads and green beans and glazed carrots and creamed corn and coffee and all the delicious food he'd eaten since he arrived. He thought maybe even the vodka was better.

That had to be it. The food. American food turned nor-mal people into superpeople.

He glanced up at the faces of the paramedics, at Cher and Running Man on the gurneys and all the others standing around who'd stopped him from achieving his goal. They looked normal, but they weren't. They were stronger, faster, and smarter than he was. Their team was better. More effective.

Even better-looking.

They had won.

And if it was one thing Vlad liked, it was to be on the winning team.

"*Cher*," he said. "*Cher*. Wait."

Phoebe leaned forward from her gurney. Vlad the Assassin wanted to talk to her? He spoke *English*? And he *knew Chase's pet name for her?*

"Vlad?"

The Russian licked his lips. "You work CIA. You said. Government."

Phoebe nodded. "Yes. I work for the CIA."

"Iz good." He paused for a moment, thinking. Then he took a deep breath.

"I want to defect."

Chapter 21

Phoebe slept soundly for twelve hours and woke early the next morning, pale gray light brightening the windows around the edges of the blinds. Her wrist throbbed faintly beneath the elastic bandage she wore, but the painkillers she'd swallowed when she got home from the hospital still seemed to be working. She'd been lucky. The emergency room physician had said her wrist was only sprained.

Chase slept on, his back to her, a square gauze bandage covering the stitches he'd received in the hospital, a huge purple bruise covering all of his shoulder and part of his back. She gulped, thinking about what could have happened if Vlad had struck Chase's head rather than his shoulder. As it was, he was hurt badly enough, but not as badly as he could have been. His throwing arm would be as good as new.

They both had been lucky.

She slid out of bed, trying not to wake him, and went around to his side to find her shoes. And then she sat on the footstool where she could see his face to put them on.

He was beautiful in repose. Even relaxed in sleep, he looked like a gladiator. His injured shoulder and arm rested on a pillow, his biceps strongly defined, his fingers long and graceful, callused from physical work. His chest was broad and heavily muscled, his skin tawny from the sun. A shock of unruly dark hair had fallen across his forehead, giving him a raffish appearance and also, somehow, making him seem vulnerable.

If that garage bomb had gone off when he was directly in front of it—or if that box bomb had exploded a couple of seconds sooner—

None of that had happened. But if it had, what would she have done?

He meant everything to her.

As her gaze lingered on him in the soft morning light, her breathing slowed and a deep calmness suffused her mind and seeped into her bones. She felt peaceful. Serene. Centered. Rooted to this place in this moment. With this man.

She felt infinite, expansive and powerful. As though the puzzle pieces to a jigsaw she hadn't known she wanted to assemble had fluttered down from the sky into place before her. As though she'd found the answers to questions that she hadn't known she'd asked.

Everything in her universe understood and accepted.

Chase meant everything to her.

A rush of tenderness flooded her heart, and she reached out, brushing the hair away from his forehead. He opened his eyes and smiled at her.

"*Cher*," he said.

Her heart ached with love and the fullness of destiny.

"Will you marry me?" she asked.

That was quite the morning conversational opener.

Chase grinned, reaching out to touch the engagement ring on her finger. "Thought that question was asked and answered."

She lifted one shoulder in the smallest of shrugs and glanced away, not returning his smile.

His heart almost stopped. He laced his fingers through hers. "You mean soon, don't you?"

She turned back and nodded, the smallest of motions. Her eyes seemed to fill half her face, her skin pale. Was she worried that he'd say *no*?

"I'd love to marry you," he said. "When did you have

in mind? Today? This morning?" He was mostly kidding, but he'd move heaven and earth to marry her in the next *minute* if she wanted that.

She smiled then, and her lips trembled a little bit, everything she felt in her eyes, her soul laid bare.

She was offering him her heart, her most precious gift. In that second, he felt his own heart expand to accept it, and he vowed always to protect and cherish it, to love her and be the husband she deserved.

"Today, then," he said. "Let's get married today."

"I'd like that," she said. "If it isn't too much trouble."

Over breakfast, Phoebe was surprised to see how enthusiastically everyone agreed to pitch in. Evidently, planning a wedding made a nice change from figuring out how to thwart a Russian assassin.

"I want to get my family here," Chase said. "My folks said they'd come. The sibs, too. Let's make flight arrangements for private or commercial carriers, either is fine. Whatever gets them all here today by, say, five o'clock at the latest."

"I'll make the calls," Kristin said. "I'm not the VP of operations for nothing! Are we going to city hall? We could probably pull some strings and get squeezed in there even without an appointment."

"I have a better idea." Chase took out his phone and tapped in a number.

"Hey, Muriel," he said. "It's Chase Bonaventure. I have a favor to ask. What are you doing this afternoon around five o'clock?"

Five minutes later, the mayor of Washington, DC, had agreed to officiate at their wedding.

Phoebe was incredulous. "Do you know everybody in the whole *world?*"

"Muriel and I go way back." Chase grinned at the memory. "She trash-talked me a few years ago before my first playoff game, told me her team'd make me eat crow. So when the Snakes won, she sent me a turkey. She's great."

After that, everything fell into place. They decided on the blue parlor for the venue because it had the best afternoon light and was large enough to hold all the guests. In addition, the blue parlor was farthest away from the damage to the garage and was therefore relatively dust-free. Big plus there.

They made other quick decisions, too—on the dress, the guest list, and the food. They needed the license and rings, so after a few minutes, Kristin shooed them out of the house to buy them. When they returned several hours later after a celebratory lunch, preparations were well underway.

"Your whole family is here already," Kristin said. "They flew private, because I couldn't get enough seats commercial, and the timing was bad, too. I can't believe how easy it was to get them here. I mean, you wave a credit card around, those planes are ready to go. Your folks are in the kitchen having a snack or helping with the food, I'm not sure which."

"I have set up the Zoom connections," Sanjay said, fiddling with a laptop that was poised on the plant stand in the corner of the room. "We are broadcasting for anyone at the Venture Automotive plant who wishes to attend. Also the Snakes team. Also my mother. I hope you don't mind. I believe everything is set to go here."

"Thanks, Sanjay," Chase said. "Your mother is very welcome."

Sanjay nodded, looking gloomy. "I believe she might have invited also my Uncle Boo-Boo."

Chase grinned. "Your Uncle Boo-Boo is welcome, as well. As long as he doesn't use any wedding images on the promotional material for his real estate business. Or any of his other projects."

"In anticipation of that possibility, I have made his signing a nondisclosure agreement a requirement for attending. You'll find that document in your email inbox."

Chase laughed. "Nice work. Sounds like you've covered all the options."

Sanjay turned to Phoebe. "I called your friend Nattie Wilkinson at the CIA, which was most uncooperative when it came to participating in a Zoom event."

Phoebe nodded. "There are a million protocol restrictions on something like that."

"Yes, so the security officer informed me. I was momentarily rather concerned that he might have aspirations to arresting me for some breach of the regulations. However, Nattie promised to leave work early to attend in person. She should be arriving at any moment."

And just then, Nattie appeared in the doorway.

"Phoebe!" she said. "Congratulations! Chase, you, too. I'm so happy for you guys."

Phoebe hugged her friend. "I'm so glad you could make it on such short notice. I've got somebody you want to meet. Amos Glenwethering. Retired CIA field officer, Russia desk. He's got stories."

She took Nattie over to meet Amos as Brenda bustled into the parlor with a cloud of white fabric over her arm. "The dresses are here! And the wedding planner ladies!"

The blond women of Tresses to Dresses entered the room, looking dumbstruck.

"Are you sure you want to wear one of these wrecked gowns?" Blonde #1 asked Phoebe. "For your *wedding*? To *Chase Bonaventure*?"

"Because we could get you a nicer dress," Blonde #2 said. "A cleaner one, anyway."

"The dresses are here?" Claire Bonaventure, Chase's mother, entered the parlor. She hugged Phoebe. "I'm so happy for you and Chase. Thank you for getting us here so quickly! What do you mean, a wrecked gown? How did they get wrecked? Can I see, too?"

"Of course," Phoebe said. "So glad you could make it, Claire! Yeah, the dresses got a little messed up, but a damaged dress will be a good memento." She turned to the wedding planners. "Let's see what you brought."

"Okay, well, I'm just saying," Blonde #2 said. "You are one lucky girl."

"That's what *I* was saying!" Brenda said.

Phoebe glanced at Chase, who gave her a rueful grin.

"The only one who's lucky around here is me," Chase said. "*Cher*, you good for now? The insurance adjuster pulled into the driveway. I want to find out when we can start on repairs to the garage."

"Go." Phoebe reached up to kiss him. She was getting married *today*. In, like, practically no time. She was amazed that everything had come together so smoothly.

"He really is the lucky one." Ancel, Chase's father, had followed his wife into the parlor and hugged Phoebe.

"Thank you, Ancel. I'm so glad you think so." Phoebe beamed at him, but she *was* lucky. Lucky that she'd barged in on Chase that day months ago, lucky that he'd needed a translator. Luck hadn't always been on her side, but today it felt like everything had changed. She was getting married to the guy she loved, the only guy who would move his car company across the country for her, and the wedding would be perfect no matter what happened.

"Sure, sure, everybody's lucky," Blonde #1 said. "Now, about the dresses."

"Your mom said something simple." Blonde #2 spread the gowns out on the bright chintz sofa, and Blonde #1 held up a sleeveless, boat-necked dress made of raw silk.

"That's the one," Phoebe said.

"I love that one!" Brenda said.

"Really?" Blonde #2 said. "The first one? Because there's a few others, and this one has a big tire mark on the back."

"I like that one," Phoebe said. "The tire mark won't show in the pictures. Unless we want it to. Which I think we might want it to, on a few of the photos, at least."

"I like that one, too," Claire said. "It's a beautiful dress, even with the tire print on it."

"Can you show it to me?" said a plaintive voice from the computer screen. "I'd like to see it, too. Why does it have a tire mark?"

"Megan!" Phoebe held the dress up in front of the computer screen so the receptionist at the Venture Automotive plant could admire it. "The story's too long to tell now, but

I'll fill you in later. We've been having quite the adventure here. How's your view to the front of the room?"

"Pretty good," Megan said. "Maybe you could point us a little more to the left."

"How's this?" Sanjay scootched the laptop a little to the left. "I want to make certain that you will be able to see all important events as they unfold."

"That's it," Megan said. "Perfect."

Amos helped Sophie into a comfortable chair. "The string quartet will be here any minute," he told Phoebe. "They're Italian, so they have a rather elastic concept of time, but I was firm with them."

"You know an Italian string quartet?" Phoebe asked. "Personally?"

"Well, they provided an invaluable assist to our country," Amos said. "So, yes."

"You would not believe the food that restaurant delivered for us," Jamal said, coming in from the kitchen. "The shrimp! The pasta! Unbelievable. We got a twenty-five percent off coupon for next week, too. They said anything for Chase Bonaventure."

"Told you." Kristin followed him, licking her fingers. "You say *Chase Bonaventure*, and doors open." She grinned at Phoebe. "The cake is here. Sort of a chocolate mousse with raspberry filling. It is *heaven*."

"And you know this how?" Phoebe asked, but she was laughing. Kristin wasn't licking her fingers for nothing.

"When I called the bakery, I said *Chase Bonaventure*, so in addition to the cake that we *bought*, the bakers, who are football fans, *gave* us two dozen cupcakes," Kristin said. "Now reduced to twenty-three cupcakes."

"Twenty-two cupcakes," Claire said. "I had one when you weren't looking."

The Italian musicians arrived and clattered around, setting up chairs and music stands and opening their instrument cases.

"Подождите! Давайте сделаем снимок!" Yuri said, charging up the stairs from the basement, holding a camera in his good hand.

"I remember this guy," Blonde #2 said. She lowered her voice. "He's *cute*. He doesn't speak any English?"

"He can say *no poleets*," Phoebe said. "Otherwise, nothing." Blonde #2 thought Yuri was *cute*? It just showed how there was somebody for everybody.

"No English could be handy," Blonde #2 said. "What did he say just now?"

"He wants to take a photograph." Phoebe eyed the camera that Yuri held. "And he told me yesterday that he thinks you're pretty."

Trouble, his white bow slipping under his ear, charged through the front door into the foyer, followed by Chase.

"The insurance adjuster says that since the construction crew is already in place, he'll expedite the claim and we can get started on the garage," he said. "And the detectives are here. They're poking around. I invited them all for the ceremony. Why not, right? It's your thing, and we've called them a million times. I feel like we're old friends. I invited Mateo and Doolie and the rest of the crew, too."

"Great!" Phoebe said. "And it's always good to have friends on the force. In case something ever happens here that *isn't* federal. Is Yuri our photographer? How can he do that with one arm in a sling?"

"You'd be surprised," Chase said. "Just watch. I think he's more than a Russian data hacker. He seems awfully familiar with cameras, especially small ones."

"Hmm," Amos said. "Interesting."

"Well, let's shoot us some pictures, then." Phoebe grinned at Yuri.

"Идти," she said, and Yuri aimed the camera and shot a photo of her. Then he took several more of them and the room.

"Looks like we'll have a lot of photos," Jamal said.

"As long as they don't wind up in any secret agency databases," Phoebe said.

Kristin glanced up from arranging a vase of flowers on the mantel. "Maybe the pictures won't be in focus."

"I wouldn't count on it," Amos said.

Phoebe laughed. "If they turn up at the CIA, I'll delete them myself. Okay, I'm going upstairs to get ready."

"We'll come help with your hair," Blonde #1 said.

"And maybe we can lighten up that dirt streak on your dress," Blonde #2 said.

"Hang on," Chase said. "I was thinking about asking you to drive over my tux a couple times. You know, put some tire marks on the jacket. So Phoebe and I would match."

Phoebe grinned. "Absolutely not. Anyway, the dirt wouldn't show up as much on your tux. We'd lose the effect."

"Jeez, you two," Blonde #1 said. "Let's go up already, okay?"

"I'll help!" Brenda said. "My little girl!"

"If you're not going to drive over my clothes, I guess I'll just have to get dressed, then," Chase said. "At least we've got a spare bedroom."

"Plenty of room for everything and everyone," Phoebe said, smiling at him. "A nice, big house."

"A strong one," Chase said. "Like us."

Less than an hour later, everyone was packed in the blue parlor. It was more crowded than they'd expected, because the wedding planners, construction crew, detectives, and insurance adjuster now stood around the edges of the room, beaming. The mayor, looking poised and official, stood at the front near the fireplace, waiting for them. Yuri darted around, snapping photos, even a photo of the laptop with the Venture Automotive and Rattlesnakes teams peering out.

Brenda, seated next to Amos and Sophie in the front row, twisted her hands together. "My little girl is getting *married!* Can you *believe* it?"

"You could tell they were crazy about each other even back in Vegas," Nattie said from the other side of Amos and Sophie.

The musicians struck up *Pachelbel's Canon* as she and Chase walked down the stairs together. They paused for a moment in the foyer.

"This is it," Chase said. "You ready?"

"Yes." She was absolutely sure. She felt rock-solid about him and more confident about their future together than she'd ever felt about anything. "I'm ready. *More* than ready. I want this marriage to get started."

Chase laughed, making all heads turn toward the entry-way.

"I'm relieved to hear it," he said. "I'm not sure what I'd have done if you'd said you needed more time."

Phoebe laughed, too, and he leaned down to kiss her cheek.

"I love you," he whispered. "Now and forever."

"I love you, too," Phoebe said, taking his arm, glancing into the blue parlor. Their house. Their friends and family.

Their future.

"Everybody's here," she said. "This is it. This is *us*."

He nodded. "This marriage will be good. *We'll* be good."

Phoebe smiled, loving him with her whole heart. "Now and forever."

ABOUT THE AUTHOR

Kay Keppler abandoned the freezing climes of northern
Wisconsin where she was raised for northern California,
where she lives in a drafty old house with wonky plumbing.
Now if the duct tape holds, everything will be perfect.